THE RULE OF 3

WILL

TO

SURVIVE

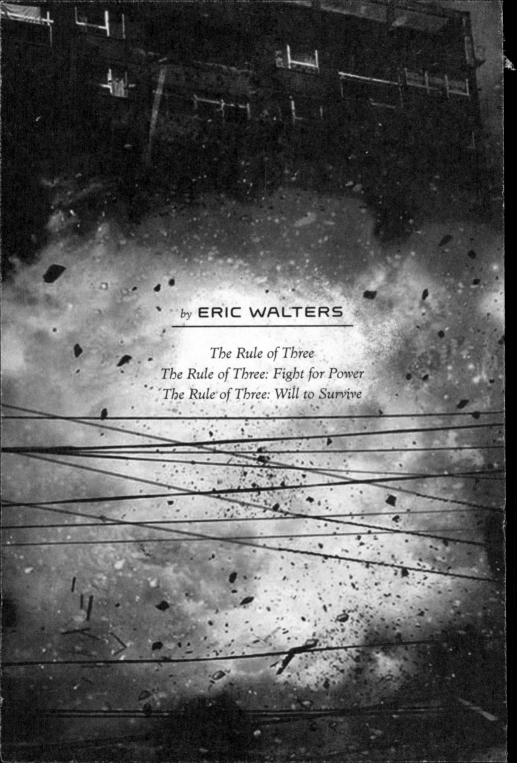

by ERIC WALTERS

The Rule of Three
The Rule of Three: Fight for Power
The Rule of Three: Will to Survive

THE RULE OF 3

WILL

TO

SURVIVE

ERIC WALTERS

Farrar Straus Giroux

New York

Farrar Straus Giroux Books for Young Readers
175 Fifth Avenue, New York 10010

Printed in the United States of America
Designed by Andrew Arnold
First American edition, 2016
1 3 5 7 9 10 8 6 4 2

fiercereads.com

Library of Congress Cataloging-in-Publication Data

Names: Walters, Eric, 1957– author.
Title: Will to survive / Eric Walters.
Description: First American edition. | New York : Farrar Straus Giroux Books for
   Young Readers, 2016. | Series: The rule of three ; 3 | Summary: After a global
   blackout, teenager Adam Daley and his neighbors have turned their middle
   American community into a fortress, defending against countless enemies, but
   what is lurking in the dark is a greater danger than ever before: somebody who
   wants to destroy the neighborhood and Adam at any cost.
Identifiers: LCCN 2015026920 | ISBN 9780374301811 (hardback) | ISBN
   9780374301835 (ebook)
Subjects: | CYAC: Survival—Fiction. | Neighborhoods—Fiction. | Electric power
   failures—Fiction. | Science fiction. | BISAC: JUVENILE FICTION / Action &
   Adventure / Survival Stories. | JUVENILE FICTION / Action & Adventure /
   General. | JUVENILE FICTION / Social Issues / Violence.
Classification: LCC PZ7.W17129 Wi 2016 | DDC [Fic]—dc23
LC record available at http://lccn.loc.gov/2015026920

Our books may be purchased in bulk for promotional, educational,
or business use. Please contact your local bookseller or the Macmillan
Corporate and Premium Sales Department at (800) 221-7945, ext. 5442
or by email at MacmillanSpecialMarkets@macmillan.com.

To those who survive
against all the odds

THE RULE OF 3

WILL

TO

SURVIV3

"I . . . I killed them," I stammered. "They were going to take me and . . . I shot them."

I was standing in a parking lot, in the dark, in the middle of the night. Beside me, inside the plane, were the two people I'd shot. *The two people I'd killed.* That rattled around in my head.

I'd killed them. Shot them dead before they could shoot me.

"Adam . . . what happened?" my mother demanded.

She, my father, and the twins were there with me. We stood in a huddle, with my family trying to calm and comfort me.

Howie, my mom's lieutenant, stood nearby.

My whole body had started shaking, as if I were standing out in the freezing cold. But it was actually just a cool late-summer night.

In the lights cast by the several patrol cars that had gathered, the whole scene was now as bright as day. Here I stood in the parking lot of the strip mall—the mall where I used to go to get an ice cream or to run an errand and pick things up for my parents at the grocery store or the drugstore, or the bakery. The place I'd come to get a slice of pizza.

Although the stores were mostly abandoned, the mall looked pretty much the same as it always did. The differences were the nearby high fence that marked one edge of our community, the armed guards at the gate, and of course the airplane with the two bodies inside it.

Those things were more different than anything I could have even imagined a few months ago, before the blackout hit.

I tried to gather myself.

The twins—my younger brother and sister—were holding on to me, crying.

"I didn't have any choice," I said. "I shot them. I had to."

"You shot who?" my father questioned.

"Two of the prisoners, Owen and Tim. They were trying to force me to fly them away."

"Oh my lord!" he exclaimed.

"They killed the guards and they all escaped and—"

"Brett has escaped?" my mother asked.

I could tell by her expression how shocked she was. More than that, there was fear.

"Yes, all of the prisoners. He and the others are probably already over the walls and gone."

My mother launched into police-captain mode, barking out orders to Howie, who rushed off to notify the guards on the walls.

She turned her attention back to me. "But why were you even out here to begin with in the middle of the night?"

"It was Brett," I said. "He was in our house."

My sister gasped.

"In my room. He had a knife." Even as I said the words it didn't seem real, more like a bizarre nightmare. "He told me if I didn't come along quietly he'd kill me and everybody else in the house. I had to go with him. There was no choice."

"But why? Why did he want you to go with him?" my father asked.

"He didn't want me. He wanted the plane. Once we were outside the house, we met up with six others, and he ordered two of them to come along with me. They tried to make me fly it out for them and—"

Then I remembered.

"We have to get to Herb!"

"What?" my mother asked.

"They shot Herb . . . We have to get help . . . We have to bring the doctor! He could still be alive!"

I broke free of my family and started running.

I heard them shouting out after me, but I couldn't stop.

I raced through the parking lot, dodging the abandoned cars, and ran out into the street. I pounded down the hill back toward Herb's house, where I pictured him lying in a pool of blood, having been shot in his bed by two of Brett's militiamen.

My feet and legs, which moments before had been so shaky that I could hardly stand, were now pulsing with power, carrying me over the pavement like I was really flying.

Coming up the hill toward me was one of the community go-carts, its converted lawn-mower engine roaring as one of the mobile sentries raced to investigate the gunshots from my battle with the prisoners. I jumped out in front of him, waving my arms in the air, and the driver skidded to a stop, fishtailing as he just avoided hitting me.

"I need your vehicle!" I screamed to the guy, whose name I had forgotten. "Please!"

Before he could react I grabbed him and pulled him right

out—the adrenaline giving me superpowers. I jumped into the seat and slammed my foot on the gas pedal, squealing around and tearing down the street.

There was a slideshow going on in my head—Brett in my room, the knife to my throat, the blood and smoke and explosions in the cabin of the Cessna.

Then I pictured Herb in his bed, bleeding from the assassins' shots. While he held me hostage out on the street, Brett had sent two men into Herb's house to kill him, and they'd run out saying they'd shot him while he slept.

There was no chance that he was still alive.

Why hadn't I done something quicker?

If Herb died, it was as much my fault as that of the prisoners who had fired their automatic weapons stolen from the guards they'd killed.

I swerved onto my street and felt the go-cart tip onto two wheels. Forcing myself to lift my foot off the accelerator, I steadied the vehicle, then bumped up the curb and across the sidewalk, ripping a path through recently harvested soybeans where the front lawn used to be. I slammed on the brakes before I smashed into Herb's garage.

Leaving the engine on, I leaped out and burst through the front door, which Brett's men had left slightly ajar as they'd fled.

"Herb!" I yelled.

The house was dark. I hurtled up the stairs, only to trip and fall, but I kept going on all fours, clawing my way up.

"Herb!"

In the dark I could make out a partially open bedroom door. I crashed through it.

I could see him . . . in the bed . . . under the covers . . . not moving . . . a dark shadow.

And all at once the adrenaline rush disappeared, leaving me shaking.

Slowly I eased forward. Reaching over, I grabbed the covers, afraid of what I knew I was going to find. I'd seen enough dead bodies over the last four months, but not one of somebody I considered family.

I pulled back on the covers and in the dark could make out a lump on the bed. It didn't move. *He* didn't move. My heart skipped a beat, but I had to do more than just stand there. My arm reached out, as if of its own accord, and touched the shape. It was soft, almost like—

A light came on, suddenly blinding me, and I spun around, my hand shielding my eyes.

"Adam."

It was a voice I knew all too well.

"What are you doing?"

He was standing there, a pistol in his hand, a look of mild surprise on his face.

I blinked, staring at the gun, and then at the man himself. Herb.

Before he could say anything more, I staggered forward, burst into tears, and collapsed into his arms.

I held on to the mug with both hands and slurped down the coffee. Coffee was in short supply, and when we ran out that would be the end of it. Knowing that made it taste even better. The shaking had mostly subsided, but I still had flashes in which my whole body seemed to convulse—fear, shock, disbelief all combining to make me feel like I'd been dumped into a pool of ice water.

So much, so sudden, so enormous, so immense, and so deadly. It was that same slideshow but now on fast-forward, a lifetime's worth of nightmarish images rushing at me in an endless loop as I sat sipping sweet, warm coffee at my kitchen table.

Herb sat with me. Somehow he had managed to get me down the stairs of his house—I think he had to practically carry me. Then when my family arrived we'd all gone over to our house, next door. I had only been able to tell them bits and pieces of what had happened.

Now my father was upstairs with the twins, trying to settle them down, and my mother had gone back to the scene of the killings to do the things she needed to do as the neighborhood's commander.

Four months ago, before our world had gone dark—my mother had been a police captain at a nearby precinct. Now she and Herb were our leaders, in charge of the safety and well-being of all sixteen hundred residents in our fortress neighborhood.

"You need some more food in your stomach," Herb said.

"I'm not hungry."

"Hunger isn't what this is about. You need to line your stomach. Just have a piece of bread."

He walked over to the counter, opened a much-used plastic shopping bag, and sliced off a piece of bread. The bakery was in full operation now and was producing some strange-tasting but still wonderful breads. They were made of various grains and seeds that were being harvested from the woods and fields outside our walls.

He handed me the piece.

"It feels like I'm being served by a ghost," I said.

"I guess if Brett had gotten his way that's what I'd be."

"I still don't understand," I said. "Why weren't you in your bed?"

"I've been sleeping in my safe room," Herb said.

"Is that the little room with the one-way glass in the basement?" I asked. I'd been in that room but didn't remember it being big enough for a mattress.

"Any room with a glass window isn't very safe. I have another room, hidden—steel door, cinder-block walls, with a separate ventilation system. Bulletproof and so solid it's practically soundproof. Remind me to show it to you."

"And that's where you've been sleeping?"

"Call it paranoia, but I've been unable to get to sleep in my room for the last few weeks, ever since we took Brett and his rebels prisoner . . . Been worried that somebody might try to harm me."

I couldn't help but laugh. "Somebody did try."

"A little paranoia goes a long way. I thought that if Brett escaped he'd come looking for me first thing."

"It wasn't him," I said. "He sent in two men to do his dirty work. They told him that they *had* killed you."

"They certainly did kill the stuffing in my bed. But they didn't pull back the covers to make sure, or they would have known. Probably too unnerved or scared or crazed to think to check," Herb said. "I didn't hear them come in, and it looks like they used pillows as crude silencers to muffle the shots."

"But you heard *me* come in," I said.

"You came in so loudly you could have woken the dead. Wait—you *did* wake the dead." He gave me a small smile, and I tried to smile in return, but I think it was more a grimace. "I'm just sorry I wasn't roused soon enough to save you, Adam."

"I saved myself," I said. I shut my eyes, trying to block the memory of firing my gun at the two men in the cabin of the Cessna. Was it my imagination or could I still smell the gunpowder from those blasts?

"I meant saving you from having to take those lives," Herb said gently.

"I did what I had to do."

"That doesn't make it much easier," Herb said.

"Brett told them that he didn't think I had the guts to pull the trigger."

"Brett doesn't understand that killing somebody is about a lot more than just guts. You always had the guts, but you also have the courage not to abandon your morals. You took those two lives with regret and remorse."

I shook my head. "I don't feel either of those things right now. All I feel is, well, numb."

"Numb isn't bad today. Tomorrow will be different. You need to come and talk to me and—"

We both heard the front door open and reached for our guns—being paranoid wasn't being paranoid anymore.

Then we heard voices—my mother's and Howie's.

"In here," Herb called.

My mother and her lieutenant came into the kitchen. Mom walked right over and wrapped her arms around me for a moment. Then she and Howie sat down at the table while Herb fixed them each a cup of coffee.

We sat in silence for a while. I could hear the faint murmur of my father's voice from upstairs as he read the twins a story. I was drowsy and may even have drifted off for a second right where I sat.

Eventually I snapped awake and looked up to see my father standing in the kitchen as well.

"How many casualties on our side?" Herb asked.

"Five of the six prison guards are dead, and the sixth is up at the clinic being cared for by Dr. Morgan," Howie said.

"But I thought he was just tied up," I said.

"Tied up and then forced to watch as each of the other guards was executed. He saw them all being killed, and then Brett put the gun to his head and pulled the trigger, but the gun didn't fire," Howie said. "The guard pretty much lost it at that point. The doc had to give him a heavy sedative."

"Poor guy, but I guess he's lucky to be alive. Did the gun jam?" my father asked.

"No, it was a fake execution," I explained.

"What?" my mother asked.

"Brett only pretended he was going to kill him."

My father stared at me, surprised. "What sort of person would do such a thing?"

"A sociopath," Herb answered.

"He would have to be a sociopath to just kill men in cold blood who were tied up and completely defenseless," my dad said.

"Brett didn't kill any of them," I said.

They all looked at me again.

"They—Tim and Owen—told me Brett made the others do the killing."

"Why would he do that? They were tied up," my father said. "They weren't a threat."

"He did it so there was no way back for any of those men," my mother said.

"The same way terrorist groups force children to kill their own parents before they kidnap them and make them into child soldiers," Herb added. "That way the children can never return to their homes."

"But why didn't he just have his men kill them all?" my father asked. "Why did he leave one?"

"So that there was a witness to tell us who had done the killing," I guessed.

"But more than that, they wanted to spread terror," Herb said. "Has anybody heard of the Gurkhas?"

"Aren't they an ethnic group in India?" my father asked.

"They are warriors from Nepal known as some of the bravest and most ferocious fighters in the world. For generations they have been professional soldiers. One of their ancient tactics was to steal into an enemy encampment at night. They would go into tents and slit the throats of all the men as they slept . . . except for one or two people. Those soldiers would awake to find everybody else in their camp dead."

"But why wouldn't the Gurkhas just kill them all?" Howie asked.

"Because it was more effective to leave witnesses who would spread the terror of what went on. Those survivors infected countless comrades with those horrible stories, filling them with fear."

"And you think that Brett is trying to terrorize us?" Howie asked.

"He wants us to fear him," Herb said. "And we should."

"How much can he hurt us?" my dad asked. "It's just him and those four men, and they're probably going to get as far away from us as possible."

"You're wrong," Herb said. "We're going to see him again."

"And it's not just five of them," I said.

It was time to share the last bit of news I had been keeping to myself since my encounter with Brett earlier that night. In a way, it was the most frightening news of all.

"Brett has formed an alliance with the colonel and the remains of the Division." That was the group of ruthless bandits who had tried to destroy us weeks before—the enemy we had attacked more than once. "They're back at their original compound again. That was where I was being forced to fly the plane."

"That can't be true," Howie said.

"It is."

"Are you sure?" Herb asked.

"I'm sure. Tim and Owen told me before I—"

I couldn't even say it.

"Before you *escaped* from them," my father said.

"This has suddenly become much worse," Mom said.

"Much worse," Herb agreed. "Brett is now part of a force that we already know is big and lethal enough to present a threat to us. He knows the way we operate, our defenses, the positions on the line, the number of armed men, the level of training, our weapons supply. He knows everything, and on top of that he now wants revenge."

"Then we have to start by changing what we can," my mother said. She turned to Howie. "I want the guard stations switched, the times that the sentries are changed to be altered, the weapons on the walls to be reinforced. I want everything to be done differently."

"I'll get right on that," Howie said. "I already have some ideas."

"There's something else we have to do immediately," Herb said.

"Do you want to call an emergency meeting of the committee?" my mother asked.

"We don't have time for that. We have to act now."

"What do you have in mind?" she asked.

Herb didn't answer right away, and the seconds painfully passed. Finally he spoke. "They're expecting the Cessna to land in the compound. We have to give them what they expect. And a whole lot more."

3

A half hour later, my father stood with Herb and me beside the Cessna. We'd taken the old plane from the Division weeks before, when we raided their compound and found they'd all fled. The plane, the engine not working, was left in a warehouse. Our mechanics and engineers had gotten it running and made sure that the plane was airworthy.

Mr. Nicholas, one of our neighborhood's engineers and top mechanics, had been roused from sleep to give the plane a quick check. He was just finishing up now.

"I still think it should be me flying this thing," Dad said.

"If this were a jet, you would be flying it. Adam has more hours at the controls of a Cessna," Herb said.

"I just wish . . ."

My father looked lost for a second, and I had to turn away. I couldn't afford to be undone by emotion. Not now.

Herb laid a hand on my dad's arm. "That you could put yourself in danger in place of your son?" he asked.

My father nodded.

"He's going to be all right."

"I'm counting on you to keep your word on that," my father said.

"You checked out the plane, as did Adam and Mr. Nicholas.

It's guaranteed. We'll be back on the ground here in less than two hours."

"I just wish it could have been taken up for a few more flights before you had to go that far," my father said. "Just to be certain that it's still flightworthy."

"The bullets didn't hit anything to be worried about on the plane; they just punctured the fuselage."

He didn't mention that some of the bullets had punctured flesh before punching through the metal skin of the airplane.

"If we have any problems, we'll abort the flight and be right back," Herb said. "It's just that we don't have much time. We need to get to the compound before Brett does."

Brett and the rest of the escapees were probably still on foot. It would take them at least six hours to get back to their base—unless they'd hijacked one of the few remaining vehicles on the road.

"But why should getting there first be a problem—isn't Brett expecting you?" my father asked Herb.

"He's expecting the plane to be there when he arrives. If he gets there first, it's going to raise alarm. Our safety is predicated on surprise but also on expectations of our arrival."

My father nodded although he still looked like he was feeling uncertain.

"We'll be back soon, safe and sound. You'll see." Herb offered my father his hand, and they shook. Then Dad gave me a quick hug and walked toward the watchpost on the wall from where he could monitor the takeoff.

I understood the doubt and uncertainty. I didn't want to do what we were going to do, but there wasn't much choice. Delaying wouldn't work. It was now or never, and now seemed to be winning.

I fingered a bullet hole on the outside of the fuselage, on the pilot's side of the aircraft. I didn't even know how I could have made that shot, as it was on the side of the plane where I'd been sitting—and then I realized it hadn't come from me. It had been return fire from Tim or Owen. It had all happened so fast, in seconds, that I hadn't even realized it wasn't just me doing the shooting. One of the men had taken a wild shot or two back at me. It was probably nothing more than an involuntary twitch on their part after they had been shot, pulling the trigger and letting go a round or two before they died.

With hesitation I opened the door of the cockpit and climbed in.

Of course, the bodies had been removed and efforts had been made to clean away the blood and guts, but there was still a smell—a combination of gunpowder and something more sinister. Was that what death smelled like? As I looked over the instrument panel and strapped myself into my seat, I looked out the Plexiglas window to my left. Off to the side, next to the old Baskin-Robbins, the two corpses lay under canvas, waiting for the work detail that would take them out to the cemetery beyond the eastern wall for burial later today. I couldn't help staring at them. I couldn't help wondering if—

"Adam?"

I turned to face Herb, who was strapping himself into the seat beside me.

"Are you all right?"

"Sure . . . fine . . . I can do this."

"I don't doubt it," Herb offered. "Your passengers are counting on you."

At his feet was our second "passenger," a metal cylinder no larger than a propane tank from a portable barbecue grill but much more deadly. It contained a lot of high-powered plastic explosives from Herb's basement, part of the arsenal he'd acquired and stored before all of this happened.

We were transporting a bomb. A bomb made from explosives that had been sitting in the basement of the house beside our house. What a bizarre thought that my neighbor had grenades, sniper rifles, night-vision goggles, thousands of rounds of ammunition, and plastic explosives in his basement all those years.

"Adam, I think it would help if you turned on the engine."

"Oh, yeah, of course . . . I was just checking the controls." That was nothing but a lie—one I knew Herb would instantly see through.

I opened up the fuel line, pulled out the throttle, and started the plane. The engine roared to life and I slipped on my headset. The engine noise was muffled, and the ringing in my ears from the gunfire returned.

We bumped out of the parking lot, along the road, and through the gates. The guards there motioned us onward with a wave. They looked solemn and serious. They didn't know what we were doing or all that had happened, but they did know about the escape and the two dead prisoners and the guards who had perished at the hands of Brett and his men. Soon everybody would know. My mother was meeting with the families of the guards—bringing each family the news that their loved one had lost his life in the line of duty. Would the fact that two of the escaping prisoners had been killed mean anything to them? Would it ease the pain at all to know that there had been some form of justice?

Probably not.

I brought the plane to a stop in the middle of Erin Mills Parkway, which ran directly in front of the western wall of our heavily fortified suburban neighborhood. An open quarter-mile stretch of blacktop lay in front of me. The sun was just about to come up. It was good to have light for the takeoff and flight, but not so good for what we were going to do. Darkness would have provided cover.

I looked over at a flagpole that poked up from the front yard of a house just on the other side of our defensive wall. The flag hung there, limp. There was no wind to factor in. Instinctively I pushed the yoke in and then pulled it back out, watching the flaps respond. Everything seemed right.

I opened the throttle, and the engine raced in response, the buzzing propeller pulling us down the runway, faster and faster as we approached takeoff velocity. The vibration in the wheels stopped suddenly as we lifted off. I pulled back on the stick and we quickly gained height.

I thought about doing one lap around the neighborhood, just to make sure everything was working as it should, and then I decided against it, just wanting to get on with the mission. I banked sharply and headed toward our destination. The sooner we were there, the sooner it would be over.

We were heading almost due east, straight into the rising sun. It was still beneath the horizon, but there was a thin line of light—a reddish glow along the curve of the earth in front of us.

"Normally our advantage would be that we were coming in under cover of darkness and our enemy wasn't expecting us," Herb said over the intercom. "Today our advantage is that they *are* expecting us. Or at least they expect Brett to come back in the plane at some point."

"I hadn't even thought of that. We don't have to rely on darkness."

"Light just means more of them will come out to the tarmac as we land. More is better. Just think—Brett may be looking up at us right now from somewhere down there as he's moving toward the compound, gloating. Although he might also be wondering why it took so long for the plane to take off."

I thought of Brett and the remaining men, scurrying to get back to the compound just like rats racing back to their nests.

"If it had worked, if I had brought the plane to their compound, how long do you think it would have been before he killed me?"

"You would have been kept alive as long as you had value either as a pilot or a hostage. It could have been weeks or even months, although you might have wished you were dead."

"That wasn't going to happen," I said. "Even if they got me to pilot the Cessna into the air, I wasn't going to put it down gently at the compound. I knew I'd already be as good as dead, so I wasn't going to die alone and I wasn't going to give them the plane."

"You would have crashed it?"

I nodded. I knew for certain that was what I would have done.

"That would have been a very difficult decision, but I believe you . . . How are you feeling?"

I didn't answer right away, letting the question echo in my headset. Then I shrugged. "I'm not sure."

"There will be plenty of time to talk it over later. Assuming we live through this."

I looked at him; he had a little smirk on his face.

"You really aren't being particularly reassuring right now, Herb. What is our backup plan, by the way? You know, in case this little mission of ours doesn't work out the way we planned?"

"Well, either we make it work or we die trying."

"That doesn't strike me as the best backup plan."

"It's not much different from the plan you had to crash this aircraft—except with me it's only a backup plan."

The rising sun was revealing more and more below us. While I had no hope of spotting Brett or his men, there was so much I could see. Below us on the shadowy landscape were houses—some of whose owners had banded together to form small enclaves with fences and barricades. Other houses were nothing more than burned-out shells. Streets were without movement but not without vehicles. All modern cars and trucks had been rendered useless when the virus hit and their on-board computers self-destructed. Hundreds, thousands of computer-dependent vehicles were still scattered down there, littering the roads, unmoving and unmoved.

Within some of those houses a few families or random clusters of people remained, struggling to survive somehow among the chaos and violence that had washed over everything.

Soon those people would be out getting water or working on their gardens. I just hoped none of them—innocently trying to just stay alive—were met by Brett and his band, who wouldn't hesitate to take everything they had, including their lives.

"I understand Brett wanting to kidnap me, but I'm just not sure why he wanted to kill you so bad," I said.

"I think it was meant as a compliment."

"How is him wanting to kill you a compliment?"

"He saw me as a threat and he wanted to eliminate the threat by eliminating me. I guess in some ways that's what I'm trying to do right now, return the compliment."

"Do you think he's already at the compound?"

"If he and his crew managed to hijack a vehicle, they could be there. On foot his trek will take between five and six hours, so in that case he won't be there until long after we're gone," Herb said.

"Then we won't kill him."

"But what we do *might* result in him being killed," Herb said.

"How so?"

"This bomb will cause major destruction and take out many of the men at the compound."

"I still don't understand. If Brett isn't even there, how will it kill him?" I asked.

"When he finally does arrive to a scene of carnage I'm hoping they'll feel he's responsible—and then they will react."

"And turn on him."

"That's the hope. And I don't think any of the survivors at the compound are going to be thinking about giving him a fair trial or jail time. I'm hoping he'll be greeted by a bullet in the head as soon as he walks in."

"And you think it was our mistake for not simply killing him instead of arresting him?"

"No, it's *my* mistake. I should have done it the night we confronted him, put an end to all of it."

"But you couldn't," I said.

"Oh, I could have. I *should* have. Those guards and their families paid the price of my indecision, my weakness, my—"

"Your fairness and compassion," I said, cutting him off.

"Fairness and compassion can be a weakness. Compassion stops you from pulling the trigger. Instead of killing, though, you get yourself killed. We still don't know the full price we're going to pay for my mistake."

"Maybe he'll just leave us alone."

"He will never leave us alone until either he's dead or we're dead, or the neighborhood is destroyed."

"You can't be certain of that," I said.

"I'm completely certain. I know how people like him think, how they feel . . . or don't feel. Only a six-foot-deep grave is going to stop him from coming back to haunt us, so I hope we can help put him into one."

I'd never heard Herb sound so angry and bloodthirsty.

The leading edge of the sun was now peeking over the horizon. It was a blazing, brilliant orange fireball and it was throwing off enough light for us to clearly see the ground below. We were flying the most direct route between our neighborhood and our enemy's compound thirty-five miles away. Brett was someplace below and there was no way he could miss seeing us up in the sky, since we were the only air-craft in the area. It gave me some satisfaction to know that if he saw us he'd be confused—why were we still flying, why hadn't we reached the compound? Would he be able to wrap his head around the idea that his men were dead and I was free, that instead of being a captive to be tormented and killed, I was going to inflict a blow to him and to our enemies?

We flew in silence for a minute.

"I want you to come in low and slow," Herb finally said.

"And then?"

"If they open fire, take evasive maneuvers and get us out of there as quickly as possible. If they don't shoot, then bring us in for a landing."

For the first time in my life I hoped to be shot at.

The compound came into view off to the southeast. It was a large industrial area, with a big open road in the center that was now a runway, ringed by buildings of assorted sizes. The whole thing was surrounded by a high metal fence topped by barbed wire.

Herb was surveying the ground with his binoculars and could see the details I couldn't.

"Anything?" I asked.

"The perimeter fence has been repaired, but I can't see much else."

"Maybe there isn't anything else to make out," I suggested.

"I'm sure they're trying to keep things hidden from the air. It's not just that they want the Cessna for themselves; they want to deny us from having it."

"I'm going to come in from the north and land toward the barracks," I said.

"And will that give you enough runway to take off again?" Herb asked.

"I'm not sure. I think I might have to turn and go back over the same stretch of pavement. Do you need me to come to a complete stop?"

"The slower the better. I'd rather not bounce this amount of explosives any harder than I have to. Plastic explosives are fairly stable, but I'd rather it went off with the timer instead of with impact."

"That won't happen, will it?" I asked anxiously.

"It really shouldn't happen, but if it does and it explodes, it's not like we'll have time to regret our decision . . . We'll be vaporized in less time than it takes to blink."

"In that case I'll try to arrange it so you can gently place it on the pavement like it's a newborn baby."

"Just remember, even if they don't shoot at us on the way down they're definitely going to shoot at us on the way back up, so let's not waste too much time on the ground."

I knew the timer on the bomb would be set for thirty-five seconds. Just looking at the deadly package now in Herb's lap made me nervously wish we could set it for thirty-five minutes.

"Why not set the timer on the trigger for a little longer?" I asked.

"I want it to be just long enough for us to get away but not so long that other people can recognize the danger and escape. You ready?"

"I better be . . . here we go."

I eased off on the throttle. The slower we came in, the less runway I'd need in order to land. The compound loomed dead ahead. I could see the fences, the runway, and the barracks, the place where most of the men would be sleeping.

I focused on the runway, though I couldn't help but see two armed guards step out of the shadows and away from the fence as we passed over. Even in that flash I could see they had rifles. We were low and exposed, but they weren't going to be shooting at us as we landed. Instead we'd be just as low and exposed as we took off—and then they'd be firing.

The wheels touched down and we bounced back up in the air wildly—I hadn't been focusing as much as I'd thought. I pushed the stick forward and worked the flaps to get us back down and create enough drag to keep us on the ground. We rolled along the pavement, and I applied the brakes and eased off the throttle on the whirring blades. I needed to slow us down and I also needed to travel enough of the runway so that we would have room to take off once I spun us around. It wasn't like I was going to get a second pass if I ran out of pavement.

We started to bounce. Off to the right were buildings: warehouses that could be holding vehicles, stocks, supplies, and certainly some guards. I wondered if they also held more prisoners, more slaves, as we'd found the first time we'd attacked their stronghold. I forced that thought out of my mind.

"We don't need to get much closer. Spin us around and get ready for takeoff!" Herb yelled.

I applied the brakes and we decelerated sharply. Herb worked to push open the door, fighting the wind from the prop. He nudged the bomb toward the door until it was hanging out, getting ready to drop. We slowed down to almost a stop as the barracks loomed in front of us. I saw two men holding weapons, moving toward us. I hit the right rudder and left brake to start our turn back up the runway, spinning us around in a tight circle so that the barracks disappeared and the open expanse of the runway came into view. At that instant, as we were barely moving forward, out of the corner of my eye I saw the bomb drop to the pavement. I braced for an explosion as Herb slammed the door shut.

"Go, go, go!" he screamed.

I goosed the gas and the engine roared. At first I drifted off the right edge of the runway and had to correct to bring us back in line, picking up speed.

"Thirty seconds!" Herb called out.

"I'm going as fast as I can!"

Over to the right, I could make out more guards lining the fence. I assumed they all were armed, but so far nobody had fired at us. I opened the throttle up full—faster and faster we raced along the runway until the wheels started to lift off. The end of the runway and the guards on the fence were still far away as I pulled back on the stick, trying to get as much elevation as possible as quickly as possible.

"Fifteen seconds!" Herb said.

The plane lifted up into the air, the ground disappearing from my view as I continued to pull back hard, gaining height and distance. Still nobody had shot at us, or at least hadn't come close enough for me to even know we were being fired at. Would I even hear gunfire over the roar of the engine? The motor screamed out in protest against what I was asking it to do. I banked hard to the left and, looking down, could see that the compound was behind us. We had gotten free.

"Why didn't they fire?" I screamed.

"Probably too confused. There was no time for anybody to give an order to open fire. We have to just be grateful."

"But the bomb . . . it hasn't gone off?"

"Not yet . . . seven . . . six . . . five . . ."

His count was slightly off. Suddenly a massive ball of

flames shot up into the air to my left and behind the plane. A plume of smoke followed, and then a shock wave hit the plane and we were bucked to the side. It felt like we had been pushed by a gigantic invisible hand, causing us to slide across the sky rather than flying across it. I struggled, banking into the direction of the slide, going with the force, and the plane came back under my control.

"What does it look like back there?" I yelled.

"I can't see much through the smoke, but it looks like it had the desired effect. There's going to be a crater in the runway big enough to drop a transport truck into," Herb answered. "I want to see how much damage was done. Can you bring us around in a circuit wide enough to avoid gunfire but close enough for me to use my binoculars?"

I banked to the right so that Herb would be on the inside of the turn with the compound visible out his window. As we started to come around I could see the smoke and fire spreading out and rising up.

"It's still hard to see, but I can tell there's a lot of damage. The whole front of the one barracks has been blown off, basically peeled away. We'll be able to tell more when we fly over tomorrow."

"You want to come back tomorrow?"

"We'll circle at the same distance as today. I'll be able to see things much more clearly, but there will be another goal. I want them to see us, to be afraid that we're going to attack again. I want them to think twice before they even consider attacking us. But I've seen enough for now. It's time to go home."

4

I pulled off the covers and got up from the couch. There was no point in even pretending to sleep. This was three nights in a row that I'd been awake. How long could I go on like this?

Thinking about my girlfriend, Lori—even being with Lori—wasn't enough to ease my mind or change my thoughts. I'd seen her a couple of times since the shooting and we'd talked about it a little bit, but she knew me well enough to know when I just needed some time to myself. Besides, she had her hands full helping her dad supervising the harvest all around the neighborhood.

I took the pistol off the coffee table and slipped it into the holster. The second gun was secured in an ankle holster. It had never been comfortable, trying to sleep with it digging into my leg, but now I thought I'd never be able to sleep again without it pressing against me. Rather than being a bother, it was a reassuring bump that calmed my mind. Thank goodness I'd had it on me that night Brett escaped.

I'd even added another level to my arsenal. On the inside of my other leg I had a knife, safely stashed in a sheath. It was only four inches long but would be effective and silent and deadly and was almost undetectable unless you were looking for it.

Then again, if I was losing it, was it really wise for me to be carrying around two guns and a knife? Should sleep-deprived, paranoid people be allowed around weapons?

The house was still and quiet.

Everybody is asleep—or dead.

What a terrible thought! But it was the sort I hadn't been able get out of my head since the kidnapping.

I'd check the doors and windows and then just poke my head into the bedrooms to make sure my family was all right.

I slid the table away from the door to the hallway and moved the desk so that I could open the door. I'd taken to spending the night in the living room, barricading the door at night.

My bedroom just triggered too many bad memories that made sleep impossible. It was hard enough to go in there even during the day.

In the living room, behind the barricaded door, I felt calmer. I couldn't afford to be worrying about anybody sneaking in on me. Not Brett, but not even my family. What if I shot one of them by accident?

I went to the door, then stopped and took out one of my guns before I pulled the door open. Pistol in hand, I crept down the hall; it was nearly sunrise, still dark but light enough to see to move around. I could tell there was nothing to be afraid of except for bumping into the hall table. I lowered the gun but kept it by my side.

In sequence I checked the front door, the windows, the side door, and then the sliding doors leading off the kitchen. All were securely locked, so there was no problem.

Unless somebody had come in and then locked them after they entered.

I knew that was nothing more than paranoia, but I had every right to be paranoid—it had only been three nights since I had been taken from my bed.

Now I could just go upstairs and check to make sure that my family was safe and sound . . . No, I wasn't going to give in to the paranoia.

I doubled back to the front door and went out, locking it behind me.

I was fully dressed—as always—and I was even leaving my shoes on now when I tried to sleep.

I walked out to the driveway to where my ultralight was tethered. Even though it was still early, I wasn't alone. Up at the intersection were two guards.

Not only were there more guards on our walls than before my kidnapping, but additional sentries were also positioned around the neighborhood each night. If Brett was still alive and decided to launch an attack or sneak in, we were planning to make it harder for him to get over the wall and hopefully impossible to move around if he did.

Everything of importance had been relocated within the neighborhood. The medical supplies, weapons, food stocks, and extra ammunition had all been moved. I told myself that was what I was doing by sleeping in the living room: relocating myself to a new position. In all honesty, though, it had more to do with my just not being able to sleep in my room.

I couldn't lie on my bed and close my eyes without feeling a presence in the room, Brett moving in the shadows, coming toward me, his hand on my throat and the cold metal pressed against my neck . . .

Not that I was any more comfortable in the Cessna—the scene of the crime. I'd flown it with Herb to bomb the compound, but that was it. My father had been the one to go with Herb the following day to see the damage.

Instead, I'd been going up in my ultralight. I always did like the ultralight more. I liked the wind in my face. It was so much better than being cooped up in the Cessna.

— I didn't mind flying on my own. It was an escape. Maybe I was being paranoid—maybe I had a right to be paranoid—but when I was with the twins at the playground or on harvest duty, it felt like everybody was staring at me, thinking, "That kid's a killer . . . What's he going to do next?" Those feelings were so strong that I'd been keeping more to myself, and I hadn't even gone to eat at the community dinner at the school the last couple of nights. Instead, Ernie or somebody had kindly arranged to have the meals brought to me at the house.

I heard an engine and spun to see a truck turn onto our street. As it closed in I saw Herb at the wheel. He pulled into his driveway and climbed out. In his hand was his sniper rifle. I knew he'd been out "hunting."

"Good morning!" Herb called out. "You're up early."

"Not as early as you."

"I went to the compound."

I knew that without him saying it. He'd gone out there the last two nights, doing recon and taking shots at the sentries there.

"There are two fewer of them this morning than there were last night," Herb said. "They're getting more careful."

"Was it just you?"

"I had backup. It's always good to have a couple of people watching you."

"Wouldn't it be better to have more than just a couple?"

"Smaller is quieter and more elusive. I don't want them to know when I'm out there so that they think I'm *always* out there," Herb explained.

"But you want them to see the Cessna above during the day."

"It's the same in a different way. I want them to always feel like they're being observed by us."

"Won't that just provoke them?" I asked.

"They don't have enough men to attack us outright anymore. Ideally, I'd like them to leave the compound, go away, as far as possible, and not even think about coming after us."

"What about us going after them?" I asked. "Have you thought any more about an attack on the compound?"

"They're expecting that now, so it's the last thing I want to do. We could defeat them, but the cost to us would be too great, too many fatalities and injuries. This will do for now." He paused. "I'd like it if you could take the Cessna up over the compound today."

"My father can do that."

"He's going to be busy. He and Howie are selecting the people to be part of the new away teams."

My father was going to be leading one of the teams. I didn't like it at all, but I couldn't argue with his logic— nobody had spent more time outside the neighborhood than he had. When the blackout hit, he'd been in Chicago and had had to make his way hundreds of miles back home on foot. He still hadn't really talked about what had happened to him on that trip.

"You need to get behind the controls again," Herb said.

"I've flown it once, and you know I've been up every day with the ultralight."

"Have you seen the social worker?" Herb said.

"Not yet."

"How have you been sleeping?"

"All right . . . you know . . . about the same as always."

"And have you been sleeping in your own bed?" Herb asked.

He probably already knew the answer to that question. Herb often asked questions when he already had the answers.

"Not always. You're not the only one who thinks he needs a safe room."

"And what does your mother think you should do?" Herb asked.

"You know that, too," I said.

"I know that it's standard procedure for a police officer to seek counseling after an episode involving violence, even if it is clearly a justified incident."

"I'll see her when I can," I said. "I've just been busy . . . flying the ultralight and helping with the harvest, and now you want me to take the Cessna up."

"I do want you to take me up again, but there's lots of time for that. Let's wait a day or two. How about if you find the time for a talk today? All right?"

I looked away. "Okay."

"Promise?"

I dragged my gaze back to Herb, who was looking at me with concern. "Do you want to do a pinky swear?" I joked.

"Just give me your word. I'll never need anything more than your word," Herb said.

I gave it to him.

It turned out that the social worker didn't have time for me until the following day.

After another crappy night, I made my way across the neighborhood to a little ranch-style house where the social worker, Maureen, lived.

Soon enough, I was settling into one chair in a little room she used as her office while she settled into another. I expected her to have a pen and pad to take notes, but she didn't.

"So, Adam, how are you doing today?" she asked.

"Fine. So fine I don't even know why I'm here."

"It sounds like this wasn't your idea to be here, that you don't want to be here."

"Does *anybody* ever *want* to be here?"

"I think many people want to be here to work out issues, but nobody wanted those issues to happen in the first place."

"I had no choice in what happened," I said.

"Many times people don't have a choice. Accidents happen."

"This wasn't an accident. It was deliberate. I did what I did, but you and everybody know that."

"I know what happened," Maureen said.

I laughed. "You'd be shocked what most people don't know anything about, including you."

"You're right. There are lots of things that happened that night that I probably know nothing about."

"Probably?" I questioned. "Definitely."

"Okay, things I definitely don't know about. I do know about the shooting, though." She paused. "It must have been difficult."

I shook my head. "It's easy to pull a trigger. Remarkably easy to take somebody else's life." I made my finger into a gun and pointed it at her. "Bang, bang . . . as easy as that." I let my hand drop. "Have you ever shot anybody?"

"No."

"Have you ever had anybody threaten to kill you?" I asked.

"No, although all of us have experienced that threat in some form over the past months."

"Some *form*, some vague threat from a distance. But having a knife pressed against your neck while you're sleeping in your bed, a gun aimed at your head, looking at the person who wants to kill you—that's all different," I snapped.

"I didn't mean to minimize what happened to you . . . I didn't know about all the details. I knew you were taken from your bed—at least I'd heard that. A lot of people see you as a hero."

"A hero, is that how they see me?" I laughed. "I killed those two men because I had to kill them or I would have been killed. That doesn't make me a hero, just desperate enough to do what I had to do."

"I seem to be saying a lot of things that are getting you upset. Maybe it would be helpful if you just told me what went down the other night."

In a quick burst I told her. It all sounded like a story I'd heard rather than something that had really happened to me.

"Do you have any more questions about it?" I asked.

"There are lots more questions to be asked and things to be discussed."

"And how will the two of us talking change anything that happened?"

"It's not going to change anything. It's just that sometimes it's good to talk about things, things you can't or don't want to talk to your family or friends about."

"Or girlfriend," I said. I knew there was a lot of it I couldn't tell Lori or anybody else, not even Herb.

"Or girlfriend." She paused. "But you can talk to me. Anything and everything we talk about stays right here inside these walls."

"Everything?"

"Everything. You have complete confidentiality."

I thought about the two men I had killed, and then thought further back to the scenes of carnage at Olde Burnham after the people living in that neighborhood had been attacked; those women and children coming out of the building who we'd almost killed by accident; the bridge being blown up and hundreds of men plunging to their deaths; the massacre on the street; the looks in the eyes of children walking by our neighborhood, children we couldn't help; the burned bodies at Tent Town; cries of pain, looks of fear, the smell of death, our bomb going off at the compound—all the images I couldn't get out of my mind. I thought about them and then I started to cry.

And that's when our conversation really began.

5

After my session with Maureen, I went back home and, to my surprise, actually fell asleep for an hour or so. Then I woke up to the sound of the twins' voices coming from downstairs, low murmurs at first, like they were trying to be quiet, then rising in volume until they were in a flat-out argument. I couldn't tell what they were arguing about. And then after a couple of door slams there was silence.

I sighed, and decided to go check out the Cessna.

Like everything else of strategic importance, the plane had been relocated to a new storage area. Using a couple of our lawn-mower-engine-powered go-carts, it had been ferried from the parking lot of the strip mall to the driveway of an abandoned house a few doors down from mine. This was much farther into the middle of the neighborhood, farther from the runway, and nowhere near where Brett thought it was stored.

Presuming he was still alive—I could only imagine the reception he'd received when he got to the compound.

I opened the door of the plane and inhaled. There was still an odor—the acrid scent of gunpowder—but it was much fainter. If I hadn't known what it was, maybe I wouldn't have even noticed it. The backseat had been scoured thoroughly by a cleaning crew. Again, if I hadn't been there for the gunfight I never would have suspected anything. Even the bullet holes had been patched up by Mr. Nicholas or one of the mechanics so they weren't as visible anymore. I reached over and touched one of the repairs. They'd done a great job. Some things could be patched over.

"Do you and your plane want to be alone?"

I spun around. It was Todd.

"The way you're fondling that machine makes me think Lori has reason to be jealous."

I laughed and took my hand off the fuselage.

"Not that I'm going to tell her," Todd went on. "You know we have the bro code to uphold, so I won't be telling Lori nothing about your abnormal sexual attraction to metal objects and how you—"

"Shut up or you won't be coming up with me."

"Is that because you want more *alone* time with the plane?"

"Always the funny guy," I said. "I wouldn't have asked if I didn't want you along."

"Because, while you are my best friend, I draw the line at getting involved in some sort of twisted three-way thing with you and your plane."

I pulled the door open. "Get into the backseat."

"The backseat? What sort of guy do you think I am? I've already told you I'm not interested in any kind of—"

"You're in the backseat because *he's* in the front seat." I gestured to Herb, who was coming toward us. "Unless you want to fight him for it."

"James Bond Senior there is almost four times as old as me,

and I'm twice as big as him, but there's no way in the world I would even *consider* getting into a fight with him." Todd hustled into the backseat and the whole plane shuddered lightly under his weight.

"Good afternoon for a sightseeing trip," I said to Herb as he neared the plane. There was no cloud and an almost unlimited horizon in all directions. "I hope you don't mind that I invited Todd along."

"No problem. It's a four-seater and, by chance, I also invited someone."

"Who?" I asked.

"Quinn."

"Quinn . . . the prisoner?" Todd asked.

"Yep."

Quinn had been a Division member before we'd taken him into custody. Before they attacked us, they'd attacked Olde Burnham. We'd heard the attack in the distance, but before we'd been able to do anything it was over. By the time we'd arrived all that remained were smoldering ruins and a few survivors who had remained hidden. Mostly what we found were the bodies of the residents they'd killed in battle and those they'd captured and then executed. It was then that we discovered how deadly, ruthless, and cruel our enemy could be.

Among the casualties had been Quinn. He had been shot by Olde Burnham's defenders and then left for dead by his supposed friends in the Division when they'd retreated. He'd been rushed back to our neighborhood, undergone an operation, and then received treatment that allowed him to live. Saving him hadn't been an act of kindness by Herb and the committee but rather a way to find out more information about our enemy. Ultimately that information had allowed us to survive.

Now Quinn, recovered, had become a member of our community. Many people still didn't trust him; but Herb did, and I decided that had to be good enough for me.

"We're going to be flying over the compound. Nobody knows better about what goes on down there than he does," Herb explained.

"Are you sure you can trust him?" Todd asked, voicing my own concern.

"I've trusted him enough to take him with me the last two nights when I went out on recon," Herb replied.

"I didn't know he was going out with you," I said.

"Your mother knows, and the committee agreed to it, although reluctantly."

"But isn't that dangerous? What if he ran away and tipped off his old friends somehow, or did something to you?" Todd asked.

"First off, we weren't alone."

"Howie had your back?" I asked.

"I made sure of it," Herb admitted. "I always take care. You know that. But, still, Quinn's been a very helpful resource."

"Really? How can you be sure he isn't sympathetic to them?" Todd asked.

"Sympathetic?" I asked.

"Sure, you're not the only one who can use big words."

"No fear of that," Herb said. "He hates the Division even more than we do."

"How can that be?" Todd asked.

"It's complicated," Herb replied.

"No, it isn't," I said. "It isn't just what they did to him but also what they made him do to others that's behind his hate."

Herb nodded ever so slightly. "We'll go as soon as he arrives."

A half hour later we were airborne.

At Herb's direction, we weren't going straight toward the compound. He wanted to check all major routes leading into the neighborhood just to make sure nothing was coming toward us as we were heading to the Division's home.

"I can see the hospital," Todd said. "Or what's left of it."

From this distance it really didn't look too bad. I'd been closer, though, and knew that parts had been set on fire. Some of the windows were smashed out, and there was no telling what the inside looked like.

"Judging from the security fence, there must be people living down there," Quinn observed.

All around the perimeter of the hospital grounds a primitive defensive wall had been constructed. It looked like it was made of scrap wood and metal, as well as overturned cars and a couple of ambulances. It didn't look very formidable even from this height, but any wall was better than no wall.

I had to assume two things—there were guards on the wall and there was something worth guarding down there. It might be simply where a group of people—a cluster of families— had come together to live and provide mutual protection. I could also see that some of the hospital's lawn had been turned into gardens that were now semi-harvested. The inhabitants were making a go of it, although definitely not on as a large scale as we were.

"It's good to see so many little communities springing up," Herb said.

"Good if they're on your side, bad if they're against you," Quinn commented.

"There are a lot of them, but I haven't seen any that would be large enough to hurt us or in any other way be threatening to us," Herb said. "Adam, from what you've seen from your flights, how many would you say there are?"

"I guess it depends on how you define them. You're right—there's none nearly as big as our neighborhood, but there are dozens and dozens that could have thirty or forty houses each, and hundreds smaller than that."

"People have either left, dug in, or died out," Quinn said.

"Died out?" Todd asked.

"Less than half the people who lived in this area before live here now," Herb commented.

"And the ones who aren't here anymore—they've all died?" Todd asked.

"Died or left," Herb said. "It's worse in the cities. Probably only twenty percent of the people in larger cities have stayed and survived."

"I guess we've seen a lot of the people from the cities walking by our walls," I said.

"But I've noticed a lot less people on the road now, you know, walking by," Todd said. "The guards on the wall say that now they're seeing the same people again and again, first going one way and then coming back the other way."

"Those are people living close by going about their daily business. Things have stabilized," Herb said.

"That makes it sound positive," I said.

"Not positive or negative, just neutral. And that's the best most people can hope for."

"Will it get better?" Todd asked.

"Not before it gets worse." Herb paused. "Winter will be hard. Food supplies will dwindle, sickness will spread. Simple things like flu and pneumonia without medication and treatment will result in high mortality rates."

"Should we be worried?" Todd asked.

"We have food, shelter, fuel, doctors and nurses, medical facilities, and enough medication to combat simple illnesses. We're as prepared as we can be," Herb said.

"But most people down there don't have those things," Todd said.

"Most are unprepared or underprepared. They're waiting for someone to save them."

"And that someone's not going to come, are they?" Todd asked.

"Probably not."

"They should be more worried about who else *might* come," Quinn said.

There was no need to say anything more. We all knew. Quinn had been part of it. I couldn't forget that. I didn't know if anybody could. I knew that certainly the survivors from the Olde Burnham community would never forget and probably never forgive.

"But I guess in some ways it's good that there are so many small communities out there," Quinn added.

"How do you figure that?" Todd asked.

"Predators go for the weakest. That's why I think they'll leave us alone," Quinn went on.

"Us?" I asked—and then suddenly felt bad for the tone of my voice.

"I guess that's how I think of it," Quinn said. "I'm not *them* anymore. I hope people in the neighborhood will eventually come to realize that."

"I have," Herb said.

"Thanks. I really appreciate that," Quinn said.

"And you're right. As sad and tragic as it sounds, the weakness of others makes us less vulnerable," Herb said.

"Maybe it would be better if we could help them become less vulnerable," I said.

"You know we aren't equipped to protect everybody," Herb said.

I wanted to argue, but I knew he was right. It wasn't like we could extend our walls. But still, could we do more?

"Can you please swing us down farther toward the lake?" Herb asked, pointing in the direction of the giant body of water twenty miles to our south.

"Of course. Do you see something?"

"It's got more to do with what I *want* to see. Do you know where the oil refinery is?"

"I know exactly where it is. It's at the bottom of Southdown Road, on the lake." I banked sharply to take us farther south, away from the direction of the compound and away from our neighborhood.

Quinn leaned over the seat. "We also knew about the oil refinery being there. That place was on the radar as a potential spot to hit."

"But you didn't get around to it," Herb said.

"There were closer and easier ways to get fuel than taking on the people there."

"Obviously, your recon knew that it was well defended," Herb said.

"I don't know how well defended the refinery is, but there's still enough fuel out there that's closer and completely undefended. Along with our Cessna flights, there were always recon groups out on the ground searching for targets," Quinn confirmed. "I guess we're doing the same thing here today."

"No, we're not!" I snapped. "We're not setting out to kill people!"

Everyone on the plane went silent.

"I guess I deserved that," Quinn said after a minute or so. "I'm sorry I offended you . . . You're the last person in the world I want to offend—after you saved my life and all."

Of course I hadn't saved his life—it was all part of an elaborate con to trick him into giving us information that he knew nothing about. I wondered whether I should tell him the truth about what happened, but then decided not to. It was good to have Quinn feeling indebted to me. Still, I felt lousy about my outburst.

"I'm the one who should apologize," I said. "I'm just . . . just edgy. It's not your fault. You probably saved my life, too."

"How do you figure that?" Quinn asked.

"If you hadn't helped us find out about Brett and his men, they probably would have been successful in taking the plane, and me with it, or killing me before we found out about them. I guess that makes us even."

I turned around in my seat, reached over, and offered him my hand. "Sorry . . . Friends?"

"I'd like that."

We shook.

We continued to fly until first the lake and then the refinery came into view. It was big, a tangled mess of pipes and towering metal superstructures. Catwalks and gigantic tanks all painted white surrounded it. I counted fifteen tanks, ranging in size from big to huge.

The complex took up almost as much acreage as our neighborhood. It had always been an eyesore, and people who lived around it had objected to the fumes. Now someone had planted crops between the tanks. The plants looked sickly and small, and I couldn't imagine how bad it would be to eat food grown in soil that was probably contaminated with petroleum and other pollutants. I guess it beat the alternative of not eating at all.

The refinery had always had high metal fences topped with barbed wire. Those remained, but they'd been reinforced in places with what looked like guard towers. I could make out the small figures of sentries, weapons in hand. I was sure they were all looking at us the same way we were looking at them. We were either a curiosity or a threat, but either way we were worthy of being watched.

"The refinery isn't working, is it?" Todd asked.

"Unlikely. A refinery requires massive amounts of electricity that would be far beyond the power produced by an emergency generator," Herb said. "But from this distance I don't see any noticeable damage, so perhaps it could be put back into operation if it had power."

"Then what's the value?" Todd asked.

"If the refinery was operating normally when the blackout

hit, then we can assume that one-third of the oil had already been converted to gasoline, one-third was in the process, and one-third was waiting to be refined."

"That means that five of those tanks are filled with gas," Todd said. "That's enough gas to fuel all the gas-guzzling old cars and trucks and go-carts and planes that we have running for years to come."

"Certainly a year or two," Herb said.

"So in there would be more than enough for what we would need?" I prodded.

Herb didn't answer right away. Did he think the blackout was going to last more than two years? I was almost afraid to ask that question, and certainly wasn't going to ask it in front of Todd. Besides, I knew that even if Herb thought that, he wouldn't say it. He always talked about how you couldn't give people more truth than they could handle. Already—just judging from the way the food was being rationed, the way wood was being harvested and stacked for fires—people had started to suspect that the blackout would last throughout the winter.

"We have enough gas to run our neighborhood vehicles, this plane, and your ultralight for the foreseeable future, but not forever," Herb finally answered. "As well as gas, that refinery is also a storage facility for propane. We can use propane."

"It would be nice to have a barbecue," Todd said.

"I was thinking more about the propane heaters that could be used to heat the greenhouses and prolong the growing season," Herb said.

"I hadn't thought of that," I said.

"Neither had I," Herb replied. "That's the thinking of

Mr. Nicholas and the other engineers. That's why we have the away teams searching for abandoned tanks."

"I wouldn't think they've had much luck," Quinn said.

"Not a lot. It's not just Todd looking for a way to cook," Herb answered.

"Maybe we could work out a deal with the people here at the refinery, you know, trading gas for things they might want, like food," I suggested.

"Do we have enough food to trade?" Todd asked.

"Ultimately, we might not have any choice," Herb said.

"You might even be able to trade them for those go-carts you've been making or medical treatment if they don't have a doctor," Quinn suggested. "There might be lots of things."

"We probably can think of something to trade to get fuel from them," Herb said. "And then we could trade that fuel with other communities for other things we need. It would basically be free trade at work."

"We could even partner with them the way we partnered with the Olde Burnham neighborhood," I said.

"We saw how that worked out," Todd said sarcastically.

Of course it hadn't worked out. They'd all been slaughtered, their valuables taken, women and children kidnapped and used as slaves—and we'd been powerless to do anything except see the aftereffects. We had been useless as their partners when it came down to the crunch. We'd avenged their deaths—but did that make it any better? Did it make them any less dead? I knew the answers to my questions, but still there was something right about what we'd done in the end.

"I think we will try to make contact with the refinery at some point," Herb said. "Better to have new friends than new enemies. I've seen enough. Let's head off before they decide we're a threat and take a shot at us."

I had been so interested looking down that I hadn't realized just how close and low we'd gotten. We were certainly within rifle range. I pulled back the stick to gain elevation and at the same time banked away from the refinery. I goosed the throttle to feed more fuel into the engine and compensate for the climb and bank.

Leveling off and coming out of the bank, I did some dead reckoning and aimed for a spot where the towers of the city were just poking above the horizon, dwarfed by the distance. I thought that line would take us pretty close to the compound.

As we flew I was more aware of the little communities that appeared beneath us. Repeatedly I altered our course to get a closer look at a patch of green—cultivated land—and the fences that surrounded it. Most often the fences seemed like they wouldn't so much stop invaders as let them know that perhaps there was something inside worth taking. It made me realize just how solid our defenses were, how much bigger and better prepared we were than most people—no, better prepared than *anybody* else.

I was able to use the roadways below to correct our flight path to take us toward the compound. It wasn't long until I could see it in the distance.

"How close do you want me to get?" I asked Herb.

"Close enough for them to definitely see us, but far enough away to avoid them taking potshots at us," he said.

I adjusted our course. If I was going to err, it would be on the side of safety. I pulled us into a slow bank around the compound, circling so that Herb and his binoculars were on the inside.

"So what do we do now?" Todd asked.

"What we're doing," I said. "We observe."

"And what do you see?" Todd asked Herb.

"Nothing, I'm seeing nothing."

"Do you want me to bring us in closer?"

"Make smaller and smaller circles until I tell you to pull out," Herb said.

Once again I adjusted our flight to get closer. At the same time I pulled slightly back on the stick. If we had to get close I wanted more height. Herb kept his eyes glued to the binoculars. I looked past him to the compound. I couldn't see any movement at all—no vehicles or people were visible to the naked eye.

"I think we need to fly right over the top, low and slow," Herb said.

"Is it smart to do that?"

"There's nothing to worry about. The compound is deserted. I'm pretty certain they've left again."

I hit the pedals and flaps and tightened up the bank until we were coming straight at the compound on the same approach I'd used to land. I pushed forward on the stick and brought us lower. "Are you sure there's nobody?" I asked.

"Nobody. They're gone."

As we swooped over, I could see that the grounds were deserted. There were no guards on the perimeter, no vehicles by the buildings, nothing. I could also see the damage that had been done by the bomb. The end of the runway was marked by a gigantic crater. There was still room to land or take off if necessary, but overshooting the landing would be fatal. The middle barracks looked to be completely destroyed, with its front gone and interior exposed like a dollhouse. Two other buildings were damaged as well but still seemed to be relatively intact.

"Where would they go?" Todd asked.

I turned around so that I could see Quinn out of the corner of my eye.

"I don't know," he said. "That's the only place I'd ever been since the lights went out."

"They could be anywhere," Herb said. "I'm assuming they moved to get away from us, so they are probably farther from us and closer to the city. Right now, though, there are more important issues at hand. Adam, get us back home right away."

I had a terrible thought. "Do you think they've gone to attack the neighborhood?"

"I think they would be fools to do that—and they're not fools. They're on the run," Herb said.

"But why are we rushing back to the neighborhood?"

"I want to get an away team together as soon as possible. We're going to go back to the compound and do what we should have done the first time. Rip it apart, burn it down, and make sure they never have a place to return to."

6

I handed Lori a tray and a plate and we joined the end of the line waiting to be served. We were part of the second supper shift—there would be about four hundred of us who were getting our turn to have dinner in the school gym.

It was the first time I'd been in here since the plane . . . since the shooting. Even though I just wanted to be alone, Lori and Todd had persuaded me to join them tonight and now Todd was nowhere to be seen. I was counting on having at least two friendly faces with me.

"It's good to see you," I said.

"Sorry it's not as romantic as it could be under normal circumstances," Lori said.

"Maybe not romantic but it *is* the best place in town, I guess."

"I think it's the only place in town."

"Which is the reason it's the best," I said. "What are the odds of there being a steak waiting for us at the end of the line?"

"Slim and none and slim has already been eaten. There will be potatoes and carrots, though," she offered.

"There are always potatoes and carrots. I'm tired of

potatoes and even more tired of carrots," I said, and then instantly felt guilty for complaining.

"Believe it or not, Dad is worried we're not going to yield enough potatoes in the coming months."

Lori's dad—as the only farmer in the neighborhood—was in charge of deciding what would be planted, harvested, and ultimately eaten, beyond what we could scavenge or procure from whatever stock still remained from the shelves of the grocery store.

"I guess I am impressed with all the ways that they've been making the potatoes," I said. "Boiled, mashed, baked, fried, and made into soup."

"I heard they're working on a special potato drink," Todd said as he came walking up from behind and gave me a slap on the back. "Drink your potatoes or you can't have potatoes for dessert."

A couple of people in the line in front of us turned and started laughing. Great. Encouragement was the last thing Todd ever needed.

"You could let us have yours if you don't want them," I said.

"I'm so hungry I'd eat your potatoes and her potatoes and lick the plates if you two would let me," Todd said.

"Gross," Lori said.

"I guess we should just feel lucky we have food to complain about," I said.

"I know. Even though I'm complaining, I'm not complaining," he said.

I was glad he said that. With so many people going hungry outside our walls, with the limitations we had feeding this many people, we all just had to be grateful for what we had instead of complaining about what we didn't have. I knew he was goofing around just like I had been, but complaining was contagious and we had to make sure not to get caught up in spreading it.

"What time do we leave tomorrow?" Lori asked.

"Early. It's always best to leave early," I said.

"But not as early as the away teams," Todd added.

Lori, along with Todd, was going up with me in the plane to provide eyes in the sky for the mission to the compound.

It hadn't taken long for the committee to agree with Herb's plan. They now seemed to see the wisdom in acting fast when he thought they should.

We came up to the first server—her name was Evelyn. She had been a cashier at the grocery store and now she worked as part of the team under the former store manager, Ernie Williams, helping to cook and serve the communal suppers that took place every night.

She greeted each of us by name. Almost everybody knew everybody else nowadays, if not by name then by sight.

One by one, we held out our trays. No surprise, as she gave each of us small portions of stewed greens and mashed potatoes on our plates. But none of us complained, not even my jokey friend.

The committee had heard lots of reports about people hassling the servers and kitchen staff, demanding more food or saying they were being given less than they should be, and even blaming them for the shortages. Hungry people could sometimes be less than reasonable, and most people here were at least a little hungry most of the time.

"Thanks so much," Lori said with a smile.

"I wish I could give more to everybody," Evelyn said.

"I guess it can be hard sometimes, dealing with all the complaints," I said.

Evelyn shrugged. "It's nothing compared to the people who have to go outside the walls. Here it's just words I have to dodge, but out there it's other things. Adam, you'll be out tomorrow, right?"

I nodded.

"And you two?"

"All three of us," Todd said.

"Well, I'll say a special prayer for each of you tonight."

"We appreciate the thought almost as much as the food," Lori said.

My attention was caught by raised voices. I turned and scanned the room to try to find the source. There were just people sitting at tables eating—and then two guys at a table in the far corner jumped to their feet and began yelling at each other even more loudly.

Somebody was going to have to do something. Arguments could quickly become fights, and with all the weapons floating around, those fights always had the potential to turn deadly. I looked around for my mother or father or Herb or Howie, but they were nowhere to be seen. Did that mean I had to do something?

Just then, out of nowhere, Ernie came running across the gym. That was a relief. Ernie could take care of it. This was his part of the world and he was in charge.

In a moment, Ernie inserted himself between the two men.

I knew both of the guys—Kevin and Paul. Kevin lived two streets over from me, and Paul and his wife and kids had been invited into the neighborhood because he was a mechanic and his skills were needed. They both were okay people, so I was sure Ernie would be able to sort it out.

I looked around the room. Nobody was eating and everybody seemed to be looking and listening—in fact there was now more to listen to. The separation, with Ernie between them, hadn't settled them down, but instead they were yelling louder and the tone was angrier. This was the worst possible place for something to happen.

"Todd, I think we should— "

"Already ahead of you."

He had put his tray down on the counter and both Lori and I did the same.

"I'm going to go see if I can find somebody to help," Lori said, and she took off at a run out of the gym.

Todd and I moved quickly toward the fighters. We got there just as one of them shoved Ernie and he tumbled over to the side. I jumped in between and one of them swung and caught me by surprise, hitting me on the side of the head, sending me flying off my feet and sprawling against a table, then smashing onto the floor.

I spun around in time to see Todd and another man tackle the two fighters and knock both of them to the ground. Kevin tried to get free but Todd had him wrapped in a bear hug, locking his arms in place. A third and a fourth person got involved until there was no way either man could fight back. I looked up, staring at them, and realized that my right hand was on my gun and—

"Both of you settle down now!" It was Howie, rushing in the doorway, followed by an out-of-breath Lori.

Both men seemed to ease off, almost relax, although each was still held in place by two sets of arms. Howie hustled over and then stood there scowling. He was now the captain of the guards, but I could see the former policeman in him glowering at them. It didn't hurt that he was such a large, imposing figure. Todd was big but Howie was huge.

"Let them go," Howie ordered.

There was a hesitation but the two men were released. They didn't fight. In fact they appeared to be embarrassed. They both looked down at the floor. The entire gym was silent, all eyes staring at them.

Slowly, so nobody would notice, I took my hand from my gun. What was I planning on doing, drawing my gun and shooting them? I got to my feet, my jaw aching a bit, and I felt embarrassed to be knocked down in front of everybody.

"What was this all about? . . . No, wait, I don't want to hear it. Not here." Howie pointed at the door. "Come with me . . . And who are my witnesses?"

"I saw it all," Ernie said. "Me and Todd and Adam."

"Yeah, we saw it all," Todd said. He turned to me. "You okay?"

"Fine, good, no problem."

"Ernie, why don't you and Lori stay here and take care of things? Todd and Adam, come along with us." Howie looked around the room at everybody who was now looking at him. "All right, folks, the show is over!" he called.

Some of the people turned away or started to eat again. For others, the attraction was still too strong and they continued to stare.

Howie gestured for us to follow and then started walking. Todd fell in right beside him, and Kevin and Paul followed—two men who had just been in a fistfight, two men who were both undoubtedly carrying weapons. And Howie's back was turned away from them. Once again I put my hand back on my gun as I trailed behind them. This time I didn't care who saw it or what they thought of me.

Paul suddenly turned around to face me. "Sorry, Adam, I didn't know it was you. I didn't mean to hit you."

"It's okay," I said. "No harm, no foul."

"I'm still sorry. You're the last person I ever wanted to take a swing at."

Was he saying that because of what I'd done to Tim and Owen or—

"If it wasn't for you, me and my family wouldn't have been invited into the neighborhood to begin with."

I thought back to that day, months before, and a chance meeting on Erin Mills, when I'd found out he was a mechanic—one of the skilled people we were looking for—and had invited him in for a meal. We'd eaten together, right here in this gym.

"Of all people, you didn't deserve that," he said. "I hope you can accept my apology."

"No need for another word," I said. "Just glad you're here with us."

We left the gym, but there was no more privacy. There was a crowd of people milling around outside, waiting for their turn to eat. Howie continued into the school yard and we walked between the rows of the cornfield, which had replaced the soccer field. Finally, with some distance and cover provided by the stalks, we stopped in the middle of the field.

"So spill it, what was this about?" Howie demanded.

"Nothing," Kevin mumbled.

"Nothing? You got into a fistfight over nothing?" Howie questioned.

"It was nothing that wasn't stupid," Paul said. "Just a disagreement about a stupid card game that got out of hand."

"Stupid or not, I need you both to give me your weapons."

They looked like they wanted to argue but neither did. One removed a pistol, and the other a long knife. Both handed their weapons to Howie. I felt better knowing they weren't armed anymore.

"What happens to us now?" Paul asked.

"You're relieved of duty until you go before Judge Roberts," Howie explained.

The judge—who was also on the committee—was in charge of a weekly proceeding that dealt with all internal disputes and arguments. It was just natural that sixteen hundred people living in close quarters, under terrible threats and worries, including people who had suffered great losses, would have disagreements. It always got worse when something important—like the away team going out tomorrow—was about to happen. It was crucial not to let things brew or get out of hand. With so many weapons in so many hands, it would be easy enough for an argument to become a fistfight to become an armed battle. Could those two have drawn weapons? Could I have drawn mine?

"But what happens for us tomorrow?" Paul said. "We're both part of the away team."

"We were even hoping to be in the same vehicle," Kevin said.

"Yeah, I could see how the two of you would really be able to back each other up," Howie said.

"I'd give up my life for this guy," Paul said.

"And I'd do the same for him," Kevin added.

Somehow that didn't surprise me.

"That's what I like to hear," Howie said. "Still, you're not going anywhere until there's a hearing, and that won't be happening tonight."

"Maybe it could," I said.

They all looked at me.

"How about if I talk to Herb and my mother and ask them to arrange things with the judge for a special hearing?"

"Could you do that?" Paul asked.

"I'll go and talk to them," I said.

"Of course, they might just decide that neither of you is fit enough to go out tomorrow," Howie added.

"We'll convince them," Kevin said.

"We have to," Paul added. "Our team needs us to be there."

"I know you'll try. Maybe the best place to start is with a handshake."

The two men shook hands and then gave each other a big hug.

As we got ready to look for my mom, I asked Todd to go and say goodnight to Lori for me. As he walked off I remembered something and called his name.

He stopped and turned around. "What?"

"You can have my potatoes tonight," I said.

7

The convoy set out at first light. There were fifteen vehicles loaded with armed personnel, including both Kevin and Paul. The judge had cleared them to participate and they were both grateful and thankful to be going out. They'd even been assigned to the same vehicle, along with my father. He was going to keep an eye on them just in case. His being there was a precaution, but Herb had infected us all with a need for precaution and backup plans.

Herb was leading the team, while Howie and my mother were remaining in charge of security at the neighborhood. Every person who wasn't helping with the harvest was either on the wall or out with the away team. While Herb didn't think there would be an attack on us, he didn't want to take any chances.

I'd given them an hour's head start before I went after them in the Cessna. I'd watch their advance and do a final pass over the compound to make sure it was still deserted. I had two people in the plane with me—Todd in the backseat with binoculars, and Lori riding shotgun beside me. In this case perhaps "shotgun" wasn't the right term. On Lori's lap was a high-powered hunting rifle. She was by far a better shot than either Todd or me, and it was good to have her along in more ways than one.

We moved so much faster than the cars on the ground, of course, that I couldn't just stay above them but instead made sweeping passes. It was a delicate balance to watch over our assault team without drawing attention to them. Anybody anywhere below could see us in the sky much more easily than we could see them on the ground. Watching the plane would give anybody who was interested in knowing some indication of the progress of the convoy.

I couldn't help but think about those men they were chasing away. They were cruel, merciless killers, but they weren't fools. They were trained, some of them ex-military, and they knew about recon, ambush tactics, and hand-to-hand fighting, so they'd know how to set a trap. I wondered if Brett was alive. If he was with them, was he helping them understand us, advising them about our strengths and weaknesses?

"I don't see anything dangerous," Todd said over his headset.

He'd been taking his job seriously, eyes glued to the binoculars, scanning the ground below.

"It's good to have you both along," I said.

"It's good to be *anywhere* with you these days," Lori said.

Todd spoke as he continued to scan the roads ahead of us. "I think what she's saying is that she hasn't seen enough of you lately."

"Thanks for the translation," I said to Todd.

"Hey, no problem. You know that I understand the female mind in a way that is almost scary."

"I guess that explains your phenomenally long relationships."

"Perhaps it does. I was aware enough of what they were thinking that I knew it was time for us to break up," he joked. "You should listen to me."

"The day I take advice from you is the day—"

"Maybe you *should* listen. Todd was right about the first thing he said." Lori turned around in her seat. "Well, tell him more."

I wasn't sure I liked where this was going. No, I was positive I didn't like it.

Todd waded in. "Lori is probably thinking that you're thinking about breaking up with her."

"I've never had that thought!" I protested.

"He didn't say you were thinking it. He said that I was thinking that's what you were thinking," she said.

"Really?" I asked.

She shrugged.

"I just figure if two people were dating, they'd occasionally see each other, that's all," she said.

"We almost had dinner together last night," I said.

"You two, and me, and ten thousand other people including two guys who got into a fistfight," Todd said. "That hardly constitutes you two having time together."

"The boy is right again," Lori said.

"It's just that I'm busy."

"We're *all* busy," Todd chimed in from the backseat. "Maybe she thinks you need to see her, spend a little time, help her not be so worried about you."

"She's worried about me?" I turned to Lori. "You're worried about me?"

She nodded.

"We're all worried about you," Todd said. "Even when you're there, you're not really *there*."

"What does that mean?" I demanded.

"You're lost in thought," Lori said.

"We know how bad it was," Todd said, looking my way.

"No, you have no freaking idea!" I snapped, and instantly felt awful. "Sorry . . . you're right. There are too many thoughts in my head."

"Well, that's your problem right there," Todd said. "Me, I try to keep my head completely empty almost all the time. I have almost *no* thoughts."

There was welcome and necessary laughter.

"And I must say you seem very successful at that," I said.

"That's better. That actually sounded a lot like you. And thank you for the compliment and recognizing my success. Buddhist monks and Hindu yogis spent their whole life trying to meditate to reach a state of nothingness, and I can do that anytime I want."

"Very impressive, but I've never thought of you as either Buddhist or monk-like, although you do remind me a bit of Yogi Bear."

"A high compliment. That bear always did get the picnic basket. *Namaste*," Todd said as he brought his hands together and did a slight bow from the waist.

I laughed even louder. Todd was good for my soul.

"Now back to what we were saying—or more precisely, what Lori is thinking," Todd said. "Tonight you need to go home, get cleaned up, and spend some quality time with that poor, neglected girl."

"She is definitely feeling neglected," Lori said.

"I wonder if she would like that?" I wondered aloud.

"Of all the hardships this blackout has caused, this may be the worst: a girlfriend has to be asked if she'd like to spend time with her boyfriend?"

I nodded. "Okay, you're right . . . I will."

"Good boy—and try to be happy, say nice things, compliment her, tell her she's smart and pretty, and that you love being around her," Todd added. "And have some fun."

"I could do fun."

"You can try, although serious has always been more your strength than fun has. Tell you what—how about if we make it a double date?"

"Who would you bring?" I asked.

"I'll figure that out when we get back on the ground. There are many lovely ladies who would practically kill for a chance to spend some time with the Toddster."

"You are delusional, you know that, right?"

"It's what keeps me going. Look around our little world. Isn't a little delusion a good thing?"

That was hard to argue with.

"Then it's a date. But first things first: How long before our people get to the compound?" Todd asked.

"Twenty minutes, so it's time for us to make our pass over it."

"Are you sure we shouldn't wait until they're closer?" Todd asked.

"We need to make sure it's clear before they arrive. Don't worry. My first pass is going to be high and wide, and then I'll make smaller circuits. If I see anything—or if either of *you* see anything suspicious—then I'll pull up and we warn the away team."

I came straight at the compound. I was going to make my first pass right through the middle but at a height that would provide some protection from gunfire.

Suddenly, I had a vision of Brett down below with a sniper rifle, taking aim at the plane. I hit the left pedal and right flap, and pushed down on the stick all at once and we dropped and zagged to the right.

The g-force from the maneuver was pretty intense.

"What's happening?" Todd screamed with his face smushed against the window. "Are we crashing?"

"Sorry. We're okay . . . I was just taking evasive action."

"Um, what are we evading?" Lori asked.

"I think I was just imagining it. Sorry. I should have warned you."

Todd seemed beyond scared and Lori looked pretty unfazed. And just plain pretty.

"Although, Todd, I must admit that scream of yours was at least a little bit amusing," I said.

"If I crapped my pants, you probably would have thought it was hilarious. Just let me know when you're going to do that again," Todd said.

"Roger. Now, could you both keep looking out the window?"

The compound was now just below. There were no vehicles visible and no motion that I could make out. That didn't mean there weren't a hundred men hiding in the buildings, weapons ready for us to appear.

We did a full circuit.

"Okay, I'm going to bank sharply and dip lower," I said.

"I appreciate the warning, captain," Todd said. "Was that so hard?"

Coming back around again, I felt comfortable enough

to bring us in much lower and slower to give us a longer look.

"Well?" I asked.

"I can't see anything that we need to be scared of," Todd said.

"Me neither," Lori said. "Should we let them know it's okay?"

"No. We're maintaining radio silence, so unless there's a reason to warn them, we say nothing. They know that. I'll keep circling, and you two keep your eyes wide open."

Satisfied that the compound was safe, I broke from the bank and aimed back toward the convoy. I'd shadow them all the way in now.

An hour later, the compound was alive with movement. Our convoy had arrived and seized control of the area. We had placed guards all along the fence, weapons aimed out beyond the perimeter, as well as guards by each building. Trouble could still come from any direction.

I brought the Cessna in from the north. The strip was shorter now, with the southern end cratered from the bomb, so I reduced my speed dramatically, coming in just above stall speed, and low. We cleared the fence and the two sentries gave us an encouraging wave. The wheels touched down and I hit the brakes hard until I had us under control again.

As we rolled up toward the edge of the crater, I hit the pedals and flaps, goosed the engine, and turned the plane back around, ready to take off again.

"I just like to be ready," I explained as I cut the motor.

"No arguments from me," Todd said.

We undid our harnesses, took off our headsets, and climbed out. All around us, people were at work. The chain-link fences were being taken down, rolled up, and stacked onto the back of the trucks. Other walls were being torn down, the rocks and bricks scattered and wooden portions set on fire. A ring of flames was starting to encircle the compound.

The buildings were being systematically searched. Any valuables were removed and loaded on the trucks. So far I didn't know what had been found, but I was certain what hadn't: prisoners.

The last time they deserted the compound the members of the Division had left behind dozens of women and children, captured prisoners who had been virtual slaves. We took them into our neighborhood, offering them not just freedom but also the safety and support of our neighborhood. They were now part of us, working and living among us, but I could still tell some of them just from the look in their eyes. I knew they would never get over what had been done to them. I wasn't sure if I'd ever get over just seeing it. I understood desperation could make people do desperate things. What I didn't understand was cruelty, or evil. What the Division had done to those people was pure evil.

Todd and Lori had wandered off to join some of our people—friends of ours from school—who were trying to set fire to the barracks. With the one building it seemed like overkill to me, since the front wall had already been peeled off by the explosion.

I looked around at the chaos that surrounded me. Men

armed with guns, others with axes and sledgehammers, and still others holding torches—we looked like a mob chasing after Frankenstein's monster.

Off at the side, all by himself, stood Quinn. I hesitated for a second and then went to join him. It was as if he was in a trance, staring into space, so lost that he didn't even notice me arrive. When I got closer I realized he was crying, tears rolling silently down his cheek. I felt embarrassed for him and for me, and wondered if I should just walk away and give him his privacy. Then he looked at me and I had to stay.

"Are you all right?" I asked.

He shook his head. "I don't think I ever will be all right . . . It's so strange being here again."

"It's strange for all of us."

"Not the same way. I lived here. I was part of this, this . . . *evil*."

That was the word that had just been in my own mind. "They forced you—you told us that," I said.

"That was a lie, mostly to myself, to allow me to live with what I did." He paused. "I'm as bad as anybody who was here. Maybe worse because in my heart I knew better."

"And you're working to make up for what happened."

"I'm trying, but I don't think I can ever really make it up."

"I'm going to leave soon. Do you want to come back with me and Lori and Todd in the plane?"

"Thanks for the offer, but I have to stay," Quinn said. "I'm going to make sure that not one rock is still piled on top of another before I go. I can't change the past, but I can make sure it isn't repeated."

I put my hand on his shoulder. "Don't sell yourself short. You're a better person than you think you are."

Suddenly he threw his arms around me. That wasn't the effect I thought my lame comment would have. He held on to me tightly and started sobbing again as I stood there feeling awkward and strange.

8

Once the compound had been destroyed,
we tried to resume our regular life back in the neighborhood.
And that meant organizing and attending a mass funeral for
the five guards who had been killed by Brett's men.

It had taken a few days for all the outside issues to be
dealt with, the arrangements to be made, but now all the
families were satisfied and the bodies were going to be put
to rest. Once again we were going outside the neighborhood
to bury them. We'd established a cemetery close to the
back gate.

The procession was gigantic. Five sets of pallbearers carrying five coffins. Everybody in the neighborhood who wasn't
on the walls was here to pay their last respects. Of course,
everybody knew the guards because now everybody pretty
much knew everybody else, but it was even more personal
than that. For a time we'd gotten to the point where we
thought of ourselves as being safe within these walls. They
were strong and guarded, and we'd even withstood attacks
from outside forces. Now these deaths had happened within
our walls—and worse still, they had come at the hands of our
own people who had betrayed us when they'd joined Brett.
There was no place that felt completely safe, now that we

knew there was always the danger that even trusted people could betray us.

My mother and Howie were at the front of the procession along with the rest of the committee, just behind the families themselves. My father and others from the away team had taken up positions all around the burial site, providing some security. Herb was stationed at the top of the underpass, scoped rifle in hand, surveying all that he could see. It probably would have been good for me to be up in the air, but nobody had made that suggestion and I was tired of flying—a thought I never would have expected to have. Maybe I was just plain tired.

It seemed only natural that my eye followed the perimeter fence, checking on the guards, looking for trouble. I'd gotten to the point where I couldn't turn off my paranoid mental radar. I couldn't help but see Brett hidden behind every tree.

Then I saw Dr. Morgan off to the side. The spot he'd picked was well chosen. He was close enough to see, but far away enough to have a level of detachment. I'd assumed he'd be here like everybody else, but why was he off on his own? There was only one way to find out. I moved around the procession until I was at his side.

"Mind if I join you?" I asked.

"The company is appreciated."

We stood in silence watching as the funeral unfolded in front of us. There were five caskets, five families, a minister and a priest, and from what I estimated over five hundred people in the procession. From this distance it was less upsetting—just like when I was up in the air, I was more a witness than a participant.

"I'm happy not to get any closer than this," I said.

"Most people don't want to be too close to death. And, funnily enough, being a doctor isn't always helpful. Sometimes people get angry at you because they feel like you should have saved the life of their loved one."

"I guess. Maybe in the case of an illness," I said. "But the guards were dead before you even knew they'd been shot. This has nothing to do with you."

"I know. It's not about logic, just gut feelings. My own included. In some ways you think you could have done more, that you are responsible." He paused. "I guess you'd know what that feels like."

Of course I did. This was my second set of funerals today. There had already been one early this morning for Tim and Owen, the two men I'd killed. It was quiet, just a few people and members of the committee. Neither of the dead men had family in the neighborhood, thank goodness. I didn't know how I could have faced family members. It was bad enough that people knew them—that I knew them—and that they had some friends who still lived here.

Not that anybody was blaming me. Most people had tiptoed around the whole thing, not saying anything to me at all. Still, I knew what the doc was saying. What was the proper protocol for showing respect? Was the person who killed them supposed to be there at the burial or stay away? I just knew that I needed to be there, to see things to the finish. I'd killed them, so I needed to be there to the end.

"So how are you sleeping these days?" Dr. Morgan asked.

I glanced up at him.

"My guess is that you are having trouble sleeping."

"Trouble doesn't describe it."

"Come and see me. I can prescribe something to help with that."

I shook my head. "I can't do that. I have to be alert to fly."

"And how does not sleeping make you more alert?" Dr. Morgan asked.

He had a point, but I didn't want to take medication. "I'm meeting with Maureen, the social worker." At least I'd met with her once. "I think it's helping."

"Good. A strong man knows when he needs help."

I didn't feel strong, but I did feel like a man—a very old man.

"Maureen is good at what she does. I see her myself," Dr. Morgan said.

"You?"

"It's good for all of us to have somebody to talk to. There have been things I've had to go through that have shaken me."

Hearing him say that meant something. I really did respect him. Maybe I should schedule in a second session with Maureen. It couldn't hurt.

A loud electronic squawking made me jump. Dr. Morgan reached into his pocket and pulled out a walkie-talkie.

"It's coming!" the voice called out. "Sooner than we thought. She's almost fully dilated."

"I hear you. I'll get there as quickly as possible." He put away the walkie-talkie.

"What is it?" I asked anxiously.

"That was one of the nurses. A baby is on its way, and it sounds like it's in a hurry to get here. The house is over on the far side of the neighborhood, so I've got to hustle."

"My car is in my driveway, close by. I can take you," I offered.

"That would help."

We started off for my Omega. I was glad to help and grateful to get away from the funeral. There were enough people offering support that they didn't need me.

We walked along the creek, up the embankment, away from the crowd, and in through the gates. The guards, grim-faced and watching the procession in the distance, hardly paid any attention as we passed.

An enemy couldn't pick a better time to attack us, I thought.

Dr. Morgan was now moving so fast that I had trouble keeping up with him. We got to my house and jumped into the car. For the first time in a while I wondered if it was going to start, and I was pleased when it roared to life. It made me smile. I'd loved this car since the first day I got behind the wheel. It had been my grandfather's car and it always reminded me of him. I'd been ignoring it in favor of my ultralight and now the Cessna, but it was always going to be my first love— or, well, second love, after Lori.

I had kept our date a few nights ago. It hadn't been my best moment, but doubling with Todd and his date had made it better. Todd always had a way of killing off silence like it was a mortal enemy, and this new girl—Ashley— was still at the point where she was infatuated with him. I told him he better treat her well because it wasn't as if there were an unlimited number of girls either inside or outside the neighborhood for him to date. As it was, she was probably better than he deserved. And I knew that from my own experience—Lori was definitely better than I deserved.

I'd taken Todd's suggestion and gotten her flowers—a little bunch of purple asters that were growing just outside the neighborhood walls. She gave me back a smile that was unbelievable. It made me think I'd have to listen to more of Todd's dating advice. Before this I always thought that doing the opposite of what he suggested had a better chance of working.

"What street are we heading to?" I asked Dr. Morgan as I brought my mind back to the present and threw the car in gear.

"Drive up to Plowshare."

I bumped out of the driveway and we raced off. The street was completely deserted. We went by little front-yard plots that were either lush with produce or bare, having already been harvested. The final totals weren't in yet, but it looked like we'd produced far more food than was estimated. That hadn't been officially announced, but when it was there would also be an increase in daily food quotas and an increase in morale. People needed something good to think about.

We rolled onto the street, and I was going to ask which house it was, when it became obvious—there was a woman standing on the lawn of a townhouse waving for us.

"There's my nurse," the doctor said.

I skidded to a stop.

"Good luck," I said.

"Stick around in case I need you and your wheels."

He jumped out and I turned off the car. I could certainly provide wheels, but I couldn't imagine what else I'd be able to offer in the way of help.

It was especially quiet out on the street, with so many people at the funeral. In a birch tree by the driveway I noticed a dark bird sitting on a low branch. I could hear its plaintive song but didn't notice any answering chirp from another bird.

I closed my eyes and drifted off for a while. Sleep often was easier in any place other than my bed. A loud, piercing scream brought me awake in a flash. I jumped out of the car and headed up to the house. There was a brief silence followed by a second scream, even louder. I decided against going any farther.

I slumped down on the front porch as the screams continued, louder and louder until . . . silence. Even the bird was long gone.

I held my breath, waiting, wondering what was happening. This couldn't be good, could it?

Then there was a cry—a baby's cry! It was loud and strong, and I felt a rush of joy, along with a sense of relief.

I took a couple of deep breaths. At the sound of footsteps, I struggled to my feet.

Dr. Morgan opened the door. His jacket was off and his sleeves were rolled up.

"Everything okay?" I asked.

"Better than okay. It's perfect. Both mother and child are doing fine. Do you want to see them?"

"Could I?"

"Come on in."

I followed him through the townhouse and into a back room. The mother was in bed, another woman—the nurse—at her side and her newborn bundled in her arms.

"Could my friend Adam here see your baby?" Dr. Morgan asked.

She nodded and smiled. She looked exhausted yet happy. She peeled back the blanket to reveal the baby's face. The baby was wrinkled and bluish, and the head looked strange, sort of pointed.

"It's a boy," Dr. Morgan said. "I don't imagine you've ever seen a newborn."

"I saw Rachel and Danny when they were a couple of hours old, but that was a long time ago."

"Would you like to hold him?" the mother asked.

I shook my head. "I'm not sure . . . I'm afraid I might drop him."

"You won't. I trust you."

She held him out, and I took the little bundle of baby and blanket into my arms. He was so small and light it was like holding air. Very valuable air.

"This is such a blessing," Dr. Morgan said. "Not just for you, but for all of us who live here."

I knew what he was talking about. The whole neighborhood would be happy. A previous baby had died at birth. The last thing people needed was another tragedy, especially today. This was a miracle and I was holding it in my arms.

"Have you decided on a name?" Dr. Morgan asked.

"Joseph, after his father," the new mother said. "I just wish he could have been here."

There were lots of reasons the father might not have been here, and none of them were good.

"Her husband was away on a business trip when the blackout started," Dr. Morgan explained.

"I'm sure he's still trying to get back home," I said.

Her eyes filled with tears. "I just wish I could have been there at the funeral for those guards today," she said. "My heart goes out to anybody who has lost somebody they care about."

"You were there in spirit," he said.

She started to cry. "Were there lots of people there?"

"Pretty much the whole neighborhood except for the guards on the walls and the people who needed to help you have your baby," Dr. Morgan said.

"I'm grateful for everything you did."

"It was my pleasure. This is the best thing a doctor can be part of."

I looked down at the baby in my arms. His eyes were tightly closed. He couldn't know anything about the world he'd come into. Someday when he was old enough his mother would tell him about how he was born on the day when we buried five brave men who died defending our neighborhood, protecting him, providing for his future. His own father wasn't here any longer to do that. And probably wasn't ever coming home. But the rest of us were here. I felt such a rush, an urge, a need to take care of this baby and make sure no harm came to him.

He started to wiggle in my arms, his legs thrashing, and he began to cry.

"Don't worry, Joseph," I said. "We're all here to take care of you."

Gently I handed him to his mother and the crying stopped. Somehow he knew he was safe. I had to be part of making sure that he always would be.

9

It felt strange to be back home after attending the mass funeral and then holding the newborn Joseph, as if I should be doing something more than simply getting ready for another date with Lori. But my mother had insisted that we all come home and spend time together—we had even sat down together at the table, listening to the twins chatter about their day, about how the harvesting was going. Now the twins were playing a board game together by candlelight at the kitchen table—something that had become a regular evening ritual for them—and my parents and Herb were in the dining room, talking.

I glanced at my watch. I was supposed to drop by Lori's place in fifteen minutes; she and I were going to go to the movie showing in the school gym. It was an old movie, one I'd seen half a dozen times and didn't even particularly like, but it was the only show around. Besides, being with her would more than compensate for what we were going to watch.

I could hear the murmur of the adults' voices, but I made a point of not listening to what they were talking about. Less information was sometimes better. I needed my mind to be more quiet.

I popped my head into the room. "I have to go," I said.

"Just remember, you have an early flight tomorrow," my father said. "Unless you want me to take it for you?"

"I won't be out late, but thanks."

My mother gave me a little hug. "Just be safe."

"We're going to a movie, not on a mission."

"Do you want company?" Herb asked.

"On the flight?"

"On your walk."

"Actually, I'm going to the Petersons' house, to meet Lori, and then we're off to the movie."

Herb laughed. "So you'd rather spend time with your girl-friend than with me?"

"I guess you could go to the movie with us if you want . . ."
What was I saying?

To my relief, he laughed again. "How about if I walk with you for just a bit, and then I'll go off on my own?"

"Sure."

Herb and I stepped out of the pool of lantern light that shone from our front porch and headed into the growing darkness of the night. The sun had just gone down, but there was still some light reflecting over the horizon. Soon darkness would reign, though, the way it did almost everywhere inside the walls once the sun set each day. Generators were few and far between, and most often were used for something that had an important purpose to the neighborhood—the clinic, the warehouse, the community room at the school. Even Herb and my mom didn't run their shared generator very often. It was only at the grocery store where one was running full-time, to keep the freezers working. And that wouldn't even be needed much longer, since our stock of frozen meat was down to almost nothing. Hunting and fishing expeditions were proving less and less fruitful. It wouldn't be long until we were all mostly involuntary vegetarians.

Herb scanned up and down the street. "Nice night," he said.

"I guess. Though I could do with some light and noise and traffic."

Herb laughed. "Do you ever think that all of this was because of you?"

"All of what?"

"This," he said, gesturing around with both hands. "Your neighbors being safe and sound."

"I've helped, but everyone else has, too."

"You were the one who suggested we band together in the first place, Adam. Without your suggestion this neighborhood would have been abandoned. A lot of the people living here don't even know lives were saved by you."

"Saved by all of us working together, maybe, but mainly it was you. My idea without your execution would have been nothing."

"No, you have it backward. My ability to execute without your idea would have meant nothing. Regardless, we've created something special."

It *was* special. We were an island of calm in a sea of chaos. I had no way of knowing what was happening farther away, but in the area I had been able to see from flying around, I knew that our neighborhood was a small sliver of civilization in a land where civility had been lost. Here we were surrounded by twenty-foot walls, protected by armed guards on all sides; we had food, shelter, and a layer of order and fairness. In here was safe. Beyond was uncertain. No, not uncertain—wild and dangerous and dog-eat-dog. And really, it *had* been my idea.

Herb stopped walking and faced me. "Look up."

That rush of fear came back. Was it a plane or—no. "Stars. I see a few stars in the sky. The moon isn't even visible yet."

"Millions of stars."

I kept looking up, allowing my eyes to drink in the sky. The larger stars like the North Star had been visible since dusk. Now the lesser lights were glittering through the gathering darkness.

"Our neighborhood is like one of those stars, one of those pinpricks in the sky. And all around are other points of light."

"Other neighborhoods like ours."

"Across this country, around the world, are the other little pockets of civilization struggling to survive. You have to re-member that life goes on, that humanity always tries to find its way. We're all points of light." He paused again as if strug-gling for his words. "Before this all happened, it was as if our society was at high noon. Now night has fallen and the moon hasn't even come up yet. But as sure as there are stars in the sky, the sun will rise again."

"You sound like a preacher," I said. "You really believe it's going to happen, that we're going to recover from this?"

"I've had my doubts, and I could still be wrong, but I do believe. We humans are such an industrious breed of ants."

"You're saying we're a bunch of bugs?"

"I don't mean it in a negative way. There's nobility in being an ant. We are insignificant on our own but powerful as a collective. We are resourceful. The only thing that we seem better at than killing each other is surviving. Somehow we'll survive. Someday we might even thrive."

"I don't think I've heard you be this positive before."

"Like I said, I think you're having a positive effect on me. I'm just afraid that my effect on you hasn't been so fortunate. For that I'm sorry."

For a moment, I just looked at Herb—this wasn't sounding like him. In fact, now that I was really looking at him in the gloom, I saw pouches under his eyes. He looked even older than he had just last week. "You have nothing to be sorry for," I said.

"I shouldn't have exposed you to so much. I should have done more to protect you, shield you from what you saw, what you experienced."

"There was nobody else to fly the ultralight. It wasn't just that you needed me; everybody needed me. If there had been another pilot, if my father had been here, it would have been different."

"Your father *is* here now, and he's definitely a leader I can count on," Herb said. "And I know he'd be happy to fly more of the recon missions and give you some time off." He paused. "What would you think about that?"

"I think you're worried I'm going to crack up the Cessna."

"It's not the plane I'm worried about."

"Is it just you, or are there others who are worried about me?" I asked, although I knew the answer from Todd and Lori.

"You're far more valuable than the plane. I need to know you're going to be okay, Adam. I'm not going to be here when the sun finally does rise, when civilization patches itself together."

"You don't know that," I said.

He shook his head. "I know it."

There was a certainty to that odd statement that was shocking.

"Look, I'm old. Let's just leave it at that. All I want to say is, we're going to need people like you—not just to help us survive but to put things back together again."

"I'd like to think I could be part of it."

"What I'm talking about is more than you just leading this neighborhood. I think there's a bigger role you're going to play in the future. It's uncertain when it's going to arrive and what it's going to look like, but you're going to be part of shaping it."

I didn't know what to say to any of that.

Herb smiled. "When that time comes you'll be able to handle it. Of that I'm certain. But in the meantime, I'd like you to stay in the neighborhood, take a break, get some sleep, be sixteen years old again."

"That actually sounds pretty good to me right now."

"I'll ask your father to take up the plane tomorrow."

"You've *already* talked to him about this, haven't you?" I asked.

"I asked if he'd be willing, and of course he said he would."

"A break would be nice, and then I'll be fine."

"We all need a little downtime. Yours starts now."

Herb started walking back toward our house. After a few seconds, I called out to him. He turned around and I pointed to the horizon. The moon had come out from behind some trees. It was big and bright and full.

He waved, and then I stood and watched as he walked away. I noticed a limp I hadn't seen before, and a slight hunch to his back.

I waited until he was lost in the darkness, the sound of his feet against the pavement growing distant and then fading to nothing.

When I arrived Lori was waiting on the front porch of the house where her family was living.

"No flowers tonight?" she asked, looking peeved.

I stammered, trying to spit out an apology.

She broke into laughter and gave me a big hug and a kiss. "I'm kidding, you big goon. The ones you just gave me are still in a vase in my bedroom. You know, giving me flowers really scored big points with my mother. She started giving my father a hard time about when the last time he brought her flowers was. Do you know what he did?"

"Went and got her flowers?" I asked.

"He brought her a bunch of carrots!"

"That's probably better. You can't eat flowers."

"But you can't get inspired by carrots. My father is not exactly a romantic. I love my flowers."

She kissed me again. I had to thank Todd once more. I took her hand and we started off to the school where movie night was being held. As we got closer, we were joined by others heading in the same direction.

"Is Todd coming tonight?" Lori asked.

"Nope. He's taking a turn on the south wall."

"I guess duty calls," she said. "Speaking of which, when do you have to go up or out?"

"It was supposed to be tomorrow morning."

"Supposed to be?"

"Herb wants me to take a little vacation. My father is going to go up on recon instead tomorrow, which means I can stay out tonight as long as I want."

"I like the sound of that. Maybe I could get your father to milk the cows for me as well."

"I hadn't thought of that. Do you want me to ask him?"

For a split second she seemed to think I was serious.

"You're not the only one who can joke around," I said to her.

"I guess I can still stay out late and get up early. After all, I'm not having problems sleeping."

I knew what that meant. "So you're a big part of the 'everybody' who's worried about me?"

"It's not everybody. You always act like nothing is wrong, so some people don't know you well enough to be worried."

"I'm sorry you're worried."

"Don't be sorry. Besides, tonight I'm not worried about anything except this bad movie we're going to watch," Lori said.

"It's badder than bad. But I thought you wanted to see it?"

"I thought *you* wanted to see it," she said.

We both laughed.

"I just wanted to spend time with you," she said. "But I have a better idea. Come with me."

She led me away from the school, away from the direction everybody else seemed to be flowing. We nodded or said hello to people we passed.

"Where are we going?" I asked.

"I'm taking you to a place where we can have some privacy."

"Privacy? It's here in the neighborhood, right?" I had a terrible thought that she was going to suggest we go outside the walls.

"You're not afraid of heights, right?"

"Of course I'm not afraid of— Oh, very funny."

She laughed and led me along the street. It got quieter as we got farther away from the school and closer to the strip mall. There would be guards posted all along the walls around it, so we weren't going to get any privacy there, but rather than going through the passageway leading to the front of the stores, she took me to the back. We stopped at a ladder leaning against the back of the bakery.

"You first," she said. "Don't be afraid—I'll catch you if you fall."

I placed a hand against the ladder and gave it a little shake. It seemed pretty solid. I started to climb and within a few steps I felt the whole thing vibrate as Lori started up after me. I reached the top and climbed up onto the flat roof of the building and then offered Lori a hand as she climbed the rest of the way up, too.

"Alone at last," she said.

We walked across the roof, gravel crunching under our feet, to where there was a set of patio furniture, including a pair of lounge chairs and a freestanding porch swing. She sat down on one of the lounge chairs and I perched on the other.

"I didn't know this was up here," I said.

"Some of the kids in the neighborhood managed to drag this stuff up here so they could have a place to get away from everything. It's sort of like a secret tree house," Lori said.

"It's probably a nice view during the day." Beyond the

waist-high wall was a clear vista overlooking the parking lot, still packed with dead cars, and in daylight you would have been able to see well into the houses on the other side of Erin Mills Parkway.

"It's not safe to go out there, but it's safe to look out there," she said.

"Do you?"

"Sometimes, but I'm pretty busy between feeding the livestock, helping in the fields, and doing some guard duty."

"I'm sick of being busy. I mean, it's not so much being busy as, well, being occupied . . . in my head. I think I have too many thoughts sometimes."

"I agree." She paused. "Sometimes you just need to lie back and relax."

"Maybe we could even do that relaxing thing together," I suggested. I leaned back on my lounge chair and gestured for Lori to join me. She got up from the other chair and settled in beside me. It was a tight but wonderful fit.

"Is that a new top?" I asked.

"Yes, I didn't think you'd notice."

"I noticed. It looks nice, you look nice in it."

"Thanks. Of course, it's not new, just new to me. I got it at the swap meet."

"My brother and sister got some stuff at the last one," I said.

Every second Saturday there was a swap meet at the school gym. Clothes and shoes and other personal items that people didn't want or had outgrown or that had been brought back by the away teams were all laid out on the gym floor. People were able to take things that they could use. For lots of people this wasn't just practical but was as close to shopping as they could come.

I thought back, almost in amusement, at how some people used to spend so much time "prowling" the malls. For them shopping was like a lifestyle, or a sport . . . or like hunting. Hunting—and being hunted—had changed so dramatically in our new world.

"The stars are amazing," Lori said.

"You're the second person tonight to mention the stars to me."

"Should I be jealous?" she joked.

"It was Herb."

"Then I *am* jealous. He gets to spend more time with you than anybody else does. I just hope he wasn't whispering romantic things in your ear."

"Herb isn't so much in my ear as he is in my head, and what's he's saying is never even remotely romantic. Although he does like it when I bring him flowers."

"Uh-huh."

We lay together on the chair, my arms wrapped around her. I was suddenly tired. I laid my head on top of hers.

After a few minutes of quiet, she cleared her throat. "Have you drifted asleep back there?"

"No, just thinking."

"I thought you were going to try to avoid that," she said.

"I'll do my best to—"

A popping sound somewhere close by cut me off.

In the old days, I'm sure my first thought would have been that someone had lit a firecracker. But now I knew that sound all too well. Not fireworks.

A gunshot.

10

There was a second shot and a third, and then the general alert siren went off. The shots were coming from the section of the outer wall right in front of us, maybe fifty yards from where we were sitting. Instantly I thought of Todd; then I remembered he was on duty on the other side of the neighborhood.

I jumped to my feet, pulling Lori with me, and we crouched by the edge of the roof. From behind the shelter of the bricks, I peered out, trying to see where exactly the shots were coming from. The siren kept blaring. Soon people from around the neighborhood would be here—my mother and Herb and Howie would be on their way.

Another gunshot rang out and I caught a glimpse of the muzzle flash. It was coming from outside the perimeter, from the partially burned-out condominium tower across the parkway, at the corner of Erin Mills and Burnham. It had always been one of Herb's fears that the building could be used as high ground against the neighborhood.

The emergency lights on the wall came to life, bright greens and reds and whites, strings of Christmas lights gathered weeks ago from people's attics and basements, powered by car batteries. *Merry Christmas, everybody.* The tiny bulbs lit only the area directly in front, along Erin Mills Parkway; the light didn't reach into the houses and spaces on the other side.

I saw a series of flashes—muzzle bursts from different parts of the building—followed instantly by the sound of gunfire. One of the guards on the wall crumpled to the ground.

"Oh my God!" Lori exclaimed.

Almost before the words had gotten out a second guard was hit, his body spinning backward at the impact of the bullet. There were more and more flashes from the tower, but nobody else was hit—at least not that I could see.

"Turn off the lights!" I screamed. "Turn off the lights!"

Lori jumped to her feet and started yelling again and waving her arms in the air—and making herself a perfect target.

"Lori!" I yelled. I jumped forward, knocking her over. She groaned as we smashed heavily into the gravel.

There was a loud impact—a bullet smashing into the rooftop right by our heads—then a second. I grabbed her and rolled us back over until we were sheltered by the wall again.

"Are you all right?"

"I'm . . . I'm okay . . . The bullets . . . We were almost shot."

"Please don't move," I said. "Stay here."

I disentangled myself and started to crawl away, still sheltered by the edge of the building.

"What are you doing?" she demanded. "Where are you going?"

"I have to warn them. We can't have people heading across the open space toward the wall. The shooters have too good an angle. Don't move until I come back to get you!"

I scampered along with the protection of the bricks until

I was well away from where we'd been shot at. I now had no choice. I had to move across open roof space to get to the ladder and down. If I moved fast they probably couldn't draw a bead on me. I took a deep breath and then ran as fast as I could. Grabbing the top of the ladder, I swung myself over the edge—almost falling, desperately grabbing with my feet and hands and securing a hold. I slid down the ladder, landing at the bottom with a loud thud, almost tumbling over with the impact.

I ran along the back of the stores, completely sheltered from the snipers. People were coming on foot, their flashlights marking their arrival, like signal beacons for the shooters.

"Cut your lights!" I yelled. "Get down, get down!"

Flashlights snapped off as people took cover. In the dark they'd be safe—unless the shooters had night-vision goggles. The first of the guards joined me along the wall.

Then a pair of headlights came up the road—another perfect target, even more visible than the flashlights of the people on foot. It was my Omega, which meant either my mom or my dad was driving. I ran straight toward the car, right into the beams of the headlights, waving my hands. The car skidded to a stop in front of me. Not wanting to waste time explaining, I leaned inside the open window, over my father at the wheel, and pushed off the headlights, throwing us into darkness. My mom was in the passenger seat and Herb was in the back.

In the sudden gloom, I told them we were under fire.

"Where is it coming from?" Herb asked.

"Snipers in the condo tower! They've been picking people off. At least two guards down."

"Let's move behind the stores, get out of the sight lines," Mom said to Dad as I stepped back.

My father bumped the car up over the curb, crossed the sidewalk, and pulled in right beside the back of the buildings. I ran after them and got there as they were climbing out.

"Turn off all the lights!" my mother called into a walkie-talkie.

"We should signal for the reserves," Herb said.

"I agree," my mom said. "And let's get Howie stationed with a team at the northeast corner."

As my mother repeated that order into her walkie-talkie, I realized what they were thinking: this could be nothing more than a distraction—a prelude to a full-out attack that would come at another part of the neighborhood. That's why they were sending Howie to the exact opposite side from where the gunfire was coming.

The siren stopped and the silence was welcome, like music to our ears. And then the new signal started, a short blast every five seconds, to summon all able-bodied neighbors out of their beds and onto assigned posts on the walls around the entire perimeter. I could only imagine how frightened people were right now, knowing we were under threat of attack.

I followed my parents and Herb as they went through a passageway between two of the stores, leading out to the front of the stores, to the parking lot. We moved to avoid open spaces or any other spot where we could see the condo tower—or where anyone in those windows could see us. We finally got to the outer wall.

Three more shots rang out. I pressed myself against the

wall and froze—even though I was under cover. My dad put a comforting hand on my shoulder and I forced myself to take a deep breath. I couldn't afford to panic right now.

My mother worked to calm the guards while she and Herb asked questions and tried to gather information. Three of our men had been gunned down—the third when he tried to go out and assist the first one who had been shot. All three were dead.

"Are you sure the shots came from the tower?" Herb asked me.

"I saw muzzle flashes from several different spots over there, but that doesn't mean they aren't positioned elsewhere as well."

"That's an incredible shot," Herb commented. "You'd need to be a trained marksman with a sniper rifle."

"Do you think it's shooters from the Division?" I asked.

"We can't know for certain, but they would have that capacity, I'm sure," Mom said.

"And you think there's possibly going to be an attack and it's going to come from the opposite side?" my dad asked.

Herb shrugged his shoulders. "That would be the logical place if an attack *was* going to happen."

Another shot rang out and the front window of the clinic shattered. We had to hope that whoever was in there had taken cover in the back.

"Do you want me to lead an away team out to the condo tower?" my father asked.

My mother jumped in quickly. "It's too dangerous, honey. We don't know how many of them are out there."

Herb nodded. "This could be nothing more than a trap to

get a team or two out there and then ambush them. It's better to have our guns on the wall."

"Then what should we do?" my father asked.

"I think we're doing it. Man the walls, stay low and in the shadows, and wait for the morning," Herb said.

"And then in the light of day we reassess and make some decisions," my mother said.

A few hours later, I was sitting in the Petersons' kitchen. It was still dark out.

"Hold still," Mrs. Peterson said to Lori as she disinfected the scrapes on the left side of her face.

"Does it hurt bad?" I asked.

"Not nearly as much as a bullet wound would have."

"I should have spun or something so I landed on the bottom."

"Remember that the next time." She reached out and took my hand. The knuckles on my left hand had also been scraped by the gravel. Lori lifted up my hand and looked at the scrapes with concern.

Mrs. Peterson finished with Lori and then put the same disinfectant on my hand. It stung and I flinched.

What I hadn't told Lori or her mother was that I'd all but forgotten about her up there on the roof for over an hour after I'd left her. I was so occupied by the flying bullets and the things my mother and Herb were discussing that she'd slipped out of my mind. Finally, when I remembered, I'd gone back to the roof but by that time she'd already left and gone home.

That's where I found her. She didn't say anything about it, but I still felt bad. First for forgetting her and second for not telling her I'd forgotten. It was lying by not saying.

"And thanks for taking care of my brother and sister," I said to Mrs. Peterson. The twins were in the Petersons' living room, sleeping on the couch.

"No need to thank me for that," said Mrs. Peterson.

There was now a system in place that when both parents in a household were part of the reserve team called to defend the walls, their children were taken into an appointed house to be cared for. At the first blast of the siren, Mrs. Peterson would have come over to our place to fetch the twins. I felt secure knowing that Danny and Rachel were now in the Peterson home. Mrs. Peterson had a rifle and knew how to use it. She was the one who'd taught Lori how to shoot.

"So what happens now?" Lori asked.

"We wait," I said.

"Do you think we're going to be attacked?" her mom asked.

"If we are, we can defend ourselves." I could tell from Mrs. Peterson's expression that she was thinking of her husband, who was on duty on the west wall.

What I didn't say was that our ability to defend ourselves was dependent on the type of force being applied. Our walls were strong but couldn't withstand a hit from a rocket-propelled grenade. Or an attack by a much larger force. We had close to 250 people with weapons on the walls, but 500 men with better weapons could easily breach the walls and overwhelm us.

"We'll be fine," I said. I knew I was speaking to myself as well as to Lori and her mother. "I have to go."

"Are you going up in the air?" Mrs. Peterson asked.

"Not for at least another few hours. I'll have to wait until light."

"I thought you were sitting it out for a while," Lori said.

"There's no choice. The Cessna can't take off because it needs a long runway and Erin Mills Parkway isn't secure. I'm the best pilot with the ultralight."

"I just want you to be careful," Lori said. And right there, in front of her mother, she reached up and kissed me.

11

Just a few hours later, I was back in the ultralight, Todd beside me. We rumbled down my street and then quickly lifted off.

I kept the throttle wide open and pulled back hard on the stick to gain as much elevation as I could as quickly as I could. We were a small and fast-moving target, but we were still a target.

Once we went above the electric towers I banked sharply to the right.

Todd groaned into his headset.

"I should have told you," I said. "Be prepared for lots of tight maneuvers. I'm going to be taking evasive action during the whole flight."

"Evading what, me keeping my breakfast down?"

"Yes, and I want to make it hard for somebody to take aim at us."

"I'd rather you make it *impossible*."

"I'll do my best."

We were going to make a big circular pass around the entire neighborhood, scouting for trouble from below, and then come at the condo tower from the far side. There was low cloud cover, and visibility was limited to less than two or three miles—less than I would have ideally liked—but fine for what we needed to see today.

Meanwhile, on the ground, two of our away teams had already been dispatched and were scouting the two different frontal approaches to the tower. Then they were going to loop around and come at the building from behind. Each team had ten men. My father was leading one of them.

Once they were in place to attack and I'd reported in, our main assault groups were going to come out of both the Burnham and Erin Mills gates and meet at the tower by the two different frontal routes.

"Do you see anything?" I asked as we dipped again.

"A few more sudden drops like that and you really are going to be seeing my breakfast come up."

"If that does happen, just lean over the side, okay?" I said. "It'll be like dropping a dirty bomb."

"Very sympathetic, very caring," he joked. "I expect better from you. You've become hard and unfeeling."

"Actually those last couple of dips weren't something I did."

"Well it certainly wasn't *me*," Todd said.

"I can't always guarantee flat air."

Todd scanned the ground with binoculars and I looked over the other side. I couldn't see anything. Not that I could possibly pick out a couple of people—or even a couple of dozen. I knew our crew was down there hiding among the trees and brush, or among the houses in the surrounding streets, but I couldn't see them. Todd and I were looking for something larger and more dangerous, like dozens of vehicles coming along toward us. That was something we would be able to see.

I continued to circle. I was traveling in the direction that put Todd and his binoculars on the outside where he could see everything better. On my side, I could see the neighborhood. Clustered on the inside of the two gates were convoys of vehicles and armed reservists ready to head to the tower when they were given the signal.

"Anything at all?" I asked Todd.

"Nothing, but that doesn't mean there isn't something. I just wouldn't want to miss something and put people at risk," he said.

"It's not just you—it's the two of us who are observing. I'm going to circle the condos now."

I banked sharply to the right and we quickly approached the tower. I was now going to circle with Todd on the inside of the curve so that he was closer to the tower. It was a tall building—twenty-two stories—and held the high ground over our neighborhood. We'd known all along that that could be a problem, and the proof had come last night.

The building had been secretly set on fire by Brett several weeks ago because he said he thought it was best for the neighborhood to destroy it—never mind the innocent people who were living there, struggling to survive. However, his fire had damaged only part of the building.

"If there's a sniper in there, isn't he going to take a shot at us?" Todd asked.

"That's why I'm taking a wide pass. What do you see?"

"I see a lot of burned-out apartments and blown-out windows. I can't believe people are still living there after the fire."

"I guess they remained because they didn't think they had any better place to go."

"How are they even surviving?" Todd asked.

"They must be scavenging from the area, living hand to mouth," I said.

"And what are they going to do when winter comes?"

"I don't know." Actually I did. They were going to die of starvation or exposure. "Do you see anybody?" I asked.

"Nothing, not in any of the units or at the bottom of the tower itself."

"Good, I'm going to let them know that it's a go."

I took the walkie-talkie from the compartment by my feet and gave the all clear.

Almost instantly our gates opened and both convoys sped out toward the tower.

We kept on circling, watching as the groups raced ahead. If something was going to happen, it was going to happen soon.

"Wait," Todd said. "There's a group of men coming out of the trees just beside the tower and they're armed and . . . Wait again, I think it's our people."

"*Think* isn't good enough. Where are they?"

"That way, there," Todd said, pointing off to the side.

I hit the rudder hard to cut us in that direction and pushed back on the stick to drop down to get a better view. "Can you still see them?"

"I got 'em . . . There are eight or maybe ten . . . They're heading for the apartment . . . They're our guys! I recognize your father!"

I pulled up on the stick and we soared over top of the group. They waved at us as we passed.

Hitting the rudder hard again, I put us once more in a

circuit around the tower. We watched as first one convoy, then the second, and my father's team all reached the base of the apartment at almost the same time. It had all happened without any shots being fired. Whoever had fired at us the night before had fled—unless they were holed up in there, hiding.

Now that we'd reached the building we'd have to do a full search, unit by unit, to make sure the only people there were just the residents and were no part of the threat.

"I have to hand it to your father," Todd said. "If I had gone through all of what happened to him, I don't think I'd ever want to leave the safety of the neighborhood again to go anywhere."

"He's just doing what he knows is needed," I said.

"Still, it must be hard."

I knew it was. His sleep trouble was worse than mine. He was nervous and jumpy. It had been awful out there for him, walking halfway across the continent to get back home. Even though he'd done it, it still just didn't sound real.

I guess on some level I wanted to believe that he was all right, because he was my father and he'd always been all right, always been in charge, confident, capable. He was trying to put that front forward now for our sake, but you could see the real story in his eyes when he didn't know he was being looked at. He was still scared, and his fear didn't seem to be fading.

I put my head back into the mission. Getting lost in thought could get us killed.

"So even if we don't find anybody now, what's to stop them from coming back again tonight?" Todd asked.

I hadn't thought about that. What would stop the snipers from being there tonight or a week from now? What could the committee do about it? I wasn't sure, but I figured that none of the alternatives would be good. It was only a question of how bad the choice was we'd have to make.

———————

That afternoon, the committee gathered in our kitchen—Judge Roberts, Dr. Morgan, Mr. Peterson, Mr. Nicholas, Councilwoman Stevens, Ernie, Howie, Herb, and my mom.

Since the meetings almost always took place at our house, my father had been offered a spot on the committee, but he often didn't participate. Usually he'd just listen or give advice when asked, but he seemed more comfortable not being there. Right now he was upstairs napping.

The twins were playing Old Maid and I'd warned them to be quiet. He needed his sleep. Now I sat in a corner of the kitchen and listened as the committee discussed what had happened. Some of it was hard to hear.

In the end, another four of our guards had been shot by the snipers—three had died and the fourth was in critical condition and might not make it. That would bring the snipers' death toll to seven if we included the four more people found dead at the condo. They appeared to have been bystanders; they'd simply been living in one of the units the snipers had wanted to use.

"Who do you think did this?" Councilwoman Stevens asked.

"It involved military efficiency, a couple of high-powered rifles, and a sniper's ruthlessness," Herb said.

"So you think it was the colonel and his Division," Dr. Morgan said.

"No, I don't."

"But why not?" Howie asked. "Wouldn't it be logical to take shots at our guards—the way we've been taking shots at their guards—as sort of payback, revenge?"

"Revenge is not logical," Herb answered. "It's emotional. I think that from what I've learned through Quinn and also from the colonel's actions, I've put together a pretty accurate psychological profile of both him and his old cronies. First, he has no attachment to his men. They are only pawns to him. Their loss would not be something that he would want revenge for, because they are little cogs in the machine and can simply be replaced. He doesn't attack for pleasure; he acts for gain. And though there were seven, possibly eight, people killed, there was no real gain here for the Division last night."

"Then who do you think it is?" Judge Roberts asked.

"Brett," I said, and everybody turned to me. I felt uneasy but not because of my answer. "I think that was Brett in the tower."

"Brett and at least three other men," Herb offered.

"I agree," said my mom. "I think it was Brett, because this was completely personal. He wanted to hurt us, show us that he was still out there. I wouldn't be surprised if he spray-painted his name on the side of the building."

"I guess in some ways it's reassuring that it wasn't anything to do with the Division," the councilwoman said.

"Actually, I'm not saying it wasn't." Herb rubbed his temples. "If Brett isn't dead, it's because he's still part of them."

"I just hope he's nothing more than a rogue foot soldier and not a major player," Mom added. "Maybe he just took a few men and independently decided to hit us."

"If it *is* Brett, he knows us the way we know him," I said. "He would predict we would do the kind thing and not the ruthless and efficient thing. We can't allow his predictions to be right, so we only have one option to prevent this from happening again."

"We have to take down the tower," my mother said.

"Exactly. If we try to protect ourselves by guarding it, he will use our kindness against us and launch a full-out attack on the tower and kill whoever we send out there." Herb looked around the room. "Is anybody prepared to risk the lives of our people to protect that tower?"

The implication was obvious: Herb was proposing that, to save the lives of our own people, we destroy the tower and send its residents packing. That would mean leaving possibly a dozen or more families, from what had been reported earlier in the meeting, homeless. It *was* a ruthless proposal, almost evil, but it was probably the best thing to do. It was the *only* thing to do if we didn't want the snipers to hit us over and over.

Before anyone could respond, Herb spoke again. "I want to be clear—it's not up to me, or Captain Daley. I think the committee as a whole has to make the decision."

Silence fell. There wasn't a person in the room who didn't know what needed to be done, but nobody wanted to do it.

Finally my mother spoke. "Herb is right, but we need to

discuss this fully before we decide. In the interim, we need to secure the tower."

Something had been niggling at me all this time, and I finally realized what it was. "What if—" I stopped myself. Would they really go for this?

Everybody was looking at me.

I should have kept my mouth shut, at least until I had the whole idea worked out. But I plunged ahead. "I was just thinking . . . what if we extended the wall outward to expand around the condo tower?"

Murmurs went around the committee table, and then Judge Roberts spoke up. "If we are going to absorb those people into the neighborhood, it would be a lot easier just to invite them in to take vacant houses and then destroy the tower."

"Well," I began, "I was thinking about how a medieval castle often had an inner wall and an outer wall. What if we work with the people out there to create a secondary wall that extends along Burnham a few streets over, making a wall that parallels our wall along Erin Mills and then joins back in at our north wall?"

"If the people out there could have done that, they already would have," Herb said.

"We could help them gather material and construct the wall," I suggested.

"But even if it was constructed, it would strain our forces to guard an area that much larger," Howie said.

"The newcomers would guard it. We would train them— you could train them, Howie—and help them with basic weapons like clubs and bows and arrows. We could even give them a couple of walkie-talkies so that if there is trouble, we'd not only be aware of it but could send out reinforcements to help them. Nobody would get to the tower without us knowing and instantly surrounding them."

I could tell people were mulling over what I was saying.

"And once there are walls and guards, they could grow food because they could protect their crops. We could help them there, too. We could help them plow and plant," I suggested.

"It wouldn't take long for me to do that with the tractor," Mr. Peterson said. "And we could certainly lend them a couple of rototillers. It's only August. There's still time for an autumn crop of potatoes and onions."

"We could even help them build their own rototillers, convert some snow blowers," Mr. Nicholas said.

"We could also provide them with some medical benefits," Dr. Morgan said. "We couldn't do anything that involves using our precious supply of medication, but we could help with basic medical care, minor treatments."

I kept going. "And if Erin Mills was protected with a friendly neighborhood on that side, the people on our walls would be safer. If we just simply destroyed the tower, a sniper could always pick off our guards by firing from other houses behind the tower. This way he couldn't do it."

"And the Cessna would be protected on takeoffs and landings on Erin Mills Parkway," my father added. He must have just woken up from his nap and been listening from the doorway. "We wouldn't be so reliant on the ultralight if we were under attack. That would be much better."

Herb stood up and walked over to my side and put a hand on my shoulder. "Interesting thoughts, Adam."

"Actually, you gave me the idea."

He shot me a questioning look.

"You talked about points of light in the sky," I continued, "about how we were one of those points. And then Lori talked about constellations. Building walls is like drawing lines between points, making the individual areas into something bigger, stronger, better. We can stop being a single star and start to become a constellation of stars, the center of a series of connected neighborhoods."

"So really you're not just talking about this one neighborhood," Judge Roberts said.

"I think this is just the start," I said. "Of course, only if the committee agrees."

The judge looked around. "I think we need to put this to a vote. All those in favor of exploring the option put forward by Adam, please raise your hand."

First my mother, Howie, Dr. Morgan, Councilwoman Stevens, and Mr. Peterson raised their hands. Then Ernie, my father, Mr. Nicholas, and Judge Roberts. Everybody raised their hand except Herb. He still stood beside me, his arms at his side. Finally he raised his hand as well.

"It looks like it's unanimous," my mother said. "Let's get to work."

12

It was hard to believe that only three weeks had passed, but a combination of desperation and hope had fueled the changes. The new wall was going up quickly. All the learning that had gone into making our walls was put to use in making the new walls of our neighbors. Concrete sections were "harvested" from farther along the old noise-barrier fencing beside the parkway and brought in by one of our ancient flatbed trucks. Old wooden backyard fences were taken down and used to fortify the new section of the neighborhood.

Two hundred fifty-seven people lived in the new area. Councilwoman Stevens and the judge were working with them to establish their own ruling committee. Mr. Peterson had been over to start plowing the former park and assist them with laying out and preparing their fields with late-bearing crops. We had enough seed potatoes to give them, which would grow well into the fall. Howie had been training their guards, the people who would be on the walls, and we'd even offered them a few surplus guns to supplement the half dozen they already had. Mostly it would be clubs, knives, and bows and arrows that would be their weapons. Not perfect, not nearly as good as our weaponry, but it was better than nothing.

The work was moving quickly, and while it was being completed we had placed guards outside our walls on a temporary basis to protect them and the tower.

Herb, as always, was at the center of everything.

Right now I was listening in, off to the side, while he concluded another conversation. I was always amazed at the multiple roles he played. Simultaneously he was giving directions, asking questions, acting like a cheerleader—leading but making other people think they were in charge.

As he finished talking to this one guy he slapped the man on the back and sent him away, smiling and happy.

"This is all going pretty well," I said.

"It is, but I'm not surprised, considering the alternatives."

"I guess our people can also see the benefits for us," I added.

"Having a secure force on our west side means that we're more secure. Of course you understood that before the rest of us."

"Somebody else would have thought of it if I hadn't," I said.

He shook his head. "Perhaps. But I was ready to blow up the tower, to reduce it to a pile of rubble, and the rest of the committee was more than willing to go along with it. I wanted a simple solution, and you were there playing chess."

That made me smile. I was being praised for my game by a grand master.

"I'm just curious, if we had blown up the tower what would have happened to the people who lived there?"

"They would have been forced to leave. At gunpoint if necessary."

"You could do that?" I asked.

"Listen, I can do whatever it takes. You know that. That's

what makes it so important for you to keep doing what you're doing."

"What do you mean?"

"Keep on questioning my decisions," Herb said. "Sometimes the people on the committee are uneasy about challenging me."

"Well, you have been right most of the time."

"Just keep on questioning what I'm saying, promise?"

"Cross my heart."

Herb laughed.

"What's so funny?"

"My mother used to make me say that when I had to promise her something." He put a hand on my shoulder. "You know, it's been a long time since I thought about her." He paused. "She always made me think things through, always cautioned me not to be so impulsive."

"You're always thinking things through. You're the chess master."

"In this case, I'm glad you were able to come up with a solution that involved hurting no one. But you know that that sort of solution might not always be possible."

"I know." That didn't mean I'd stop hoping. "I'm just glad you think that this is going so well . . . that everybody thinks it was the right thing to do. It is good."

Herb turned his head slightly to the side—he looked like he was studying me. "And?" he asked.

"It's just that if it was such a good thing to expand and help one area, well . . ."

"Wouldn't it be even better to expand in a different direction as well? Right?" he asked.

I nodded. "Right now we have neighbors on our south wall and this new section to our west. Why not establish a third to the north and a fourth to east?"

"We can't afford to stretch ourselves too thin," Herb said.

"If we do it right, we won't be stretched but covered. Isn't there more strength in numbers? You know, united we stand."

"In principle, but sometimes the reality is different. You're going to have to trust me on that one."

"So we shouldn't try to expand?" I asked.

"I didn't say that. Matter of fact, I have an expansion of our neighborhood walls in mind already. What do you think about taking the plane up on a little flight?"

"I'm ready anytime."

"How about Lori and Todd? Maybe they should come along with us."

I figured they'd be happy to go, and was happy to have an excuse to rustle them up.

13

I opened up the throttle and the Cessna raced along the strip of road. It had only been five days since my last flight, but I felt a rush of excitement.

I pulled back on the yoke and my spirits rose as the plane did. I grinned over at Herb in the copilot seat, and then turned around and gave a quick glance at Lori and Todd in the back. They both gave me the thumbs-up.

After we reached around two thousand feet, my planned cruising height, I turned to Herb. "So where are we going?"

"Could you do a circuit over our new neighbors?" Herb said. "I want to see it all from above."

I did a tight bank and brought us back around so that Herb was on the inside of the circle, looking down at the expanded neighborhood.

"I'm amazed at how fast that fence has gone up," Lori said.

"I think we can thank Todd's father for that," Herb said.

"Hey, I had more than a little hand in it myself!" Todd exclaimed.

"No argument from me," Herb said.

Todd had become an accomplished carpenter and clearly cared a lot more about his building assignments than he had about his old school assignments.

"There's Dad!" Lori said, pointing down.

I saw the results of Mr. Peterson's work before I saw him and his tractor. The open areas were being plowed over, black soil replacing scrub and grass. Alongside the new fields some greenhouses were being fashioned out of windowpanes to extend the season.

"This is like a little walk down memory lane," Herb said.

"Like when you were a kid?" Todd asked.

Herb laughed. "More like when *you* were a kid. Four and a half months ago we were doing what they're doing right now."

"I hadn't thought of that, but you're right," I said.

"But there's one big difference. They have somebody to help them."

That made me feel pretty happy. We were doing something good here, and not just for the condo residents and the other members of that new community. Helping them was helping ourselves in ways that had nothing to do with protection or food or survival. This was about making the pocket of civilization just a little bit bigger.

I thought the others might be thinking the same thing as we circled in silence, watching a new world being created below before our eyes.

Finally Herb spoke. "Let's keep going."

"Where to?" I asked.

"Fly to the place on Dundas Street where the bridge crosses the river. I want to come in low and slow. Matter of fact, I want this whole trip to be that way, so we can see how things are evolving around us."

I banked slightly to the left and reduced throttle at the

same time. It wasn't far, and even at this speed we'd be over it in less than two minutes.

Herb turned around to Lori and Todd. "I'm glad both of you could join us."

"Thanks for the invite," Lori replied.

"Yeah, always good to be up in the air," Todd added.

"Hah! When did you start to like flying?" I asked.

"It's a relative thing, Adam. As bad a pilot as you are, I still feel safer in the air than on the ground." Todd leaned over the seat. "I'm hoping you brought along lunch in there," he said, gesturing to the big white bag at Herb's feet.

"I'm afraid food wasn't on my mind when I packed."

"Food is always on my mind," Todd said.

"I think that's true of almost everyone these days," I said.

"You know, for me this obsession with food has been happening my whole life," Todd said. "So if it isn't food in there, then what did you bring?"

Herb patted the bag. "Just some things that I thought we might need."

Herb was like the world's oldest Boy Scout—he was always prepared. I assumed that there were a couple grenades, and lots of spare ammunition for the two rifles he had brought on board. Of course Herb also had at least two pistols—as did I. Todd and Lori were probably packing as well.

Todd's comment about food had made me hungry. Or maybe it was the view out the window. Below us were people who had basically nothing. Many of the houses we flew over were abandoned; some showed signs of fire or other damage. I could see some people moving about in the suburban yards and walking or biking on the roads, going about their daily struggle to survive. Some of them were probably starving. Even in our neighborhood some things were in short supply or had already run out. The last of the sugar was almost gone, although we had some people who had been cultivating a special type of beet and then, after using the greens for regular meals, processing the roots to extract sugar. Anything in the way of exotic fruits and vegetables had long since been eaten or had spoiled, and there was no way we'd see any more of them. Bananas—my favorite—were a thing of the past.

Funny, I'd probably had more fantasy dreams about food than any teenage boy—other than Todd—should ever have.

Herb reached into his jacket pocket, pulled out a chocolate bar, and held it up. "Actually, I did bring along a little something."

"Wow!" Todd exclaimed.

"Where did you get that?" Lori chimed in.

You'd think he'd just performed a magic trick, like pulling a rabbit out of a hat. Although producing a rabbit for a hearty stew would have been a pretty good trick all by itself.

"I still have a little stash of chocolate," Herb said. "How about if we split it three ways?"

"Why not four?" I asked.

"Yeah, it's your bar, so you should get a share," Todd said.

"Oh, I was going to get one of those thirds," Herb shot back. "I just wasn't planning on giving you any."

I could feel Todd's shock before Herb started laughing.

"You kids share it . . . It means more to you. Me—I just want to make sure I still have enough of my secret supply of instant coffee."

"Let me do the dividing," Todd suggested.

"You can do that right after we land."

"Why not now?" Todd asked.

"I don't want you distracted. Consider the chocolate as a reward once the job is completed." Herb slipped the bar back into his jacket pocket and from another pocket he pulled out a notepad and pen, which he balanced on his knee so he could take notes about what we observed.

I wanted the taste of chocolate but it could wait. Instead I couldn't help but wonder how much coffee he still had. I had seen Herb's gigantic stockpile of food in his basement. His storage room shelves had been piled high with cans and bags. They weren't completely filled anymore, but there was still a tremendous amount left.

Right beside the storage room was Herb's safe room, which was hidden behind a wall panel, then a metal door. That's where he'd been sleeping the night Brett's assassins had attacked. He'd shown it to me a few weeks ago, as promised. In the beginning, the room had also been filled with his personal cache of weapons. Most of those—including high-powered rifles, sniper scopes, and night-vision goggles— were now being used by the guards. I knew there were a few more he kept just for himself, and I suspected there were still other things that I didn't even know about. Like any good magician, he probably still had a few more tricks up his sleeve.

"I'm glad to have three pairs of young eyes to go along with one old set here in the plane today," Herb said.

"What are we looking for?" Lori asked before I could.

"We're trying to see nothing in particular and everything

in general. I want you to observe and share what you're see-ing. Young eyes go with young minds. Maybe you can see something I can't see or think of something I can't think of when you see it."

"I can do the looking part, but I don't know about the thinking part," Todd said.

Instead of laughing, Herb said something surprising while scanning out his window. "Don't do that, son," he said.

"Do what?"

"Put down your abilities. You're a very bright young man."

Todd looked out his window. "I think lots of my teachers would disagree with that."

"*Being* smart and *acting* stupid are two different things," Herb replied. "Change the habit—ultimately we're going to need young people to lead us."

"That's what we have Adam for," Todd said. "He's the brains and I'm the—"

"Stop. I don't want to hear that from you," Herb said.

I looked over at Herb, who was glaring at Todd. He had that laser-eyed look—the one where it seemed like he could see right through you—and it was aimed right at my friend.

"Yes, sir, I understand," Todd mumbled.

There was a heavy silence for a moment. Then Herb pulled out two pairs of binoculars from the bag and handed them over the seat to Lori and Todd.

Down below there was fairly steady movement on the streets, with a few vehicles scattered among the bikes and people on foot. In fact, there seemed to be more and more vehicles all the time. Anything old that didn't have silicone chips and processors for brains was now being made new, or at least functional. Beaters that had been off the road for years had been taken from junkyards, backyards, and farmers' fields and been repaired enough to run.

All of the abandoned computer-equipped cars on the road were being scavenged for parts, their tanks drained of gas. It was getting harder for us to find usable vehicles to scavenge ourselves. Not that we didn't have a lot that had already been dragged into the neighborhood. Once again, Herb's foresight, directing us to do that before others saw the need, meant we had a big stockpile. But would it be enough?

We'd also been seeing more and more go-cart-type vehicles zipping by our walls—obviously, we weren't the only transportation-starved people who'd thought of using the simple and reliable little engines harvested from the yardwork machines stored in nearly everyone's garage or tool shed. This was good and bad. It was a way for people to get around, but it also provided transportation for those people taking advantage of others, and it was more competition for fuel.

Along with the vehicles I could also now see more patches of ground that had been cultivated, converted from lawns and parks and meadows into productive land. Surrounding them were little fiefdoms that had sprung up where people were trying to protect their crops. Almost without exception they were small and would be easily overrun by any group larger than a dozen armed men.

Over the past few weeks my father had been flying a grid pattern over the entire area, mapping these little pockets of settlement. They didn't even know how lucky they were that we were a friendly neighbor, as we could have overrun them easily ourselves and taken whatever they had.

Of course, that's what we now realized Brett and his squad had been doing when they were going out each night. They said they were heading out to "protect us," and when they returned with supplies they said they'd "found" them. We should have suspected what they were doing, but I think we all turned a blind eye; we just saw the supplies we needed materializing each morning and didn't question how they'd been acquired. If we'd asked more questions sooner, maybe we could have controlled Brett better and he might still be helping to protect us instead of us needing protection from him.

Our away teams still spent their time searching for supplies, but they weren't taking them from people who were just as needy but not as able to defend themselves. We tried not to harm others in an attempt to help ourselves. Instead they'd often look for abandoned buildings and homes to search for anything that might be of value. It was amazing how a burned-out house could still hold a treasure of canned goods or a medicine cabinet full of drugs underneath the wreckage.

I banked around our old school and flew in a path that paralleled Dundas. It was a major street, one of only two roads left that had bridges crossing the Credit River. There had been a third—Burnham Bridge—but we'd been forced to destroy it to protect ourselves in our first large-scale encounter with the Division.

It still sent a chill up my spine whenever I passed near where that bridge had stood. All that remained were two gigantic cement posts sticking high into the sky. It looked like some sort of ancient ruins—like Stonehenge or those statues on Easter Island. Below, still partially blocking the river, were the concrete and asphalt remains of the bridge and the metal skeletons of the vehicles that had fallen when we blew it up. If I lived to be a thousand I'd never forget the images of the bridge being blown, the collapse, the dozens of vehicles and hundreds of men falling to their deaths.

As we neared the Dundas bridge there was much more movement on the road. The bridge was like a funnel where everyone had to merge to cross the river.

Weeks ago, in the beginning, almost all the movement had been to the west, away from the city. Now the traffic seemed to be moving in both directions. As we flew low over them, the people on the bridge all looked up. Some just stared and others waved. We remained a novelty. Maybe representing hope or possibly fear.

I cut the bank more sharply so that we turned around and were coming at the bridge from the river valley. With the valley dropping down I dipped as well so that we weren't that much higher than the bridge itself. It was ahead of us—four lanes wide, long and soaring over top of the river below. Five solid cement-and-steel towers were the legs on which the road rested. As we closed in I had the strangest thought—I could dip down and we could fly between the supports, under the bridge.

No, that was crazy. I pulled up on the yoke and we passed right over the bridge, still so low that the people crossing ducked involuntarily as we buzzed them.

The valley seemed undisturbed below—a thin line of blue

water cutting between hills of green with a few worn brown paths leading across the grass and through the trees. Those paths were dotted by people, brightly colored plastic water containers in hand, moving to and from the river. The water was being used, as evidenced by the people carrying the containers, but the land was being left fallow. No plowing or planting. People were hungry—already starving or going to starve this winter—and here was land that could make a difference. Of course maybe no one around here had seeds or fertilizer or tools, or had ever planted crops before. It wasn't like the people in our neighborhood could have planted and grown crops without the help of Mr. Peterson. But still there should have been a way, I thought. Could we extend our influence down here? Of course we couldn't. This was too far away from our neighborhood. I had to understand where the line of kindness and caring intersected with stupidity. This was well into the negative side of the equation.

"Can we now cruise along Dundas toward the city?" Herb said.

I worked the pedals and rudder to bank us that way. "How far do you want to go?"

"As far as the compound," Herb said.

"Do you think they're back?" Todd asked.

"I would be surprised, but I want to make sure it's still unoccupied." Herb turned to look again at Lori and Todd. "Eyes open for any movement, any new settlements being established, anything at all that warrants attention."

"This is exciting," Lori said. "I always enjoyed going into the city."

"I bet it never had as much potential as this to be exciting," Todd said.

"Let's hope for a minimum of excitement," I added. "Boredom is good."

"Either way, keep your eyes open," Herb cautioned. "Forewarned is forearmed. Either today or down the road, if we know what's coming we'll be better prepared to deal with it."

There was no wind or cloud cover to speak of. We were flying through stable air, so I didn't need to pay much attention to my controls. As we hit the outskirts of the city, I kept scanning to the front and side to see the ground below. In the past—before all of this—it was only natural that the closer to the city you got, the more people and movement you would have encountered. Now it was the opposite. The sleepy suburbs and little towns had become active, and the cities had been deserted. You couldn't see many people, and you also couldn't see much cultivation of open land. There were more houses and apartments, of course, but many more of them seemed to be burned out. There were whole patches, entire neighborhoods, that seemed to be nothing more than blackened scars, completely destroyed by fire. An occasional fire could have been an accident. But there was nothing accidental about an entire city block being burned to the ground.

"There's the compound coming up," Herb said.

Todd pushed himself forward, his arms on the seat, bumping me, in an effort to see out the windshield. "Where?"

"Right up ahead."

Without being asked, I pushed forward on the stick to lose elevation and allow us all to have a better angle to see out through the front.

"Anything?" Lori asked.

"It's too far to tell for sure, but no movement from here," Herb replied.

What I could see from this height and distance was the damage we had inflicted. The buildings were burned or torn down, or bombed to rubble. The gigantic crater at the end of their runway was like a big black scar. Getting closer I could see the fences, ripped open and smashed.

I eased off the throttle to slow us even more and pushed the stick down again. I wanted to come in so low and slow that we couldn't miss anybody or anything.

"It's completely deserted," Herb said.

"That's great," Todd said.

"That just means they're someplace else," Herb said.

"Someplace else is better," Todd said.

Unless that place was in the condo tower overlooking our neighborhood, taking shots and killing our people.

We quickly passed over. "Do you want me to go back around?" I asked Herb.

"No need. Take a sweep to the north, and then come back around along Highway 403."

I had started the bank when Lori spoke.

"Couldn't we go farther into the city?" she asked.

"Yeah, that would be cool," Todd added.

I looked over to Herb for direction.

"I think a flight around the city core would be a really interesting idea . . . but not this time. I want to see the activity on the highway, especially crossing the Credit River highway bridge," Herb said.

I increased the bank and pulled up on the yoke to gain altitude and at the same time gave it more fuel to compensate for the rudder and the climb. Without realizing it, I'd gotten way too close to stall speed.

Off in the distance, just small bumps on the horizon, were the office towers of the city. In all my flights I'd never gotten much closer to them than this.

Part of me was relieved to be heading back home, but another part really wanted to go there and see for myself, up close, what the city was like. That would probably happen another time, but I already knew it would be bad there—a deserted jungle of concrete.

The other night I'd had a dream about piloting my ultralight between the giant buildings of the city. I couldn't spot any people or movement, and it had been a peaceful ride—until suddenly explosions erupted all around me. Glass-fronted office towers exploded in deadly blooms and the shock waves sent me plummeting toward the urban streets below as I woke up in a heavy sweat.

It was certainly a different view of the city from what I'd seen from commercial planes whenever we flew back from holidays and circled before landing at the airport. It was a beautiful city—or at least it *had* been.

Todd took the binoculars from his eyes. "It all looks pretty deserted down there."

"There are still people, but there isn't the infrastructure to support many. You can only live where you can grow food," Herb said.

"I haven't seen anything," Lori said. "Do you think the Division is down there somewhere?"

"Somewhere," Herb agreed. "I just hope that somewhere is far, far away. I can only assume that they're after easier targets."

"Isn't almost everybody an easier target than us?" Lori asked.

"We've worked to be the hardest target we can be," Herb said.

"Then you don't think they were behind the shootings from the condo tower?" Todd asked.

"There's no evidence it was them," Herb replied.

And no evidence it wasn't, I thought.

"Is that what people are thinking, that the Division was behind it?" Herb asked.

"Some are," Todd said.

"Others are thinking that it's Brett," Lori added.

"We don't even know if he's still alive," Herb said. His words were sharper than I'd expected. "Regardless, you two can help everybody by making sure you put down those rumors when you hear them. People need to have confidence and energy and optimism, and talk like that drains it away."

Of course that didn't mean the rumors weren't true. In fact, the discussions in the committee—which remained unknown to the general population—even gave credence to those theories. However, Herb also tried to control the way people thought, mostly for what he believed was their own good.

"But really, it doesn't matter one way or the other because that condo tower is no longer a threat," he said.

"And better than that, they're now our allies," Lori said. "I was so surprised when the committee made that decision to help all of those people."

"All of those people have Adam to thank," Herb said.

"That was your suggestion?" Lori asked.

I shrugged. "I guess so."

"No guessing involved," Herb said. "Adam came up with the idea and then convinced everybody on the committee to go with it."

I had made a point of not mentioning it because I thought it was best that it just was a committee decision. Now it felt good to have Lori and Todd know—especially Lori.

But while part of me was grateful that they'd decided on my plan, another part wondered how long it would be before one of my ideas backfired and cost all of us.

"Over there, on the road, do you see it?" Todd pointed ahead of us.

I didn't see anything except the abandoned vehicles that littered the road. And then I caught some movement. There were vehicles traveling quickly along the 403 to the west, toward our neighborhood. They were small and nimble, dodging the obstacles on the road.

I opened up the throttle and pushed back on the yoke. The plane practically jumped forward. Whoever they were, there were a lot of them, moving very fast.

"Go-carts," Todd said, with the binoculars up to his eyes. "I count nine, ten, . . . a dozen."

"Do you think they're heading to the neighborhood?" Lori asked.

"That's a long, long way off, almost twenty miles—and there aren't enough of them to pose a serious threat. Let's get a closer look," Herb ordered.

"How low?" I asked.

"Buzz them. I want to see them and make sure they really see us."

I pushed forward on the yoke and we dropped into a hard dive. Todd let out a little yelp. The pavement came rushing up toward us. At about fifty feet, I leveled off. They were no more than half a mile in front of us. I eased off the throttle. The slower the speed, the longer the look.

"Guns, I see guns," Herb said. "As we pass I want you two to look back for muzzle flashes."

"Do you really think they could fire?" Todd questioned nervously.

"I have no reason to think they will or won't. Just be aware if they initiate a hostile response."

"Will we fire back?" Lori asked.

"We'll fly away. Don't worry, though, there's no chance in the world they can hit us . . . well, hardly any."

They were dead ahead now. The little carts were driving across the whole width of the westbound highway, occupying all three lanes and both shoulders, zigzagging around the stranded cars, speeding along. The drivers were all wearing uniforms or at least the same color clothing, and I could see the rifles on each vehicle, held in place in racks along the side. We were coming up fast and, judging from their lack of reaction, they didn't know we were coming. The noise of the plane was probably obscured by the noise of their engines. Closer and closer and closer—it was like watching a video game being played before my eyes.

"They look like little doodlebugs," I said, and then we zoomed over the top of them and flew on past.

"They scattered!" Todd yelled out.

"And stopped!" Lori shouted. "They all skidded to a stop."

I pulled up, gaining altitude, and then banked sharply so that I could come back at them.

"No shots, no muzzle blasts," Lori reported.

"They wouldn't have had time to do anything," Herb said. "Take a big, wide circuit around them. I want another look, but make sure we're too far away to be hit."

I pulled back on the yoke, opened up the throttle, and eased on the rudder to start our bank. As we started the curve they came back into view. I couldn't see much, but I could tell they hadn't started moving again. They had probably taken shelter behind the stalled and burned-out vehicles along the highway.

"I wonder what they're thinking," Todd said.

"Whatever is going through their minds, it doesn't seem to be panic. They were surprised and probably shocked, but they still held their ground," Herb said.

I pulled us around them in a circle, with Herb, binoculars up to his eyes, on the inside of the bank.

"All of the vehicles appear to be identical," Herb said. "Same paint color, almost a dull camouflage brown. And it's hard to see at this distance, but I think they have some plating."

"You mean like they're bulletproof?" I asked.

"At least bullet-resistant," Herb said.

"They were all wearing helmets," Todd said.

"And dressed almost the same," Lori added. "I think I saw some body armor."

"Does that make them military?" I asked.

"Maybe not military, but certainly organized. Look at the way they're acting."

"What are they doing?"

"They're doing nothing. They have stopped, stayed in formation, and I suspect while we're looking at them through binoculars they're looking at us. Make sure you don't get any closer. We saw rifles, so a sniper scope isn't out of the question."

"Could they be Division?" I pictured Brett down there tracking us through binoculars, and it sent a chill up my spine.

"Military or police would be my guess, but that doesn't mean they're out there causing trouble . . . or that they're up to any good either."

More space was better, so I widened our bank to open up more distance. We had done a full circle and had started into the second when they finally moved, heading back in the direction they'd come from—away from the neighborhood.

"Do you want me to follow them?" I asked. "Maybe we could find out where they call home."

"They'd see that as a threat," Lori said.

"I think we already crossed that bridge when I buzzed them."

Herb chuckled. "I wanted to get close and see their reaction. Besides, I suspect they'd simply wait until we ran low on fuel before they thought about revealing where they lived. Let's go back to our original course along the 403."

We left the mysterious doodlebugs behind; they were going in one direction along the highway while we headed in the opposite.

"What do you think they were doing out there?" Todd asked.

"They certainly would have been a formidable force to many," Herb said.

"Not formidable enough to threaten us, though," I said.

"Not us, but not much out there could handle a dozen highly mobile, heavily armed opponents."

Ten minutes later, I could see the outline of our neighborhood in the distance. Our north wall was the southern wall of the highway. The black strip of the asphalt roadway was empty, all of the cars harvested. It was a wide, clear stretch that was my other landing strip if the winds wouldn't allow me to come in on Erin Mills Parkway. That wouldn't be a problem today.

"Do you think we could go farther?" Lori asked. I thought I knew where she wanted to go.

"Where did you have in mind?" Herb asked.

"Could we go farther east to our farm? It wouldn't take long, would it?"

"No more than ten minutes round-trip," I jumped in. "Have we done any scouting in that direction?"

"It wouldn't hurt to do a pass in that way," Herb said.

I could sense Lori smiling in the backseat at the idea of heading home.

As we started across the neighborhood I noted that, unlike the rest of the world, the area under our wings was in good order. I dipped so that the neighborhood came more into view out my side window. It was like we were witnessing a little miracle of civilization and activity. Some of the fields had been harvested, and others had already taken on a second planting. The greenhouses filled with seedlings and the pools holding our water supply sparkled and glistened in the sun. There were no blackened houses—the one home that had caught fire had been taken down. I could see the watch-towers spaced out along the walls and knew that unseen guards were protecting it all.

Once we were past our neighborhood, the houses started to fall away and now to my right as far as I could see were open fields punctuated by the occasional farmhouse and patch of forest. I wondered if any of the farms were still occupied, if there were tents pitched among the trees.

It was crazy. Here was land that could be used to feed everybody but instead it lay fallow. Because no one could plant and protect it, it was left useless. If only people could have come together instead of fighting, these fields would have produced plenty of food. Now there was hunger and starvation, and worse still to come when winter arrived. I brought us in lower across the fields. There was nothing and nobody to fear out here. We'd be coming in at the house so low and fast that even if there were any people there, they wouldn't have time to react, so there was no danger of them taking a shot at us with any accuracy.

"Those trees mark the eastern edge of our property," Lori called out.

I'd leveled out at no more than thirty feet above the tip of the tallest tree.

"As soon as we clear them we'll be able to see my house—" She broke off with a gasp.

I could see that the roof of the house was gone and as we got closer there were telltale remnants of the fire that had consumed it. The walls still stood, but there was nothing else. The barn was completely burned down, the drive shed and garage flattened. I banked sharply to the right so that the remains of the farmhouse were hidden and instead only blue sky could be seen out of the windows on Lori's side of the plane.

"I'm so sorry," Herb said.

"You have nothing to be sorry about," she said in a whisper. "If we'd stayed, that would have been us . . . me and my family." Then she said to me, "Wait, go back. You have to go back. Did you see it?"

"See what?" I asked.

"Go back. I don't want to say anything until I see it again."

I looked over at Herb and he nodded. I executed a fairly tight bank turn and brought the farmhouse back into view.

"Not my house," Lori said. "The field, the one between the two rows of trees. And can you bring us down lower so I can tell for sure?"

I made the adjustments and also eased off the throttle. Whatever she wanted to see, I wanted to give her plenty of time to see it. We cleared the trees and instantly I knew what she had spotted.

"The field has been planted!" Lori exclaimed. "Those are potatoes, the whole field is full of potatoes!"

"I hate potatoes but that is awesome news!" Todd said.

He and Lori and even Herb began to cheer and I got so caught up that I almost skimmed the treetops on the other side of the field before I pulled up.

"How is that even possible?" I wondered.

"The people who were here must have planted the field," Todd guessed. "And then they didn't have a chance to harvest it before they were overrun."

"So what now?" Lori asked.

"We go and dig up some potatoes," Herb said.

14

The next day we left the neighborhood just as the sun was coming up. Dawn was always the safest time. There was light to see, but most people were still asleep. There were over two hundred of us, led by Lori's father and Herb. Our convoy was made up of dozens of vehicles ranging from go-carts and motocross bikes to our two biggest trucks—one of them pulling one of the Petersons' farm wagons—and seven cars, including mine.

We had to have enough transport not just to move people there but to bring the crop back, and we needed a strong show of force to make sure nobody thought they should take us on. We also had to leave enough force behind to continue to guard the neighborhood, so we'd brought along some friends: members of the little neighborhood to the south and some of our new tower neighbors to the west. There was safety in numbers, and those people really needed the food. Mr. Peterson had estimated how many potatoes would be in that field, and he figured there were more than enough for our needs, as well as some to offer to both of these satellite communities.

As we set out, I looked up to see the Cessna, with my father at the controls, circling the area. Usually I was the eye in the sky, but now he was the one offering protection. It was also reassuring to be driving with Lori right beside me. Several other passengers were crushed in together as if we were in a clown car, but there was no laughter. Everyone was quiet. Lori turned to smile at me—she seemed fine, but I worried her calm would crumble as we neared the remains of her house. Flying over it had been hard enough. Seeing it in person on the ground was going to be worse.

The drive out was completely uneventful. Any onlookers who had seen us coming had probably scattered at our approach. I had an anxious moment when we passed through the remains of another neighborhood's checkpoint on Burnham—the place where Herb and I had once been held at gunpoint—but it was deserted.

Driving down the bumpy track toward the farm brought me back to that first day our world had slammed to a halt— I remembered driving Lori home from school when it seemed like my old car was about the only thing that still worked.

We came to a stop behind the other vehicles in front of the house. The windows were broken, the front door smashed, the roof collapsed, and much of what remained blackened from fire.

Lori let out a deep sigh.

"You okay?"

"As okay as I can be. Let's go."

We climbed out, and Lori went to where her mother and father were standing in shock, looking at the house. Her father threw his arms around both of them.

Howie walked toward them. "It's clear if you want to go inside," he said.

"Thank you," Mrs. Peterson said. Together they walked in through the empty doorway.

What now? I joined Herb, who was already giving out

orders to the guards: half were staying here, guarding the lane and vehicles, and half were going out to the fields to watch over the harvesters. There was no time to waste as our neighbors headed off with shovels and hoes and picks on their shoulders.

"Do you mind if I wait here for Lori?" I asked Herb.

"I think she would appreciate that. Please have Mr. Peterson join us when he's able."

As I waited I wandered toward the remains of the barn, now just one big jumbled pile. Boards had probably been taken for firewood or to build shelter elsewhere. I turned as Mr. and Mrs. Peterson came out of the house and went over to speak with Herb, and then the three of them headed for the fields. Lori was still inside and alone.

I walked over to the house and looked in through the doorway at the burned and broken furniture. Dirt, blown in by the wind, covered the floor so thickly that weeds were actually growing in a couple of spots. I took a few steps inside. I listened. Nothing.

"Anybody home?" I tentatively called out. There was no answer, but Lori couldn't have gone far. I walked along the hall toward the kitchen. I felt like I was intruding. There was no door or windows, and hardly a roof covering the second story, but it was still their house.

In the kitchen were a charred table and chairs, and scattered pieces of broken dishes littered the floor. I bent down and picked up the biggest piece I could find. It was a pattern with reddish flowers. I knew "good" dishes when I saw them. I wondered how old they were, how many generations they went back, and how many family meals had been shared on these plates. I returned it to the ground, wondering why I was being so careful when it was clearly already broken, and went back to the hall and up the stairs. Cascading down the stairwell was light from the gashes in the roof. With each step the light got brighter. There was more of the roof missing than still remained. Exposed to the elements, the wallpaper had all peeled away, the old wooden floors were warped and buckled, and the walls were water-stained. The floor creaked and heaved under my feet.

I looked into bedrooms as I passed. At one, the door was hanging loose from the top hinge. Tentatively I peeked inside and saw her. She was sitting on the floor, surrounded by remnants of her furniture and piles of torn clothing.

Lori looked up just as I was about to knock and gestured for me to come over. I slumped down on the floor beside her. She leaned against me.

"This isn't proper," she said. "My parents would never let me invite a boy up to my room."

I couldn't help but laugh. "This isn't the way I pictured your room."

"I had some help decorating it. It's what they call open concept . . . really open." She closed her eyes a moment.

"I'm sorry."

"I shouldn't have come up here. Before, even from the sky when I saw the roof was ripped open, in my mind my room was still the same," she said. "Everything's gone, everything's ruined."

"Not everything. You got to take some things with you when you left."

"Some. And other things we put down in the root cellar in the barn." She looked up at me. "Do you think . . ." She let the sentence trail off.

"There's only one way to know for sure."

I stood up and pulled Lori to her feet. Hand in hand, we went down the stairs, out the front door, and over to the remains of the barn. Lori led me to a spot that was buried beneath a mountain of beams and boards and rubble.

"I guess we really can't check," I said. "Sorry."

"Don't be sorry. Be helpful." She grabbed a board and pulled it free. "That's one down, a few others to go." She tossed it to the side.

I came over. "It'll take too long. We better go and help with the potatoes."

"There are lots of people here to dig potatoes."

"What exactly did you store in there?" I asked.

"I'm not completely sure. My father was doing it as we were rushing to pack before we left for the neighborhood. He took some of our things from the house, but I think it was mainly farm equipment."

"Like tools?"

"Things he thought we'd need when we came back."

She turned to pull another board, then dropped it. "Maybe this is too much—we'll never be able to clear it away by ourselves."

I grinned. "Maybe not the two of us. Let's go talk to Howie."

———

It was amazing what six people and a truck could accomplish. Howie, with Herb's agreement, had assigned four of the guards. They rotated in and out two at a time in thirty-minute cycles. For the most part they were happier to be doing something than just standing around watching and waiting.

Now a thick rope was tied to the trailer hitch on the truck. The other end was already looped around a large section of the barn's roof. The driver started off slowly until the rope went taut and the truck came to a stop. Then he gave it more gas and the truck crawled forward in low gear until the section broke free, other pieces noisily collapsing around it as it was dragged away. With the section removed, we went back in with the chainsaws and sledgehammers and began breaking up the next piece to be dragged away.

After an hour or so, Herb came in from the fields and stood by the pile of debris that had been removed. He waved Lori and me over.

"Looks like you're making some progress," he said.

"Not bad," Lori said. "How are things in the field?"

"Better than expected. There are so many potatoes we might not even be able to harvest them all today."

"Should we be working out there instead?" I asked.

"No point. We'll have a hard time transporting what we do get. We might have to come back tomorrow anyway," Herb said. He looked up at the sky, where the late-afternoon sun was already starting to sink toward the horizon.

"That's good, right?" Lori asked.

"That's better than good. What we've got here will provide for all three communities. In fact, we might have enough that we can afford to trade away some food for other supplies," Herb said. "And that's because of you." He pointed at Lori.

"Me?"

"You saw the field. You were upset about your house, but

you didn't lose sight of what was important. Remember what I said in the airplane about how we need young heads and eyes? Well, this is a better example than anything I could have imagined."

Lori's dirty, sweat-covered face blushed. It made her even more beautiful.

"Your father said there are a lot of things down there in that cellar that we can definitely use," Herb continued.

"Assuming they're still down there," I said.

"We can't afford not to investigate. If all we lose is a little sweat and effort, it's a minor price to pay, even if it doesn't pan out."

"I know there are more than just personal things," Lori said.

"A great deal more. Your father said there was additional seed, some extra equipment for the tractor, and extra tools. Don't worry that this is just about getting your family dishes."

She *was* worrying—and in typical Herb fashion, he was able to read the situation and make her feel better.

Overhead, the Cessna was making another pass to the north. Just as it flew by, Herb's walkie-talkie crackled to life. It was my father.

"Herb, Howie, possible situation. I've spotted a small party moving through the woods at the north end of the western-most field."

Herb grabbed the radio and pressed the transmit button. "How many do you see?"

"I picked out at least six . . . Could be more lost in the trees . . . I saw weapons."

"Copy that." It was Howie. "I'm leaving sentries here,

but I'll send three squads to establish a perimeter and contain."

"Roger that, Howie," Herb noted. "I'll take some of the guards from here and meet them head on. Let's try talking first."

"Roger. We're on the way."

Herb quickly gathered up the men who'd been helping us clear the barn.

"Do you want me to come?" I asked.

"You stay here with Lori and keep working."

"Are you sure?" I asked.

"Positive. You take care of business here and we'll take care of business there. It's probably nothing at all and certainly nothing to worry about," Herb said. "I'll leave you this." He leaned his rifle against the fence.

"But what about you?"

"I have my pistol and lots of other people have rifles. Besides, it's often better I don't appear armed," he replied.

He and the others quickly left. A few more guards were still posted at the vehicles in the driveway, but now Lori and I were alone by the barn. I would have readily gone with them had I been needed, but truthfully I was happier to stay.

Lori had ducked under the wreckage and was scraping away with a shovel in the dirt.

"How close do you think we are?" I asked when I joined her.

She dug the shovel in again and there was a dull hollow sound. "I think we're basically on top of it."

I grabbed a shovel and we both continued excavating until a section of wood was revealed. Together, we cleared off an increasingly bigger section until the handle of the cellar door became visible. I reached down and grabbed it, but it didn't move no matter how hard I pulled.

"It's still stuck. I think we have to clear it a little more," I said.

Lori continued to scrape away dirt. I tossed my shovel aside, grabbed a rope, and attached it to a last beam that covered a corner of the door.

"Come on, you have to get out of here," I said.

Lori dropped her shovel and we walked over to the truck. The other end of the rope was already tied on to the trailer hitch.

"I'll drive," Lori suggested.

She got into the truck and I went off to the side, well out of the way. She started forward slowly and in a moment there was a loud snapping sound. The section broke loose and was dragged across the courtyard clear of the pile.

That did it. We brushed aside the remaining dirt and uncovered the whole of the trapdoor.

Finally Lori grabbed the handle once more and gave it a little pull, enough to raise the door an inch or so. I got a grip on it and helped lift it up.

The door groaned in protest as we opened it all the way, and dirt and light tumbled onto the first few stair treads. Lori took a few tentative steps down and then turned and looked back up at me.

"I can see the barrels at the bottom. I think it's all here!"

I felt a wave of relief wash over me and was about to follow Lori down.

Then we heard the gunshots.

15

There were three shots, followed by a loud silence.

"What direction did that come from?" I asked.

Lori shook her head. "I couldn't tell." She climbed back up the steps.

"What are you doing?" I asked.

"I'm going to investigate." She walked straight to the fence and picked up the rifle. "You don't have to come, but I have to do it. It's still my farm," she said as she started off.

"Neither of us has to go, but let's at least go in the right direction."

She gave me a curious look and I pointed up at the sky. My father was doing a tight circle off to the right. Whatever was happening would be taking place beneath him.

"He's over the western fields, right?" I asked.

"Of course. I wasn't thinking."

We ran across the rough, broken soil of a field. Although it had been plowed, clearly nothing had been planted here. A string of trees separated one field from the next.

"How about if we go along that line of trees before we head into the open?" I suggested.

We worked our way through the trees, using them as cover.

We hadn't gone far before we ran into one of our guards. He was lying on the ground hiding behind a stump, and we surprised each other. He swung his rifle around before he recognized us, and for a brief second his deadly weapon was aimed right at us.

"Get down!" he whispered, and we both dropped to the ground and crawled to his side.

"What's happening?" I asked.

"Out there in that stand of trees," he said. "We have them surrounded on all sides, but they're armed and already opened fire."

"We heard the shots."

"Not as close as I did. That first round whizzed right by my head."

"Do you know how many there are?" I asked.

"I saw close to a dozen."

"Were all of them armed?"

"Not all of them. Some were just kids carrying water containers."

"They were probably just headed to our well," Lori said.

"Maybe. It wasn't like we could ask them."

"Where's Herb?" Lori asked.

"Over there." He pointed to a narrow part of the field; there wasn't much space between the stand of trees where the strangers were hiding and the cover along the edge.

"Thanks." Lori and I retreated across the field we'd first crossed and moved in a wide arc toward Herb.

"If they just want water, we should let them have it," Lori said.

"If they just want water, they shouldn't have shot at us."

"What would you do if you suddenly bumped into a bunch of strangers with weapons?" she asked.

She had a good point.

We could hear Herb before we could see him. He was yelling out across the opening, trying to establish contact with the other group.

"Sorry if we got off to a bad start there!" Herb called out.

Even though he was yelling across a field he still sounded calm and reassuring.

"We must have surprised you, and for that I'm sorry. We don't wish you any harm."

There was no response. I settled in beside him on one side, and Lori on the other.

"I hear there were at least a dozen of them," I murmured.

"Could be a lot more than that," Herb answered. "We only know what we have seen."

"And some of them are children," Lori said. "They might just be trying to get water."

"Let's find out." Herb got up but stayed behind cover. "If you want to get water from the Petersons' well," he shouted, "we won't stand in your way!"

For maybe thirty seconds there still wasn't a response. Maybe they hadn't heard him or maybe they'd fled. No, with my father up above and the open fields all around the stand of trees where they were hiding, there was no way they could get away without being seen.

"How do you know the Petersons?" a man's voice finally rang out across the field.

"That voice," Lori said to Herb. "I know who it is!" She

scrambled to her feet. "It's me, Mr. McCurdy, it's Lori Peterson!"

"Lori, is that really you?" the voice called back.

"It is, Mr. McCurdy, and my parents are here, too. Over in the eastern fields!"

There was no immediate response. I wondered if the other group was talking things over.

"I'm coming out!" the man announced. "I'm not armed."

An older gentleman stepped out from the trees. His arms were in the air.

"Is that Mr. McCurdy?" Herb asked Lori.

She nodded.

"I'm coming out, too!" Herb replied. He stood up, placed his arms in the air as well, and walked into the field from our side.

Slowly the two men approached each other. They lowered their arms as they met and then they shook hands. Herb turned back toward us and called for Lori. She took a step and then realized she was still carrying the rifle. She handed it back to me, and I placed it on the ground. Then I followed her from the trees.

Mr. McCurdy threw his arms around Lori and, as she hugged him back, burst into tears.

"It's like seeing a ghost," he sobbed. "I thought you and your father and mother were just gone, dead."

"We're fine, Mr. McCurdy. Is your family okay?" she asked.

As if on cue, a woman and some children and another man came out of the woods—the man and the woman both had rifles.

"Everybody, hold your fire!" Herb called out. "We're all friends here! Rifles aimed to the ground, and everybody come on out . . . slowly . . . No need to be worried!"

All around us people started to emerge from cover, many of them our people from the neighborhood, but about another half dozen I didn't recognize. I did a quick count of their weapons. Among them they had two rifles and two shotguns.

Lori greeted the women and children, and there were lots of hugs and tears. She pulled me over.

"This is my boyfriend, Adam," she said.

I exchanged handshakes and nods with everybody. Other than Mr. McCurdy's, the names went in one ear and out the other.

"Are you still staying on your farm?" Herb asked Mr. McCurdy.

"We're on the farm property, but not at the house. We were driven out of that long ago. We've built a small shack in the woods about a half mile that way. We've even been using some of the wood from your barn." He looked over at Lori. "Sorry, we would have asked if we could have."

"That's all right. I understand, and so will my parents."

"And you've been safe there?" Herb asked.

"It's hidden and well off the road. Nobody has noticed. It's not much, and winter is coming, but we'll manage."

"It'll be tough," Herb said. "Even if you can keep yourself warm, the smoke rising from any fire will draw attention."

"I hadn't really thought of that," Mr. McCurdy said.

"And this is all of you?" Herb questioned.

"There's another five. They're guarding the homestead. Are you all coming back here to stay?" he asked.

"No, we're just here for a day," Lori said. "We've come to harvest potatoes."

"From the field in the middle of the forest?" Mr. McCurdy asked.

"Yes, that's the one."

"Did you plant that field?" I asked.

He shook his head and I felt relieved.

"We've been digging there anyway, though. That's how we hoped to get through the winter, with those potatoes. But now . . ." He let the sentence trail off.

"There's enough for all," Herb said. "Why don't you and some of your people come on over? I'm sure Mr. and Mrs. Peterson would be happy to see you again."

"Really happy!" Lori exclaimed.

"Lori, why don't you take them over?" Herb said. "Mr. McCurdy, take a couple of your men with you, and we'll radio over so that your appearance doesn't startle anybody. Surprises can lead to bad things."

"They almost did," Mr. McCurdy said. "I'm sorry we took a couple of shots at you."

"We would have done the same thing," Herb replied. "But enough. This is not about bad things that could have happened but about good things that did happen." He shook the man's hand once more, and then Mr. McCurdy and Lori and the others left to find her parents.

Herb made the radio call and then reassigned the guards back toward the farm and vehicles. Herb and I stood alone for a second.

"I was wondering—" I began.

"Yes, it probably would be the smart thing to do," Herb interrupted.

"What?"

"To invite them to go back with us. Our new neighbors to the west could certainly use a farmer or two to help them with their crops come spring."

I smiled. "How did you know I was going to ask that?"

"It's the thing that makes the most sense. Even more, it's the kind thing to do," he answered.

"Do we need to get the committee's approval?"

"This one is preapproved. We've been hoping to find somebody else with agricultural experience, and the timing is perfect. We have a new area that needs help, and because of the potato crop we have the resources to feed them," Herb explained.

"Do you think they'll come along?"

"That'll be their decision. All we can do is extend the invitation. Do you want to do that yourself or do you want me to talk to them?"

"I think it would be even better if it came from the Petersons," I suggested. "How about if I talk to them first?"

"Perfect. And then you can get back to excavating the root cellar."

"We're already done. The cellar's open and filled with things we can use."

Herb slapped me on the back. "This might just be the best day since this all started."

"Do you really think so?"

"Which day would be better?" he asked.

"Some people might say the day we blew the bridge." I pictured the vehicles plunging into the gorge as the bridge collapsed around them.

"True, we wouldn't be here if it wasn't for that day," Herb said. "But today, well, this is just so much better. That day was about surviving. Today is about *living*. Survival isn't enough anymore."

16

The backseat of my car was stuffed to the roof with personal things from the Petersons that we'd recovered from the root cellar. There were dishes, a couple of paintings, and winter clothing. We'd even squeezed in some of Lori's favorite books and souvenirs from their travels, which didn't take up much space and made her happy.

That made me happy, as did the potatoes in my trunk. There had to be six or seven hundred pounds of them, and my springs and shocks sagged under the weight. There wasn't a lot of clearance, so I'd have to take it slow along the lane leading out of the farm or I'd leave my muffler behind. It wasn't like I could stop at the muffler shop and get a new one, though I was pretty sure that, between them, Mr. Nicholas and the rest of the engineers and the mechanics would come up with something if it was needed.

Every vehicle, including the hay wagon, was filled to capacity with potatoes. Mr. Peterson did a rough estimate. He thought we'd pulled out close to thirty-eight thousand spuds. Everybody was sore and dirty, and their fingers were blistered and bleeding. Despite it all, there was almost a euphoric feeling. These weren't just potatoes—they were survival. A person could live on four potatoes a day even if he or she had nothing else to eat. What we'd done today was expand the basic diet of everybody in our neighborhood, and provide survival for the other two satellite neighborhoods.

Also, we were bringing back other things from the farm, including more seed, fruit preserves, tools, and additional farm equipment that had been stored in the root cellar. And, of course, there was one more "prize": Mr. McCurdy and his group had agreed to accept our invitation. They were going to take today and tomorrow to get themselves ready to leave their shack. Howie would come back with an away team and vehicles to transport them and all of their possessions and anything else that could be of value. We had to come back anyway to finish harvesting the rest of the potatoes. Herb was right—this had been the best day. Not just because of what we already had, but what was still to come.

Mr. McCurdy had told Herb that he knew of some other farm fields where there were carrots still in the ground, and he'd scouted out a deserted orchard that was heavy with apples. As produce that would last through the winter if stored properly, potatoes, carrots, and apples were hard to beat.

In preparation for the winter, root cellars had been dug under some of the houses to store food. There was already talk that with the potato harvest these would have to be expanded by a factor of two.

There were teams as well that were being created to can food in order to preserve it for the coming months. Not quite the same as being part of an away team, but just as important for our long-term survival. Sometimes the best tool or weapon wasn't a shovel or a gun, but a can or a bottle and knowing how to store food.

Lori climbed in and the car's springs groaned loudly.

"It might be time for me to go on a diet," she said.

"If it's a potato diet, you're all set."

She leaned over and gave me a kiss on the cheek. "Has anybody told you lately that you're cute?"

"Cute makes me sound like a stuffed animal."

"Keep in mind that I *sleep* with my stuffed animals."

"Okay, cute it is, that's definitely me, cute as a button."

She gave me another kiss as the vehicle in front of me started moving. Regretfully, I turned back to the wheel and put the car in gear. We inched up the lane, and I tried to steer around all the potholes to avoid bottoming out. We got to the road with just a few scrapes.

As we rumbled over the highway and left the country behind, I felt my anxiety level rise. It was late in the day, so more people would be out and about. And since we'd already passed this way our return wouldn't be unexpected, and we were now carrying a fortune in food. We had to hope that the size of our caravan made it unwise for anybody to risk attacking us. Desperation can overpower wisdom, unfortunately, and times were becoming more desperate.

Just as that thought occurred to me, the vehicle in front came to a stop. I coasted right up to its bumper and halted as well.

"What do you think is happening?" Lori asked.

"I don't know. Probably nothing. We might just be tightening up the convoy."

Herb got out of the lead vehicle and started to walk down the line. Whatever it was, we were going to find out soon. He stopped at the window of the first vehicle and spoke to the driver, then proceeded to the second and third. His pace was deliberate, unhurried, his expression, as always, neutral. That didn't mean it wasn't something serious.

He came up to my open window. "Your family is safe," he said to me.

A chill went up my spine.

"There was an attack on the neighborhood."

"*Was?* Is it over?" Lori questioned.

"It appears to be."

"What happened?"

"Initial reports are that three RPGs were launched. One took out part of the northeast wall and guard tower."

"Was anybody hurt?" Lori asked.

"Four wounded . . . I don't know how seriously."

And then I remembered that my best friend was stationed at one of the towers today. "Was Todd one of the wounded?"

"I don't know who was wounded, but if Todd was one of them I think your mother would have relayed that info."

"Are you sending back some of our guards to man the walls?" I asked.

"Negative. They're needed here more than there. It was an isolated attack, but that doesn't mean that we won't be targeted next," Herb said.

I knew what he meant. We were exposed out here. "That's smart. Somebody could think that by attacking the walls they would force us to send some of our guards back to the neighborhood from our convoy and make ourselves even more vulnerable," I said.

Herb nodded and I glanced over at Lori. She looked as scared as I felt.

"Listen, we don't know anything for certain," Herb said, "except that it wasn't an attempt to invade the neighborhood. Somebody just fired grenades at us. If it wasn't a diversion, it was just about causing havoc without any hope of gain."

It could only be one person.

"I understand. I'll stay tight to the vehicle in front of me," I said.

"I want you to do the *opposite*," Herb said. "I need at least fifty feet of clearance between each vehicle. I don't want one RPG to take out two vehicles."

Herb reached in and placed a hand on my shoulder. "It's going to be fine, you two." He went to talk to the next vehicle in line.

"Do you think it was Brett?" Lori asked.

"It could have been anybody."

"Do you really think that?"

I shook my head. "Of course not. It only makes sense that it's Brett."

"Why doesn't he just leave us alone?" she demanded.

Rage rose up inside me. "If I'd known what would happen, I would have killed him myself."

"Really?"

"I should have just shot him in the head when I had the chance."

"I don't think you could shoot someone like that," she said.

I laughed bitterly. "I already did, remember?"

Lori looked stricken and I felt awful. Me killing those two men was one of the things we never talked about.

"I'm sorry . . . I didn't mean to upset you." I reached over, but she pulled away to face out the window.

I didn't know what else to say. Before words came, the vehicle in front of us started moving. I gave it a few seconds to get some distance; then I put the Omega into gear and we were off again.

The sun was just setting when we entered through the western gate. It felt good to be on the right side of the walls. Not that the walls were any protection if somebody lobbed another missile at us. I knew the power and the range of a rocket-propelled grenade. There were only a few places in the whole neighborhood that would have been completely safe, and we weren't in one of them this close to the perimeter.

Still, it was better to be inside than outside. We'd encountered no problems, but that didn't mean the remaining ride hadn't been tense. Lori hadn't said more than a few words to me, and the times I'd tried to initiate a conversation were met with little more than a word or two.

Once we were inside the walls, the guards on go-carts and motocross bikes raced off, along with Herb and Howie, heading to the northeast gate. The trucks and cars turned into the shopping mall parking lot, where they were going to be unloaded. As they turned I kept going straight.

"What are you doing?" Lori asked.

"I'm going to park in your driveway so you can unload your family's things. Can you then take my car back up to the mall so the folks up there can unload the potatoes, please?"

"And what are you going to do?" she asked.

"I need to know what's happening, what's going to happen. I need to talk to my mother and father and be there when the committee meets." I knew the committee would gather automatically this evening, because of the emergency. We turned onto Lori's street, and I pulled to a stop. "It's probably best that you leave the car running while you unload. You know it can be hard to start sometimes."

I went to get out and she grabbed my arm. "I'm sorry for being, you know, not very talkative. I was just scared," she said.

"Of Brett?"

"Of you."

I leaned back on the headrest and she put her head on my shoulder. We both stared out the windshield. We sat like that for a little while, not saying a word.

"All right, get out of here," she said at last.

We kissed, and then I climbed out of the car and she slid into the driver's seat.

———————

As I approached the site of the attack, the sun was below the horizon and daylight was fading fast. At the breach in the wall there was a hive of activity. I recognized many people but didn't see my mother or father, or Herb or Howie.

Then I spotted Todd. He was standing by a section of the wooden wall that was reduced to a pile of toothpicks.

One of the guard towers had collapsed, and I could see a scorch mark where an explosion had taken place. There was a crater inside the wall that marked the impact of another explosion. If nobody was killed, it wasn't due to lack of effort by the shooter.

"Are you okay?" I asked as I came up to Todd's side.

"Twenty-five minutes later and I would have been in that guard tower," he said. "I guess it was lucky we altered the schedule on the shift change."

"I'm just glad you're okay."

"Okay, but a little annoyed. You know I practically built that guard tower, and now it's gone. You remember how angry I used to get when somebody would destroy something I was building with Legos?"

"I remember. I think I did that to you once in kindergarten."

"Well, think of this as a really, really big Lego tower. I guess I better get to work. Talk to you later."

A construction team was already putting together a temporary wall, more a pile of debris than anything fancy, and Todd walked over to join them. Todd's father was leading the repair crew, but he was too far away for me to talk to him.

"Does anybody know where my mom or dad is?" I called out.

One construction person stopped working and turned. "I haven't seen your father, but I think your mother's out there," she said, gesturing beyond the wall. "We sent two teams out."

That wasn't the reassuring message I was hoping for. "And Herb?"

"What do you think? He and your mom are leading one team; Howie is leading the other."

I thanked her for the info and hustled right over to the gate—or what was left of the gate—and slipped through.

I zipped up the vest of body armor that I'd been wearing

most of the day. That made me feel a little more secure, although I knew that it couldn't stop anything of too heavy a caliber and it didn't protect my head at all. I might as well have been completely naked if a sniper had me in his scope. Actually, that's how I thought of myself—completely exposed, completely naked.

Then I thought of something else that made me even more upset. My mother was out here, too. What better way to hurt me than to hurt her?

As I got closer to the woods beyond the wall, I could see movement among the trees and recognized a dozen or more of our people, my mother and Herb in the lead.

I scrambled down the slope, sending rocks ahead of me. It wasn't a quiet or graceful slide, but noisy was better, anyway. You didn't want to sneak up on a bunch of people with weapons, especially when they were probably more than a little edgy.

They all turned at the sound of my advance, and my mother waved.

"What are you doing out here?" she asked.

"Looking for you. What are you doing out here?"

She seemed taken aback. "Excuse me?"

"You shouldn't be out here with Herb and Howie. Don't you understand how vulnerable—"

Herb raised a hand to silence me, and I stopped. He turned to the dozen guards with him. "Can you please fan out and give us a perimeter of thirty yards, no more than fifteen yards apart, behind protective cover. Go."

They set off. Herb turned back to me with a stern look, but before he could say anything my mother jumped in.

"Adam, I might be your mother, but I'm also a leader of this neighborhood, and you should never, *ever* question my judgment in front of the people I'm commanding. It completely undermines my authority."

I felt like I was six years old. "Sorry," I mumbled.

A transmission came over her walkie-talkie, and while she dealt with that I took a few deep breaths and settled myself. When she finished, she turned back to me and gave me a deep look.

"Apology accepted. And please accept mine."

"For what?" I asked.

"You're right. I shouldn't be in the open with Herb and Howie. I could have stayed within the walls to help if there was another attack. But I couldn't send people out if I wasn't willing to go out myself," she said.

"Everybody knows you're willing and able. It's just that you're too valuable to risk," I said.

"I don't think any of us should be out here," Herb said. "If this was Brett's doing, the three people he wants to kill the most are all standing in one place: right here." He pointed to the ground.

"Of course he doesn't even know you're alive," I said to Herb. "And it's probably better that it stays that way."

"Point made and taken," Herb said. "How about you two head right in with all the scouts? I'll be in shortly."

"Why not right away?" I asked.

"I have a couple of things to do before the committee meeting," he replied. "Can we convene at seven? I should at least have some interesting questions to put forward then— if I haven't come up with the answers yet."

17

"Sorry I'm late," Herb said as he entered our crowded living room and settled into a seat at the corner of the table, next to Howie and my mother. Everyone else on the committee had arrived. I was sitting on the couch with my dad, talking about a minor mechanical issue on the Cessna we both had noticed.

"We haven't quite started," Judge Roberts said.

"I was just making a last round of the wall. I wanted to make sure people were all right."

"And?" Councilwoman Stevens asked.

"A little spooked, but they'll do their jobs. They're just worried about the people who were wounded. I haven't had a chance to go to the clinic. How are they doing?"

"Two have already been released, and the other two will be fine . . . although it's going to be a little while," Dr. Morgan said. "I guess we got lucky—considering the seriousness of the attack."

"Imagine how much worse it would have been if it had happened twenty-five minutes later, at shift change," Howie added.

"But instead it happened when the shift change *used* to happen," Herb pointed out.

A pregnant silence spread over the room.

"It's hard not to think it was deliberately done by somebody who knew our schedule," Mr. Peterson commented.

"I don't believe much in coincidence," Herb said. "It could only be one person."

There was no need to even say his name. In fact, it seemed like people went out of their way not to say his name out loud, almost like saying it might make him appear.

Brett had become the bogeyman of more bad dreams than just mine.

"The real question involves looking forward," my mother said. "What are we going to do to protect ourselves from another similar attack?"

"Could we strengthen the walls?" Councilwoman Stevens asked.

"If we made them into earthen berms they'd be better able to withstand an explosive impact," Mr. Nicholas said.

"What exactly does that mean?" the judge asked.

"We take massive amounts of dirt and pile it up into an extremely steep hill to form a wall," Mr. Nicholas explained.

"That would involve a tremendous amount of work," my father piped in from the corner of the couch.

It was rare for him to talk in these meetings.

"But if that's what has to be done, I'll be part of it," he added.

"It would be a lot of work," Howie agreed. "And it still wouldn't stop anybody from firing over the earthen walls at the houses."

"So that isn't a solution," Judge Roberts said. "What if we put more patrols or guards out into the forest?"

"Then they'd be susceptible to attack," my mother argued. "We need the walls to protect people, not have people protecting the walls."

"I'm open to other ideas," the judge said.

"Actually, I think you're all correct," Herb said. "We do need to make our defenses stronger, and the way to do that is to expand the walls. But instead of making them thicker, we have to make them farther out. What I suggest is a simple extension of Adam's plan, the one on the western and southern walls of our neighborhood. Perhaps it would be better to show you rather than try to explain it."

Herb got up. For a moment he seemed unsteady on his feet, almost a little wobbly. Again I thought about how much he'd aged over the past few months.

Herb had a very large piece of paper in his hand. He unfolded it and then taped it up to the wall beneath a photograph of my father's parents that was hanging there. It was a hand-drawn, artistic map of our neighborhood and the area around it extending as far east as the Credit River, south all the way to the lake, west as far as the Petersons' farm, and several miles north, well past Eglinton and even Britannia Road.

"I've been making progress on our little map project," he said, tapping a small square area at the center of the map. "Here we are, of course."

Inside the walls of our neighborhood, there wasn't much to see on the map. The streets were marked, but that was it. The detail was in the surrounding areas. Herb had marked not only streets but also distances, boundaries on smaller neighborhoods scattered throughout the area, the two bridges that remained across the Credit, the hospital complex well to the north, and the refinery well to the south just by the lake. And he'd added on dozens of other buildings and landmarks as well. It was a map that showed the reshaped world around us in the wake of the blackout: the pockets of life, the decimated areas, the potential threats.

"As you're all aware, for the last few weeks we've been working on a survey, marking off all the territory surrounding our home," Herb said.

"Are we to assume your diagram is completely accurate and to scale?" Mr. Nicholas asked.

"We've done our best. Misinformation is worse than no information," Herb replied. "We are fortunate to have a pilot in our midst who has the eyes of an eagle."

For a second I thought he was referring to me, but of course he meant my father.

"Could we have a round of applause for our senior pilot?" Herb asked.

People clapped, and my father looked a little embarrassed but a lot pleased. I felt happy for him. I guess this explained why he was here this evening.

"There are many reasons that the committee recommended that this survey be done," Herb said.

As I recalled, it had really been Herb who had recommended it and everybody else had simply approved it.

"The first places I'd like to draw your attention to are the two communities that adjoin our neighborhood." He tapped the area just south of our Burnham border. "With our assistance this has become a completely vital community. They have water, sufficient food to get through the winter, techniques and equipment to grow food next season, and the ability to protect their borders. They are operating under solid leadership and could be completely self-sufficient with the exception of defense."

"And they provide some additional defense for us from the south," my mother pointed out.

"Yes, an excellent point that I'm going to double back to." Next he tapped the new community we were helping to build to the west. "Soon they will have their walls in place. With the potatoes from the harvest, combined with the farmers from the Petersons' property who will join them tomorrow, they now have a significantly greater chance of survival." He paused. "And to emphasize the excellent point made by the captain, they will provide us with a security buffer to the west."

"The latest attack happened on the northeast corner, away from where both these communities are located," Howie said.

"Exactly, and that leads me to what I'm going to say next," Herb said. "We need to further extend the idea that Adam championed when we provided support for this fledging community to our west."

"Do you mean we're going to set up communities on the north and east as well?" I asked.

He nodded. "I want to work with the people who live north of Highway 403 to create a third buffer community. There are enough fields and open land among those houses to allow them to ultimately grow enough crops to sustain themselves."

"But most of those fields aren't planted," Mr. Peterson said. "*Ultimately* is a long way away, and the growing season is pretty much shot unless they planted last week. Who knows if those folks have a cache of food?"

"Then we're going to have to help them survive. Food is power, so we have to offer them food to entice them to join us," Herb said.

At this, Ernie Williams, our man in charge of all the food stocks, cleared his throat. "I'm sorry to say this, but even with the potatoes we really don't have much in the way of a surplus to give to anybody else."

"Not to mention that even with the root cellars and ideal storage we have to count on a percentage of those potatoes rotting before they're used," Mr. Peterson added. "There's always waste."

"That's an even better reason to offer some now of what will go to waste eventually," Herb said. "We have to find or grow more food."

Councilwoman Stevens spoke up. "Mr. Nicholas, you had mentioned to us in an earlier meeting that you were thinking of a way to heat the greenhouses so they can produce food throughout the winter."

"I've been playing with a few ideas. Last week I was able to get the first part of that plan off the ground. I built a little windmill out of scavenged bits and pieces, and I believe it can be used to convert wind power to electricity to heat the greenhouses. If I had enough of those windmills, I could heat more and more greenhouses."

"That is nothing short of genius," my mother said.

Everybody burst into applause again. Mr. Nicholas looked suitably pleased.

"We've also been gathering propane heaters, the sort that people use on their patios to take away the evening chill," he added.

"Aren't we basically out of propane?" Ernie asked.

"They've been searching for full or partially full tanks as well. Technically if we had enough fuel for those heaters, coupled with windmill-driven electricity generators, we could extend our growing season throughout the winter."

"In that case, get what you need to make enough windmills and find more propane," was the judge's verdict. "Talk to the scavenger crews and let's make this a priority. You, Mr. Nicholas, are a jewel."

"We're going to offer those communities food and the ability to grow food—we're going to offer them hope." Herb took a deep breath. He sounded a bit shaky and I tried to catch his eye, but he looked straight ahead and went on to outline his plan to incorporate a satellite neighborhood to the east that could stretch all the way to the west bank of the Credit. As he pointed out, the river was a natural defensive position, with a wide swath of land between us and the waterway, plenty of room for a new community.

Herb ran his hand over his head. "We need to find people who'd be willing to become part of that community and offer our support to help them organize and survive. I also want us to establish a walled corridor to lead from our northeast gate along the 403 and all the way to the river. We need to control this crossing, to fortify it so we can decide who is allowed to cross or not cross."

"It would give us access to a secure and plentiful water source at the Credit River as well as navigation right down to the lake," my mom observed. "Ultimately the river might become a highway again."

"I also think we need to create partnerships with two other communities: the refinery in the south and the hospital in the north," Herb said.

"You don't expect us to extend our walls that far, do you?" Mr. Nicholas asked.

"Not our boundaries. I just want us to consider forming a partnership built around trade and mutual security. We need what they have, and we have to hope they need what we can offer."

"I understand that we could use more medicine, but don't we have enough gasoline to last for years?" the judge asked.

"Years may not be enough," Herb said.

All the planning we had done, and all the work, had allowed us to think beyond today and into the immediate future—like into the coming winter, and next spring—but nobody really wanted to talk about anything beyond that. Except Herb.

"While without electricity the refinery wouldn't have the capacity to process oil to gas, those tanks should have massive quantities of fuel from before the blackout," Herb said. "As well as gasoline they will most likely have propane. We could solve our need for propane with one significant trade. They have fuel but basically there is almost no cultivation going on inside their boundaries."

"They probably *can't* grow anything," Mr. Peterson said. "The land around the refinery would be so contaminated that even if anything grew it wouldn't be fit for human consumption."

"That means they're undoubtedly already trading fuel for food," Herb said. "If they're doing that with others, there's no reason why they wouldn't do it with us. We can develop a trading partnership."

"And it would be incredibly important to create that same

link with the hospital," Dr. Morgan said. "I'm assuming you believe they have stashes of medicine."

"I can't think of anyplace that would have greater potential," Herb said. "You've kept us informed about the dwindling stock of medication we have. How are our stocks of medicine holding up at this point?"

"Some better than others."

"What's most needed?" my mother asked.

"Insulin," Dr. Morgan said without hesitation. "We're going to be out of insulin within two months."

"How many insulin-dependent diabetics do we have in our community?" my mother asked.

"Fifteen. Unless we secure more insulin, they will all be dead in six to twelve months."

"Then getting insulin is a priority, not just for the lives of those people but also for the life and spirit of the community," the judge said.

"I just hope we're not trading with food we don't necessarily have to spare," Mr. Peterson said.

"Food will be part of the deal, but not all of it. They need additional security, and perhaps more important they will crave a sense of connection and community," Herb said.

"We all need that," my mother said. "We all need to feel that we're not alone, that there are others out there to help, to stand by us, to offer support."

"It's like we're creating a neighborhood of neighborhoods," Herb said.

"It can be bigger than that," I said.

"It has to get bigger," Herb said.

"This all sounds wonderful," Howie said, "but I don't know

how effectively we can offer security to communities that aren't right on our borders."

"I'm suggesting that we create a joint security force," Herb said, "made up of members from all the communities that we ally with. A force that is well armed, in communication, and highly mobile."

"Like those go-carts," I said under my breath.

Herb pointed at me. "Exactly. We need to create a new fast-response defensive force, with fifty people from each of the new communities and the majority from Eden Mills."

"This is all going to take a lot of diplomacy, a lot of discussion," my mother said.

"It will. In the meantime we need to get working on the physical task of extending a walled, guarded corridor along the 403 all the way to the river so that we can control all access across the river."

"But what about the bridge across Dundas? Do we expand to there as well?" Judge Roberts asked.

"That's too far to expand or even provide protection for guards who would be placed there. That's why we have to destroy that bridge."

The judge gasped and said, "Destroy it?"

I could see the same shocked look in the expressions of others around the table.

Herb nodded solemnly. "We'll do it the same way we destroyed Burnham Bridge and basically for the same reasons. Except this time we can't afford to wait until an enemy appears."

"But don't a lot of people use that bridge?" Councilwoman Stevens asked.

"Hundreds use it each day," Herb admitted.

"But what will happen to them?" she wondered.

"People on foot will still be able to cross at the bottom, but vehicles won't," Herb said. "It's vehicles, carrying large groups of men, that we have to be afraid of."

"But the last two attacks have simply been by a small group of individuals. Destroying the Dundas bridge or controlling the one along the 403 won't protect us from that," Judge Roberts said.

"We are providing some protection for our core neighborhood by the expansion of the surrounding areas, but we can never have control over small-scale attacks. Those attacks can wound but never kill us. We have to take measures to make sure that nothing large scale can come at us from the city. Right now danger can come only from that direction."

"But there are other bridges across the river," my mother said.

"With the removal of the Dundas bridge and the control of the 403, the next-nearest bridge is almost thirty miles to the north. That distance gives us some protection. We can't eliminate threat; we can only make it less desirable and more difficult for any enemies who might choose to attack us," Herb explained.

There was complete silence around the room as everybody tried to digest all of what Herb had just suggested. I knew there would be a need for people to talk and argue, weigh the alternatives, think things through. Then after that had taken place, I was equally sure it would all happen. Herb was right, and everybody knew it.

18

It was four days after the meeting and I was back in the Cessna, with Lori beside me. We were heading for the refinery. I would have felt more comfortable going out in the ultralight, but it was agreed the plane was more impressive—and we wanted to make an impression.

After our little fight, I had been trying to patch things up with Lori, and last night I had gone over to her place to spend a few hours with her and her parents. Her father had filled in Lori and her mother on the committee's decisions. Without hesitation, Lori asked to come up with me, to help out on this mission.

"Can you go any slower when we make the drop?" Lori said.

"Any slower or lower, and we'll *be* the drop."

She had in her hands the invitation we were going to send down to whoever was living at the refinery—a weighted parcel tied to a homemade parachute. Originally it was going to be Herb at my side as well, but he was feeling under the weather.

Nobody except my family, Judge Roberts, and Dr. Morgan knew anything about him needing to rest. Herb being strong gave everybody else strength. His confidence gave everybody else confidence. Even so, his absence was easy to hide because it always seemed like he was everywhere, so everybody just assumed he was simply someplace else. And since the decision had been made to put his plan into effect, he had been almost everywhere all at once, hurrying from place to place inside and outside the neighborhood trying to put everything into motion. Today we were going to put two more parts into play, trying to arrange meetings with the refinery and the hospital.

The flight had been less than a smooth one. Right after takeoff we were buffeted by strong winds. I had to work the controls pretty hard to keep the plane steady, and it helped that Lori stayed calm beside me, even when we had one drop that was so sudden and severe that we both rose up in the air, our seat belts the only things that stopped us from hitting against the ceiling. Lori's only response was to giggle. Todd would have screamed. Heck, I almost screamed.

Repeatedly I'd changed elevation looking for calmer air, but there was none to be found at the lower range. Technically I could have tried to go above the turbulence—the ceiling of my plane was ten thousand feet—but there was no point in doing so when we were going such a short distance and needed to be low when we arrived.

Now the refinery loomed just up ahead, its metal superstructure towering into the air. It looked impressive and intimidating and a little unreal, like something made by a giant kid with an equally gigantic Erector set. It also made for difficulties with this drop. I needed to come in low enough to drop the parachute and make sure it landed on their grounds but high enough not to hit anything.

The first drop, at the hospital, had gone off without a hitch. As we circled back around we saw that a group of men had retrieved it; they even waved to us as we passed over. I'd wiggled my wings in response.

The refinery didn't look as friendly. Positioned all around the grounds were two dozen gigantic spherical storage tanks, streaks of rust marring many of them. The whole complex was ringed with razor-wire fences, earthen berms, cement walls, and guard towers. I couldn't see the guards yet, but there was no question that they could see us. Almost instinctively I dipped and banked to the right to evade anybody who had us in their rifle sights.

Lori popped open her side window, and a rush of air filled the cabin and the engine noise increased. We swept past the fences, the rigging rising right ahead of us. She chose a spot and dropped the package out the window, and I hit the rudder hard right, pulled out the throttle, and eased back on the yoke. Instantly we gained speed and height.

I craned my neck to try to pick up the little parachute going down but couldn't track it.

"You see it?" I asked.

"Direct hit," Lori replied. "That makes us two for two."

If both groups accepted the invitations, we'd meet with one tomorrow and the second the day after. I just had to hope that Herb was feeling well enough to take part in the meetings. Regardless, though, they were going to happen. We couldn't very well reschedule.

"So how would you feel about extending our flight?" I asked.

"How about a tropical vacation?"

"Close—a flight to the city."

The committee had requested that my father and I widen our air patrols, looking for potential allies and dangers that were farther afield. So I'd informed them that I was going to travel closer to the city on this flight.

"I'm more than okay with that. I love being up here." She reached out and placed a hand on my leg.

That sent a jolt through me. Luckily, it didn't cause me to put the plane into a nosedive right then and there.

"Good, then let's both keep our eyes wide open," I said, although right then it was the last thing I wanted to do.

Slowly, so as to not disturb that hand, I put the plane into a long bank, bringing us well out over the lake before looping us back around toward the city.

"So pretty," Lori said.

"The water is beautiful from up here, although I can't help but think of all the untreated sewage flowing into it."

"You really know how to say the most romantic things." Lori stared down at the lake below. "Look at all the sailboats."

I could see lots of watercraft, including motorboats. That made sense. Anything with just a basic outboard still could work because they were all simple engines that didn't require computers, like the lawn mowers, old cars, and even the Cessna.

In the distance, just on the horizon, I could make out the tallest of the downtown office towers. They were in the core of the city and I could use them as dead reckoning to get there. On the way home I'd take a different route, probably following along one of the highways leading out of the city and ultimately right by our neighborhood to the south.

"It's so peaceful up here," Lori said.

"It's maybe the only peaceful place around."

I pulled back a little bit more on the wheel. I wanted to get even more cushion between the safety of the sky and the turmoil below. It meant we wouldn't see as much detail on the ground, but I was willing to make that trade.

Lori leaned in closer, and I thought the flight was going to get even better, but then she jerked back suddenly.

"What's wrong?"

Eyes wide, mouth open, she pointed past me.

Another plane was flying parallel to us—no more than fifty feet off to the side! I had to consciously think to not jerk the controls and put us into a dive or bank.

"Whoa, that's a World War II Mustang P-51!"

"What?"

"An old U.S. military plane."

It was silver, with large numbers and a big white air force star painted on the side. It looked like it had flown out of the past and right to my port wingtip. This was unreal. And then the unreal became even more so as a second Mustang materialized on the starboard side! I was sandwiched between two antique fighter planes, the second even closer than the first.

We flew along in a little formation, both planes so close that I could see their pilots. And then one of the pilots starting making hand gestures.

I knew what he was saying, I just didn't want to believe it. "He wants us to go down, to land."

"Land where?"

I shook my head. "I don't know."

"Can't you just ignore him or outrun them?"

"Not a chance. This is a Cessna 172 with a top speed of about a hundred and eighty miles per hour and that's on a very good day. The Mustang's top speed is more than twice that. Plus it has a range that's longer than mine, a higher ceiling, and can make turns tighter than I could even imagine."

"What if we just ignore them and keep flying?" she asked.

As if in answer there was a short burst of machine-gun fire that came out of the wings of the port plane.

My heart was pounding. "The Mustang also has six fifty-caliber machine guns and was one of the most dangerous fighter planes of the war," I added mechanically.

"How do you even know all of that?" she asked.

"I love planes. I know things . . . things like that. We have no choice but to do what they want."

The pilot to my left gestured for me to follow. I nodded. He accelerated and took up a spot in front of me. The second plane dropped back until he was right on my tail—the perfect place to use those machine guns to blast me out of the sky.

The front plane started a slow bank and I followed his lead. My mind raced, looking for a solution, but there was none. I couldn't outrun, outlast, outturn, or outfight him. All I could do was follow.

We were too far from the neighborhood to send a distress call over the walkie-talkie. So we were really on our own.

I looked over at Lori, who smiled back tentatively. "I'm so sorry, Lori, so sorry."

"It's not your fault."

We continued to turn, circling the office towers and descending at the same time. I played with the idea of hitting the rudder hard and cutting through the towers, but what then? If I did shake my tail for a moment, they'd just be waiting for me on the other side. How long did I think I could dodge them, how long before they'd simply lose patience and shoot us out of the sky?

I stayed true to the course he was setting. Whatever was waiting on the ground had to be better than being shot down, I hoped.

As we descended, I noticed we were doing a big pass over the lake, and then I remembered: there was a small airport on the island that formed the outer barrier of the city's harbor. Was that where he wanted me to land?

We came back around, and I knew I was right: the little airport, with its two black runways, appeared before me.

"I've landed here before, with my dad at the controls of a Piper Cub he'd borrowed from a friend, years ago, when I was a little kid."

"What's down there?" Lori asked.

"I'm not sure what's down there now, but it used to be just a small private airfield, a few dozen houses people used as summer places, and an aviation museum." Then it came to me. "They had old warplanes at the museum. It was a group of air enthusiasts who bought and repaired old planes."

"Like Mustangs?"

"Like Mustangs. I've probably sat in the cockpit of one of those planes." I wished I was at the controls of that plane right now. We'd have a fighting chance, or at least a chance to fight back. Here I was, defenseless. What were we supposed to do, crack off a rifle shot at one of them?

Lower and lower, the first plane led the way. I thought

about overshooting once he landed, but there was nothing to stop him from skipping back up, a quick touchdown and takeoff, and then there was the problem of the plane still on my tail. He'd backed off, but that was just to keep a better eye on me. There was no way I was flying away from this.

"When we land I'm going to keep going, taxiing along the runway to get as close to the end as I can," I said. "As soon as I come to a stop, jump out and start running."

"Where are we running to?" she asked.

"Away from the runway, into any cover we can find. We have to try to hide. I can see a wooded area at the end."

She nodded. "I'm scared."

"So am I," I said. Would Herb have said that? No, he would have said something to inspire confidence. "But we're going to get out of this. I promise."

The runway came up fast. People and vehicles were moving around just off to the side, and as we came down I could see that the surrounding ground had been cultivated, some fields brown and harvested and others still filled with crops.

Without taking my eyes off the controls, I told Lori, "Run as soon as I come to a stop. Head off to your side and I'll be right behind you . . . Remember, we're going to be fine. They don't want us, they want the plane."

"So when they have the plane what are they going to do with us?" she asked.

That question was too close to the truth. "We're not going to find out because we're going to get away."

With one hand remaining on the wheel I used the other to unsnap my harness. Lori hesitated then did the same. I also did a touch check of the pistol under my arm and a second of the weapon strapped to my ankle. I also had the knife strapped to the other leg—not that it was going to do me much good. There was no point in bringing a knife to a gunfight, especially when that gun was a .65-caliber machine gun.

"Take the pistol," I said.

"I'll take the rifle."

"No, I'll take the rifle."

"I'm a better shot than you," she said.

"That's not the reason. If they're going to shoot us they're more likely to shoot at whoever has a weapon. They won't see the pistol from a distance, but they're going to see the rifle. Please?"

She reached over and removed my pistol from its holster.

"And whatever we do we can't give them information about our neighborhood," I said.

"I didn't think they were going to catch us."

"They're not . . . But if they do, we say nothing that's true. We're from up north, small community, and we just happen to have a plane . . . right?"

She nodded.

"Here we go."

The lead Mustang had slowed down to almost stall speed. He skimmed along the runway but didn't touch down. He wasn't going to give me the opportunity to touch and go. My wheels were just above the asphalt—I wanted to stay in the air as long as possible to get to the end as quickly as possible.

On both sides there was a burst of activity. There were men and women and even kids and I could see weapons in the hands of some of the adults. Our wheels touched down and we bounced lightly, and then they settled in and we rumbled along. I didn't hit the brakes hard. I wanted to keep moving away from the center, away from the tower and all the people. We raced along dangerously fast, and the end of the runway and the woods beyond came rushing toward us. The woods meant safety and danger both.

"Hold on!" I yelled.

I applied the brakes hard, the plane jerked, and we lurched forward, the steering column holding me in place and the dash holding Lori. The woods were coming closer and closer. I wasn't sure if we were going to make it, and we skidded sideways and then came to a stop. I quickly scrambled to open the door, but when I looked up we were surrounded by a small army with rifles pointed directly at us.

19

"Hands up!" one of the men yelled.

They had us surrounded, and the thin metal skin of the Cessna was no defense.

"Carefully drop the pistol to the floor," I murmured to Lori.

As I slowly put my hands in the air, Lori half bent down to drop the gun, then straightened up, hands in the air. Two men, one on each side, came to the doors of the plane while the others continued to train their rifles on us. The doors were flung open and the two men reached in and grabbed me from my seat. I heard Lori scream out from the other side. I was thrown onto the ground, the asphalt biting into the side of my face.

I struggled to move, to turn over, to try to see Lori, but a foot was pressed into my back, pinning me in place.

"Search them!"

Hands were running all over me. Deliberately I pressed my ankles together so that the pistol and knife were protected from prying hands.

"He's clean!" one of the men yelled.

"The girl is, too."

"There's a pistol on the floor and a rifle inside the cockpit!" another voice called out.

In their minds finding two weapons meant that there were no more to be found. That assumption only worked in our favor.

Still pressed to the ground, I could hear a vehicle coming, getting louder and louder, and then the squealing of brakes. Then there were footsteps on the pavement.

"Let them up!"

"Yes, sir!"

A man leaned down close to my face. "No sudden move, tough guy, or it will be your last," he threatened.

Despite my fear, my brain registered the smell of toothpaste on his breath.

Strong arms pulled me to my feet and held my arms in place. I looked over at Lori, who was flanked by two men.

"Have they been searched for weapons?" the man demanded. He was gray-haired and tall, his back ramrod straight. It certainly sounded and looked like he was in charge.

"Yes, sir. And we have confiscated their weapons from the plane."

He nodded in acknowledgment. "Release them."

They let go, and Lori moved over to my side. I put my arm around her shoulder, somewhat uselessly.

There was a military precision to them, like what we'd encountered with troops from the Division. The fear that I'd been feeling suddenly increased. Had we stumbled into the new compound? Was this man the colonel? Could I expect Brett, like a monster in a nightmare, to jump out at us any minute?

The older man walked forward. "You're bleeding." He pulled a white handkerchief from his pocket and held it out. Lori took it and placed it against the cut on the side of my face.

"Did you do that in the landing?" he asked.

"It happened when your men threw him on the ground," Lori snapped.

Her feistiness gave me renewed strength.

"We can't be too careful," the gray-haired man said. "We aren't used to unexpected guests."

"Guests? Is that what we are?"

"Perhaps 'guest' is the wrong word, but we still need to take precautions when you land at our airfield."

"Your planes forced us to land," I said. "This wasn't our idea."

The man seemed unperturbed by our anger. "Actually it was mine," he said smoothly. "I gave the order when they radioed in your presence. Seeing your plane over the city caught us unaware."

"Seeing your two Mustangs wasn't what we expected either."

He smiled. "Please accept my apologies for the manner in which you were forced to come here, as well as for your injury, but we felt it would be wise to talk to you and you didn't respond to our attempts to radio you."

"I didn't have the radio on," I admitted. "It wasn't like I was expecting a call."

I needed to think. What would Herb do if he were here?

"This is nothing," I said, pointing up to the scrape. "Apology accepted." I held out my hand. "I'm Adam and this is Lori."

He held out his hand. "Robert Wayne," he said as we shook hands.

"Pleased to meet you, sir," I said. If they called him "sir," then I should as well.

Lori understood what I was doing and changed her tune as well. "Do you think they could put down those rifles?" she asked. "I don't usually expect apologies to come with weapons involved."

Mr. Wayne motioned for his men to comply and looked at us closely for a moment, as if memorizing our features. "I think it was equally unexpected that the pilot and passenger of a plane would be two young people." He paused. "But since you're our guests, why don't we continue this conversation over a cool drink and some food?"

"If we're guests, are we free to decline your invitation and climb back into our plane and leave?" I asked.

"After that rough landing and hard braking I think it would be wise for our ground crew to have a look at your plane before you take off," he said.

"And if I don't want that?" I asked.

"I'm afraid it would be unwise, and inconsiderate for me to force your plane to the ground and then not take responsibility for making sure it was airworthy. As such, I must *insist* that you join me for a drink. I could never forgive myself if I sent you up before the inspection took place and something happened to you." He paused. "We definitely would not want anything to happen, would we?"

"No, we wouldn't want that," I agreed. What choice did we have?

He turned directly to one of the men who had held us at gunpoint. "Take care of their plane, and, please, be more delicate than you were with the pilot."

He ushered us toward the truck he had driven up in.

"Why don't you ride in front, Adam? And, Lori, would you share the back with me?" he said. These were more commands than questions.

Two of the men opened the doors and we climbed in, me beside his driver, a large man with a stern expression and a pistol strapped to his side. As we drove away, we left behind a dozen men with rifles. The odds had shifted in our direction. Of course they both had on side arms, but I'd taken on two armed men before and won.

We drove in silence. Casually I reached down and let my hand brush against the gun strapped to my ankle. It was reassuring and frightening to feel the bump. I looked out the window, at all the people, many of them women and children, and my thoughts raced.

Shooting the two of them couldn't be done without drawing attention to us and couldn't possibly end well. I had the knife, but pulling that wasn't going to give me a better result. Better to keep both hidden. Surprise was our only chance. And besides, it wasn't like I could just pull out my gun and force them to drive us to safety. We were on an island. Even if we got off the island we were close to forty miles away from our neighborhood and would have no way to get there except on foot and through potentially hostile situations every step of the way.

I forced my thoughts away from escape and to our immediate surroundings. I could see at least a dozen planes parked out on the side of the runway, and there were probably others tucked away in the hangar. I wondered how many of them were actually airworthy. I noted a few Cessnas, a glider, and a collection of other old military planes, including what looked like a Lancaster and a Spitfire. There was also an old passenger plane.

They had their own little air force right here.

The car came to an abrupt stop in front of a low building. Almost instantly two guards opened up the doors to the vehicle, let us out, and ushered us inside the building. As we walked along the hall, a couple of the guards actually saluted Mr. Wayne. We reached an office, and he called out to one of the men to bring refreshments before he closed the door behind him.

"Please take a seat," he said.

We sat down on two seats and he circled around a large desk and took a seat himself, gazing at us kindly as if he really were just our host and we were simply having an impromptu get-together.

"So tell me about where you live," he said.

"It's not much," I said, sensing that Lori wanted me to take the lead. "I'm much more interested in this place."

He smiled. "What we've done is rather impressive."

"How many people live here?" Lori asked.

"Just under three thousand call this place home—a home, I should mention, that has sufficient food, medical facilities, and secure boundaries."

"I guess it helps being on an island," she responded.

"It helps, but that wouldn't be enough on its own. There are lots of people who have boats and guns out there," he said.

I gestured outside. "But not many places have their own air force."

"We were fortunate to have had the warplanes museum right here."

"I've visited it before with my dad," I said.

His gaze sharpened. "Your father—is he a pilot, too?"

I'd obviously given away more than I wanted. "Yes, he's a pilot."

"So you followed your old man's footsteps," he said. "Just like my two boys who followed in my footsteps and joined the marines."

"So you're not 'Mr.' Wayne . . . Should we be calling you Major Wayne or Colonel Wayne?" I asked.

"If we're going to be formal, it would be Colonel Wayne."

Colonel! This pushed me even more on edge. Could this be the Division's leader, the infamous "Colonel"?

"So that puts you just one step below a brigadier general."

"One big step. How do you know about marine rankings?" he asked.

"Who doesn't think about being a marine when they grow up?" I asked.

I sensed Lori looking at me in surprise, but I didn't turn her way.

"A marine pilot," I added.

"That was what I did," the colonel said. "F-16s. It's not quite the same being in a Mustang, but it's still flying. How long have *you* been flying?"

"Not long. I was just getting ready to solo when the blackout happened."

"So you don't even have a pilot's license?" he asked.

"Not technically . . . I would have had one by now."

"I'm sure you would have. I saw you land. You came in long deliberately. Were you going to try to run away?"

"That was sort of the plan," I admitted.

"We're pretty good at keeping people off the island, so please believe me it would be very, very hard for you to have done so. We're not quite an army here, because we have so many civilians, but we're still pretty secure."

Was that another threat—telling us we weren't going anywhere—or just a statement of fact?

He seemed in no hurry to direct the conversation back to us, so I continued my questions. "Where did all of the people who live out here come from?"

"Mostly they're people who escaped the city. We felt an obligation to take them in—up to a point, of course. It didn't hurt to have a few retired military pilots, some police officers, and three dozen other military men." He paused. "My wife and I just wish our boys were here."

"They're not?" Lori asked.

He shook his head. "They were stationed overseas."

"I'm so sorry," Lori said.

He shrugged. "At least they were in the same unit. I know they're all right. They're marines stationed with other marines. I would imagine that the most stable places in the world are built around military divisions and bases. Or those who behave like military units. Including around here."

"You know of others?"

"We've discovered that we're not alone. There are other groups, some small, and some large, that we've been able to connect with."

There was a knock on the door, and a man entered with a tray. I could smell the coffee and just about grabbed a cup before the colonel motioned for us to help ourselves. I hadn't had a cup in a couple of weeks. The man smiled, and I smiled back as I realized there was even milk and sugar. That first sip tasted incredible, and the colonel must have noticed my blissful expression.

"Do you still have sugar?"

"A little. Also, my father has been able to use beets to make sugar," Lori said. "He's a farmer, so he runs the agricultural part of things where we live."

"We have a couple of people with farming experience. The land out here is very fertile. We've also established some trade with a community to the west, and they have been able to get supplies of sugar from much, much farther away. Perhaps we can even trade with you? Tell me more about where you two live."

I was feeling pretty relaxed. Colonel Wayne was being friendly and open and had given us a lot of information, so maybe we should share with him as well. We were trying to establish more allies, so this was just perfect—unless the colonel was just trying to get us to let down our guard. My heartbeat quickened. On the one hand, I knew he could tell us anything he wanted—it wasn't like we were going to leave without his permission. On the other hand, I couldn't "unsay" something, so it was better to share as little as possible.

"There's not much to tell," I said carefully. "We're small, a couple of dozen families on a farm about seventy miles north of here. I guess all the open space gives us the same protection the lake gives you. I don't really know if we have anything you'd need. We're just trying to survive."

"We all are, but together we have a better chance of doing that. You flew a long way."

"This is all my fault," Lori said. "I nagged and nagged Adam to take me down to the city because I wanted to see what it looked like these days. If he hadn't listened to me, this wouldn't have happened."

I smiled back at her, playing along. "I fly the plane, but she's the pilot, you know?"

The colonel leaned closer. "And your father was all right with you taking the plane to the city?" he asked.

I tried to look sheepish. "He knew I was taking it up, but I didn't really tell him about where we were going."

There was a knock on the door, and the man who'd brought the coffee reappeared. "Everything checked out, sir. Their plane is flight-ready."

"Excellent." Colonel Wayne stood up. "Your plane is ready, Adam and Lori, and has even been refueled."

"We can leave?" I asked.

"Of course. Did you think you were prisoners?"

"Well . . . you had us a little worried," I said.

"I guess I understand your fears. There are a lot of danger- ous people out there. Here, though, we try to live by that." He pointed to a plaque on the wall.

The first three words were enough for me to know what it was. Written in large letters it read, "We the People." It was the Constitution.

"We can't live it by the letter these days, but we try to live it by the spirit."

"It's hard to do that," I said, "with everything that's going on out there."

"It is, but we try," he said.

"So do we," I said.

"You'd better get going. I'm sure your parents are going to be wondering where you are, and they'll be more than a little bit worried the longer you're away."

I hadn't even thought of that. We should have been back

long before this. "I'll radio them as soon as we get in range," I said.

"And now that the plane has been checked out we have to take care of you," the colonel said.

"Me?"

"Your face. It's still bleeding."

I reached up to touch the spot. It was tender and my hand came away red with blood. "It's nothing. I'm fine."

"We can't send you home all scraped up without treatment. What would your parents think of us if we did that?"

I almost said I'd have Dr. Morgan look at it when I got home, but that would have been revealing more again.

"Thanks, that would be great," Lori said. "It's not like we have anybody who can do things like that back home."

She hadn't missed a beat.

———————

"Should I call you Doctor?" I asked the woman who dabbed my face with a cotton swab containing antiseptic.

"You should probably call me Ellen. I'm a nurse, not a doctor."

"Don't you have any doctors?" I asked, fishing for information.

"We have three, but I don't think we needed them for this. Do you?" she asked. "Besides, one of them is a surgeon and another is a coroner. Your injury doesn't seem to require either of those two."

"He really is a big suck," Lori said.

"Most men are," Ellen agreed, and they both chuckled.

"So where were you when all this started?" Lori asked.

"The power outage?" she asked.

"The everything outage," Lori replied.

"I worked at a hospital downtown and lived in a big condo right by the lake. If you go to the north side of the island, you can even see my condo tower across the harbor."

"And you came here right away?" I asked.

"My daughter and son and I. On that first afternoon we paddled over in a canoe and camped out. I thought it was going to be a little adventure for a day or two, until they restored the power. I guess it's been a little more adventure and a lot longer than anybody could have imagined."

"And you've been part of this colony right from the beginning?" I asked.

"It didn't exist in the beginning, but we got involved early on."

"And it's a good place for your kids?" I asked.

"About the best place they could be. They're safe, secure. We've even started a little school. You might even see it on your way out."

"That would be nice," Lori said.

"I'm sure you'll also see my kids because they aren't too far away. You two dropping in was pretty exciting for people."

"It was pretty exciting for us, too," I said.

"There you are, all cleaned out and taped up and ready to go," she said. "You must be anxious to get going."

"Our parents will be worried," Lori said. "The colonel said we could come back if we want to sometime."

"You should. This is a good place." She paused. "I guess that's what you've really been asking all along. *Are these good people, can we trust them?*"

"And?" Lori asked.

"Yes and yes. In a world gone wild we've found ourselves in a safe little sanctuary."

Ellen had been right. Both her kids were waiting right outside the examination room. The daughter, Emma, was about thirteen or fourteen and the son, Ethan, was about the age of the twins. They were as friendly as their mother and seemed, well, to be just kids. The three of them walked us down a corridor and said goodbye at the door. It had all seemed so normal, it was almost unnerving.

I was surprised but happy to see our plane sitting on the tarmac right outside the building. Somebody had taxied it all the way down the runway. The colonel and two other men were waiting beside it.

"Should we tell him about us?" Lori whispered. "About our neighborhood?"

I shook my head.

"But why not? He's letting us go."

"We're not in the plane yet," I said. In my mind I still wondered if our courteous reception was all nothing more than an elaborate ploy—even being treated by the nurse and talking to her kids—to gain our confidence in order to get us to talk. Was Colonel Wayne really going to let us get into the plane and fly away?

"So both you and the plane are all ready to go," the colonel said. "I don't mean to delay you any longer."

"Thanks. Thanks for everything," I said. I offered him my hand and he took it.

"I'm really grateful that you didn't feel the need to pull that gun," he said, still holding my hand.

"Gun?"

"The one strapped to the inside of your left ankle. I didn't notice it at first, but then you reached down a couple of times to touch it. You weren't thinking of using it, were you?"

I hesitated for a second and then answered, "Only if I'd had to." He hadn't mentioned the knife, so either he didn't know about it or didn't see it as a threat.

He released my hand. "I understand why you would be concerned, but there was never any need. What I'll have to do, though, is talk to my men about being a little more thorough in their frisking. Your other pistol and rifle are in the plane. I also want you to know that you're welcome to visit if you ever want to come back."

"Thank you, sir," Lori said, shaking his hand.

"If you wanted to bring somebody else, including some of the leaders of your group, they would also be welcome."

"I know my father would enjoy coming here just to see the planes."

"We might even let him go up for a patrol. We have more planes than pilots and nobody at all qualified to fly that old passenger plane."

"My father was a commercial pilot."

"Interesting. And, I hope, at some point you'll feel comfortable enough to tell me where you really live and how your group is doing."

I didn't know what to say. Obviously we weren't very good liars and he'd seen clear through us.

"We all need partners if we're going to get through this,"

Colonel Wayne said, then stepped back to let us get into the Cessna.

We both settled in our seats, strapping on our harnesses and headsets. I flicked the ignition and opened up the throttle. The engine roared to life, the propeller a nearly invisible blur. The colonel waved and then gave a little salute.

When we were racing down the runway, I noticed the two fighter planes that had escorted us down were now parked at the side of the runway, and more of my worries slipped away. I reveled in the smoothness of the runway surface and the seeming endlessness of the strip. This was how planes were meant to take off, not from makeshift strips on roads and fields.

We lifted off, I pulled back on the yoke, and we soared into the air. We were now aimed almost perfectly toward our neighborhood.

I hit the right rudder and aimed the opposite direction. I was now almost positive I could trust the colonel, but still I wanted them to see me heading north. Home would have to wait a little bit longer, and I'd be watching to make sure no plane was following us.

20

We waited just down the road from the refinery, me at the wheel of my car and Herb in the passenger seat. We had guards with guns flanking us on both sides, hidden among the houses and trees. Up in the sky, low on the horizon, making large, slow circuits, my father was in the Cessna. With him were two of our sharpshooters. Todd was also along for the ride. He wasn't much with a rifle, but it was reassuring to have him up there watching me in a different way. I could just imagine him making jokes and keeping things light. We could have used that in the car right now.

"It's time," Herb said, and I set the car in motion.

Herb had been looking and acting more like himself the last couple of days. All he'd needed was some rest and sleep, and he was back on top of his game—although I did still notice that slight shaking in his hands.

Yesterday, he and Dr. Morgan, along with Councilwoman Stevens, had met with the people running the hospital. It had gone well. It certainly helped that Dr. Morgan knew some of the men and women in charge—other doctors.

They had large quantities of medicine and our two communities had already made a food-for-medicine trade to start off our new relationship. There were medicines that the hospital had that we couldn't get from raiding cabinets in abandoned houses.

They were also going to start preliminary talks about forming an alliance for security purposes. I just had to hope that today went as well as yesterday. Or at least well enough that we didn't get shot at.

"Do you remember the first time you and I went out in a car after the blackout hit?" Herb said.

"It would be a little hard to forget you loading down my car with two thousand dollars' worth of chlorine."

Herb laughed. "You must have thought I'd lost my mind."

"I don't think I was the only one. All of your predictions in the beginning sounded crazy . . . Of course, the craziest thing is that most of them have come true."

"I would prefer to have been wrong," he said.

"I guess we all would," I agreed.

"Now we just have to stay focused on the present."

"I'm focused, Herb."

"I think I was talking more to myself," he said. "You have to do me a favor and keep an eye on me, make sure I don't slip up."

"You're the most focused person I know," I said, defending him against himself.

"That focus has slipped on more than one occasion. Both of us have gotten older since the world fell apart."

"You make it seem like that was a hundred years ago," I said.

"Doesn't it feel that way?"

I had to admit that it did seem like years ago instead of months.

"You've grown up, and I've grown old."

"I'd still rather have you here beside me than anybody else I can think of," I said.

"Even Lori?"

"Especially Lori. I wouldn't want to put her in harm's way again. She does enough of that for herself."

"From what I can tell, she handles it all like a champion," Herb said.

"She does. I think she is more in control than me."

"That girl is definitely a keeper. You're lucky I'm not two hundred years younger or you'd have yourself some competition."

"I still feel bad having to put her through all of that the other day."

"You shouldn't still be feeling bad about being forced down by those Mustangs. It wasn't like you had any choice. I'm hoping we'll have a chance to drop in and talk to those people at the island when things calm down a bit."

"Has the committee approved it?" I asked. There'd been a meeting the night before last that I hadn't been around for. I'd chosen to hang out with Todd and Lori. We went over to the basketball court by the school and played horse for hours, until we couldn't take any more of Lori embarrassing us with her varsity ball-shooting skills. It wasn't just a gun that she was better at aiming than we were.

"That's one other thing I wanted to mention. I'm going to request that you become a permanent member of the committee."

"Me?"

"Well, you're there almost every meeting anyway, but

I think it's just time for you to more formally take on the leadership you offer already."

"We already have a lot of leaders."

"We do, but only one who's going to be here in twenty years," Herb said.

I was going to say something about Herb being here, but he was right—that wasn't realistic. Still, the judge wasn't as old as Herb was, and my parents were still relatively young. Then another thought hit me.

"Twenty years?"

"I'm optimistic we can make enough changes to provide stability—a new normal if you'd like—but I've seen nothing to indicate we're going to go back to where we were. There is a very long end game here," Herb said.

"I can't even imagine what else could happen," I said.

"It might be beyond anybody's imagining. The hardest part is being able to react to more destruction while still trying to figure out how to put the shattered pieces back together again."

"Isn't that what we're doing today?"

"Yes . . . We're going to have to rebuild by making our world larger. This still has to be about survival, but it also has to be about more than just survival."

I rounded the corner and the refinery came into sight. Herb rolled down the window and raised a white flag on a short stick. In the message Lori had dropped had been all the necessary information for this meet: time, type of vehicle, and even that we'd have the white flag. We had to hope that the people living at the refinery would honor our request—or at least ignore it, not open the gate, and not shoot at us.

At Herb's direction we'd also deliberately left our body armor behind, as well as our weapons. I felt next to naked.

As we closed in on the refinery, I could to make out guards behind the fence at scattered locations. I slowed down and was about to come to a stop right in front of the gate when it opened partway, allowing a gap wide enough for us to pass. Slowly, with both hands visible on the wheel, I inched us up to, and then through, the gap. My anxious feelings morphed into awful feelings. It was like my stomach was one gigantic knot. We were no more than halfway through the gate when two armed men appeared on both sides of the car.

"Keep your hands in plain view!" one of the men called through the open car windows. Herb brought the little flag into the car and placed his hands on the dashboard.

I saw in my rearview mirror the gate close behind me. That awful feeling got even worse.

"Can we get out of the car?" Herb requested.

"Slowly," one of the men said.

"Son, at my age, slowly is the only way I can move," Herb said.

He climbed out his door. I turned off the engine with one hand, while I placed the second on the dashboard. Very slowly, very deliberately, I opened the door and climbed out, too. I was frisked, as was Herb on the other side. If we had had any weapons they would have been discovered and taken.

"Do you treat all your visitors this way?" I asked.

"We don't have a lot of visitors."

"Maybe you'd have more if you treated them more hospitably," Herb suggested.

They finished patting us down and led us away from my car. We now had four guards, one leading and three behind.

I took a quick look back at the car. There were more armed men standing around it. I had the strangest thought that I should have rolled up the windows and locked the doors so they wouldn't go inside.

We went farther and farther into the guts of the refinery. It was a fascinating collection of metal pipes, tanks, and soaring superstructure. As a kid when we drove by, I'd always gawked at the eerie-looking place and wondered about it. Now I was seeing it closer than I probably wanted to. I just hoped I'd be able to see it from the outside again after this meeting.

All along the way we passed working men and women wearing hard hats. It looked like they were still processing something. Were they able to turn oil into gas even in the absence of electricity?

"Good afternoon," a man called out from the scaffolding above our heads.

"Good afternoon," Herb called back.

The man disappeared from view and reappeared a few seconds later at a ladder. He came down and extended his hand and there was a quick series of introductions and handshakes. His name was Payton Mondoux.

"Let's get down to business. You want to trade food for fuel," Payton said.

"Yes, that's part of what we want," Herb replied.

"Part?"

"We were also hoping to forge a more extensive partnership."

"And what would this partnership involve?" Payton asked.

"A great deal of that depends on what you need," Herb

said. "Our community is about fifteen miles north of here. Our settlement has sixteen hundred people, and we're affiliated with other settlements who have become our allies. In total we are almost three thousand people strong. We have medical facilities, medicine, food, air support, security, and numerous people with engineering skills."

"We have over a dozen engineers here," Payton said. "Mainly those engineers are folks who worked at the refinery before this all happened. Medical care is an ongoing issue, although we've been able to trade for some medicine."

"We can have one of our doctors come here, but it might be better to have anybody who's ill come to our clinic or even the hospital."

I noticed how Herb offered the resources of the hospital we'd only just connected with, just like I'd heard that yesterday he'd offered the hospital a fuel supply from the refinery before we even had met with them.

"We have security and transportation to get your people safely to and from our medical facilities," Herb continued.

"We were impressed with the airplane," Payton said. "There aren't many of those in the sky."

"We have two aircraft," Herb said.

I guess calling the ultralight an aircraft was stretching the truth a little, even though it was technically one.

"You must be doing something right if you have that many people and you're able to produce so much food that you can trade," Payton noted.

"And you yourselves must be doing something right to allow you to trade enough fuel to provide food for your people," Herb said. "It isn't like you're growing much of anything here."

Before he answered, Payton took his hard hat off and scratched his head. "I guess you'd know that from your flyovers."

"We're aware of many things on a wider scale than it might seem," Herb offered, saying something without really saying anything. "But you know this has to be about more than just survival. We've established a day-care center, a school, and a newspaper. We have movie nights, and I think we're providing our children with as normal a life as we can . . . given the circumstances."

"It's hard to believe that those things are happening anywhere these days."

"Seeing is believing, and I hope you'll have a chance to visit us. How many children call this place home?" Herb asked.

"We have fifty-six."

"I can't decide whether this is hardest on the children or easiest, because we manage to protect them from some of the realities," Herb said.

"It's hard to protect them from some things. I never thought my wife and kids would be living here at the refinery. It's not a place for children. I wish we could provide more for ours . . . the way it sounds like you've been able to for yours."

There was a wistful quality in that last response. I knew Herb would follow up on it.

"I'm not sure exactly how this is all going to work, Payton, but I think we can help each other. We can offer some things that can make life better for your people, your children." Herb placed a hand on the man's shoulder.

"I know there's no choice—we need to have our families here because there's really no place safer—but being here is like sitting on top of a bomb." He stopped talking and I got the feeling that he knew he'd said something he shouldn't have.

"It sounds like you've had some difficulties," Herb said. "I know you don't know me, you don't know us, but believe me, if we can help we will."

"I don't know if there's anything you can do."

"We won't know unless you tell us what the problem is," Herb said.

Again more silence. Payton was thinking this through. I knew the smartest thing he could have done was to say nothing. He'd just met us and really shouldn't trust us at all.

He let out a big sigh. "We trade with a lot of people, like you said; we give fuel in exchange for food."

"That fuel, does it include propane as well as gasoline?" Herb asked.

"We have fairly significant quantities of propane. Are you planning on using it for cooking?" he asked.

"We can cook with wood. We were thinking that we could utilize propane heaters to keep our greenhouses going to extend the growing season."

"You have greenhouses?"

"We build them. We can show you how. You could even bring in soil from outside and grow more of your own food without needing to trade for it."

"That would help us . . . but wouldn't that make your trading hand weaker?"

"This is about more than just us. It's about all of us. If you become our partner we want you to be stronger. Your strength can become our strength and our strength can become your strength. I've noticed you've also traded fuel for weapons."

"That's how we've been able to provide the security we have."

"That's smart—you've been playing to your existing strength," Herb said.

"But that same strength is our weakness," Payton said. "We're being blackmailed."

"What!" Herb was incredulous.

"How are you being blackmailed?" I asked.

"We were approached by a group . . . Unless we give this group a certain amount of fuel, they've threatened to destroy the facility."

"But you have a fairly solid defense," I said.

"There's no defense against a grenade being launched at one of our fuel tanks."

"They have RPGs?" Herb asked, and of course I knew what he was thinking.

"They gave us a demonstration," Payton said. "They destroyed a building on the outside of our facility. If they had aimed their weapons at a storage tank, the whole place would have gone up."

"Do you know much about these people?"

"There are a lot of them, and they're well armed and mobile. We know they can carry out their threat."

"You're caught between a rock and a hard place. But maybe we will be able to help," Herb said. "Why don't we sit down and work out some details about starting to do business?"

Looking relieved, Payton offered his hand. "Perhaps we can do even more than just business."

The two men shook on it.

21

I lifted off, gained altitude, and then banked to put the Cessna on course for the city and the island airport. It had been just over two weeks since we'd been forced to land there. I wondered if Colonel Wayne thought he'd ever see us again.

Herb was sitting next to me, and Lori was in the seat behind him. She'd convinced him that she had had a good connection with the colonel and should be one of the people to return.

I didn't know how Herb could counter a couple of Mustangs and a large group of armed men on the ground, but having him along made me think that somehow we had them at a disadvantage.

"Okay, take us toward the city, but first could we go by the refinery?" Herb said as we finished our circle. "I want to just wave hello to them."

I broke off the bank and aimed us south.

The partnership with the refinery had developed as quickly as the progress that was being made around the neighborhood. We'd done our first food-for-fuel trade, but so much more than that had happened as well.

Delegations had gone from one place to the other. Payton

had sent people up for medical treatment. They'd inspected our school, and there was talk of two of our teachers going down to help them set up something similar for their children.

Most important, there had been preliminary talks about joint security. Next week there was a meeting scheduled in which the leaders of all seven communities—us, the four surrounding neighborhoods, the hospital community, and the refinery—would meet. They were going to be discussing the creation of a united defense force.

We flew in companionable silence all the way to the refinery. I circled around the grounds, and the guards looked up and waved their arms. I wiggled the wings in answer.

"It's good for them to know that we're here," Lori said.

"Even if we can't do much to help them right now?" I asked. The refinery was awaiting the next extortion demand, and there was little we could do to stop that. Not yet.

We had little doubt that Brett and the Division were behind the threat, even though there was no hard proof. In some ways, we hoped it was them, because we didn't want to believe there were other cutthroat groups nearby with RPGs in their back pocket. Still, we didn't expect to get confirmation out of the blue on this very flight.

I had just broken us off the bank and aimed us toward the island colony.

"Does Payton know when the raiders will be coming to extort fuel again?" Lori asked.

"They show up about every two to four weeks," Herb said. "It's been about three weeks, so they'll be back soon."

"Do we really think it will stop when we destroy the Dundas bridge next week?" I asked.

"It will help a lot of things, but nothing can stop a few people with RPGs from coming across the river. They'll still be at risk."

We hadn't flown more than a few minutes farther when we got our surprise.

"Hello up there, Cessna," came a call over the radio. I had it on to communicate with the control tower at the island but was shocked to hear from them so soon. "We've got eyes on you."

They couldn't possibly see us from here, could they? Then it came again.

"Cessna, do you read me?"

I looked over at Herb. He motioned for me to get it.

I picked up the receiver and pushed the talk button. "Hello, ground, this is the Cessna. I read you. Who am I talking to? Over."

There was static and then a laugh. I'd know that laugh anywhere.

"Is this the little prince?" It was Brett.

Herb made a gesture with a finger like he was cutting his throat. I took my finger off the radio to make sure Brett couldn't hear us. "Answer him," Herb said quietly. "And remember, I'm dead as far as he thinks."

I nodded and pressed the talk button. "I didn't think I'd be hearing from you," I said.

"Did the little prince think I had gone away for good?"

"I could always hope you crawled into some rat hole and stayed there," I said.

"So the little prince thinks I'm a rat. I'm so insulted."

I was going to respond when Herb motioned for me to silence our transmission again.

"Keep it up. The best way to get somebody talking about things they shouldn't talk about is to get them angry."

"Okay."

"Enraged is even better. The more he says the more likely he'll say something we can use, something he doesn't know will help us."

I nodded. What could I say to really get him going?

"It's only an insult to rats to call you that." That was lame. "A rat isn't half the coward you are."

His laughter came over the radio. "Come on down and see if I'm a coward."

"I guess I could invite you up here, but I know you're afraid of heights . . . and of a fair fight. Only a coward would attack somebody in the middle of the night or send other people to do his dirty work."

"Poor baby, crying. I should have taken care of you when I had a chance," he said.

"Sneaking into my room while I was asleep. That's sure brave of you, Brett. You don't have enough guts to approach me face-to-face."

"Believe me, there will be guts the next time we meet. I'm going to gut you like a fish."

I couldn't let him hear the fear I was feeling. I couldn't hesitate.

"Brave words from somebody who hides in the woods and takes potshots at innocent people," I said.

"There are no innocent people, especially not in Eden Mills."

"So it *was* you with RPGs," I said.

"Sorry I didn't send a card to claim credit. I figured you'd know."

"Oh, we knew. It was the classic act of a coward. It had to be you," I said.

Again that laughter. "Big words."

His replies were becoming more static filled. I was flying toward the island, leaving him behind, and we'd soon be out of radio range. But where was he, why was he down there?

I hit the left rudder hard to bring us back around. Herb was scanning the ground with his binoculars.

"You just wait . . . Sooner or later we're going to meet again," Brett said.

"I'm assuming it will be later because you're such a powerless little nothing," I said. "What's the problem, little Brett, didn't your mommy love you enough when you were a baby?"

"My mother loved me just fine," he said, but there was genuine anger in his voice.

I'd hit a tender spot. "The poor old bat probably figured you out long ago and realized you were nothing more than a sociopath. She felt ashamed that she'd raised such a piece of—"

"I'm looking forward to the day we meet," he snarled.

As we came around the voice became clearer and clearer.

"My guess is that your parents ran away from home to get away from you. They couldn't stand having a piece of crap as a son. They probably—"

He roared at me like a wounded animal. I'd scored a direct hit.

"I'm going to make you regret ever meeting me. Everybody you know is going to regret it. Your mother, your father, your brother and sister will all pay for it. How's Princess Lori? I'm going to make her pay as well . . . although she might enjoy it, you know, being with a real man."

I had to think fast. "She's all yours. Do what you want with her—she dumped me." I quickly turned back to see what Lori thought, but I needn't have worried. She smirked and gave a little thumbs-up.

"Poor little prince. I guess you just weren't man enough for her."

"You'd know all about not being man enough. I figure you disappointed your girlfriends as much as you did your mother."

There was no answer for a while, just static. Had I gone out of range again?

"You're going to pay. I'm going to put you in the ground just like I did Herbie."

"*You* put him in the ground? You mean you had to beg somebody else to do it because you were too afraid to try it yourself. Are you ever brave enough to handle your own dirty work?"

A stream of swearing came over the airwaves. I forged ahead. "I'm sorry I didn't get you that night I dropped off that little explosive present at the Division compound."

"I was impressed by that, little prince. Didn't think you could respond without Herb there to hold your hand. It looks like I underestimated you," Brett said.

"I hope I impressed your ratpack's little leader, the captain or maestro or whatever you call him."

"You did more than that. I guess I owe you for that one. If the colonel hadn't been injured so badly, it would have been harder to take over."

"You're in command?" I exchanged a glance with Herb.

"Ever since I put a bullet in him to finish what you started."

I felt sick. "I'm sure you had somebody else pull the trigger, but I'm so glad you're in charge. I guess we have nothing to worry about from the Division anymore."

"You'll see . . . soon enough, you'll see," he said. His voice had become low and calm, which made his words seem more frightening.

"Anytime, anyplace," I said. "I'm not worried about you and a couple of dozen misfits."

"How about four hundred trained soldiers?" he bragged.

"We killed twice as many as that the last time."

"We won't be charging across the bridge this time."

"I wouldn't expect that. You'll be doing it like a snake and not like a man, and that's too bad because you were right about one thing: I killed Owen and Tim—without a single regret—and I'm going to enjoy killing you. But I want to be able to look you in the eyes, the way I looked them in the eyes."

That laughter again. "Welcome to the dark side, little prince. I didn't know you had it in you."

"It's there and it's out and it's waiting for you."

"Do you really think you can take me?" he asked.

"The real question is, do *you* really think you can take *me* on when I'm not sleeping? Or will you be sending somebody else?"

"It will be me, looking you in the eyes, and it's going to be soon. Very soon."

I was going to answer when Herb tapped me on the arm. He was still looking out the window through the binoculars.

"I see something," he whispered. "I see him and some of those go-carts, the ones we saw on the highway—the doodle-bugs."

"How many?" I asked.

"Three, no four . . . there among the houses."

"Where, where?" I asked.

"They've gone out of view, behind the buildings," he said. "They'll come back into view in a few seconds and—"

There was a loud *ping*, followed by a second and third, as something hit the left wing.

"We're being shot at!" Lori said.

I pushed the yoke in and hit the left rudder hard to pull us out of the bank and away from the shooters. We dove and turned so quickly that for an instant the plane started to slide and I had to back off to avoid losing control. I opened the throttle full to get some distance. Safe, I grabbed the radio, which had dropped to the floor.

"Just what I expected, taking a shot because you don't have the guts to face me man to man," I yelled into it.

There was no answer. Had I gotten us out of radio range as well as rifle range?

"You probably didn't even fire the gun because I know you're not much of a shot," I said. My mind flashed back to the time Brett and I had gone hunting together. We'd shot a couple of deer, but in the end it turned out his was shot by somebody else. "It took a kid to put down the deer you shot at."

The radio crackled.

"The next time will be in person," Brett said in a rock-steady voice. "I promise that."

"Your promises mean nothing, but mine do. I'll take you out . . . Count on it, Brett. I'm going to kill you myself. You're mine."

There was a garbled response that faded to complete static. We were now out of range.

"Do you want me to circle back?" I asked.

Herb shook his head. "We got what we needed. Much more than Brett meant to give us. Let's go on and complete our mission."

22

"You are clear for landing on runway one, the left runway. Over," the controller at the island's airport said through the radio.

"Roger, commencing landing."

It was wonderful to actually have an air-traffic controller in the tower. It was also wonderful to be speaking to someone sane after that conversation with Brett. We'd radioed in on the frequency they'd told me to use to request permission to land if I ever returned. I looked forward to a friendlier greeting than the last.

As I came across the water, straight at the runway on the left, I had a sudden stab of doubt. What if I was wrong about these people, what if this was just an elaborate trap to get us back and find out about our neighborhood so they could exploit it? Worse, what if they were partners with Brett?

Once again, it was as if both Herb and Lori could read my mind.

"It's going to be all right," Herb said.

"I know." I laughed a bit sheepishly. "I'm just nervous about this landing."

"It's funny how coming into a real airport with a real air controller makes you feel nervous," Lori observed.

All of my flights had truly been solo, with nobody watching or judging. Here there were other pilots around and pros manning the control tower. I wanted this landing to be buttery soft and smooth. It felt like I was auditioning, especially after the hard landing I'd deliberately made the last time.

I aimed the nose for the yellow midline of the asphalt, pushed in the throttle to reduce speed, and lifted the yoke to change altitude and get the nose slightly up. There was no turning back now. I put the wheels down so gently that I wasn't sure for an instant if I'd touched down. We rolled along the runway. It was a smooth ride compared to the roads and paths I'd been landing on. Gently, evenly, I applied the brakes and we slowed to a crawl.

Off to the side I caught sight of other planes. Only one of the Mustangs was on the ground along with the big Lancaster bomber.

Waiting for me was a ground controller with wands, waving me forward. That was certainly better than men with guns. He motioned me over and I applied the brakes to follow his directions. I turned onto the other runway and taxied along. Waiting ahead was another ground controller who directed me into a spot beside the hangar, between two other vintage planes.

As we rolled to a stop Colonel Wayne appeared and offered a big wave and a friendly smile. I shut down the engine and we climbed out.

We shook hands, and the colonel hugged Lori like she was a long-lost relative. I introduced him to Herb.

"Pleased to meet you, sir, and so glad you two decided to

come back," Colonel Wayne said. "So are you the person who runs your show?" he asked Herb.

"I'm one of the people."

"Well, that's great. I'm assuming since you came back, you're here to tell us a little more about yourselves."

"We do want to talk to you," I confirmed. "Honest talk. I want you to know that I didn't have the authority to tell you anything at our first meeting."

"Nor should you have, since you were in such a vulnerable position," he said. "Let's sit down and have a discussion."

He shepherded us into his office and, after being treated to more of the islanders' amazing coffee, we settled in for a long conversation. Herb plunged right in, explaining the size of our community, the resources we had, the alliances with the hospital and the refinery. I saw the colonel react with particular interest when the refinery came up. I think Herb saw it, too.

The conversation went back and forth for several minutes. Finally, Herb stood up. "Adam told us about how you run your community," he said. He walked over to the copy of the Constitution on the wall.

"We thought that if it was the foundation on which our great country was built, it was a good enough place to start our community," the other man said.

"None better," Herb agreed.

"We wouldn't have survived without Herb's expertise and foresight," I said.

"Are you a former military man?" the colonel asked Herb.

"Intelligence."

The colonel laughed. "Some people think military intelligence is an oxymoron."

"What you've done here would certainly prove them wrong," Herb said.

"We're just trying to do the right thing."

"That's our goal and our strength," Herb said. "And part of doing the right thing is trying to help other people."

"Perhaps we can help each other," the colonel said.

"I would assume that fuel is a problem for you," Herb said.

The colonel didn't answer.

"Those old planes must be pigs on fuel. And while being on an island gives you protection, it limits your ability to get gas," Herb continued. "I think we could help."

"Do you have enough fuel to spare?"

"Fuel is always going to be an issue, but we need our friends who believe in fairness and justice to be secure."

"From what you've told us, it sounds like we don't have anything you need, so what could we give you in return?" the colonel said.

"This isn't about trading," Herb said. "This is about us helping our neighbors. It's just good to know we're not alone."

"You have a friend here," he said. "And it isn't just us. There are other communities out there that have the same vision. We've established a loose alliance of sorts. There were a dozen of us, but now with your neighborhood and its allies there are thirteen of us."

Herb smiled. "Thirteen . . . like the thirteen colonies that formed this country." He paused. "It happened once. I wonder if it can happen again, this time in miniature."

"Why couldn't it?" the colonel asked.

"When I go back, I'll talk to our committee to make it official," Herb said. "To formalize the partnership."

"I'd also invite you to join with us when we meet with our other allies."

"We'd welcome the chance to be part of that," Herb said. "Right now, though, do you think you could give us a tour?"

"I'd be proud to show you what we've accomplished."

"While that's happening, do you think you could also have one of your mechanics go over my plane with me?" I asked.

"Certainly. Are you having mechanical problems?" Colonel Wayne asked.

"We were shot at," I said. "I think a bullet or two went through the wing as we were passing over the city."

"Was it random fire from the ground?" He sounded concerned.

"From the ground but not random," Herb said. "We knew the person doing the shooting. He raised us on the radio before he took a couple of potshots at us."

"So not somebody you'd count as a friend," the colonel said.

"That's a bit of an understatement. He was a member of our community who violated our code and had to be expelled."

"What did he do?" the colonel asked.

"He's a murderer. He killed innocent people outside our neighborhood. He was up for trial when he killed his guards and escaped."

"And he radioed up to let you know he was going to take a shot at you?"

"More a combination of taunting us and trying to keep us in rifle range. What he didn't realize is that he gave away more information than he should have," Herb said.

"What sort of information?"

"For starters, up until we heard his voice we didn't even know for sure if he was still alive. Now we know that, if what he says is correct, he's the new leader of the Division."

"The Division!" Colonel Wayne exclaimed.

"You know them?" Herb asked.

"We were told stories from survivors coming out of the city. From what we heard they were run by ex-military, and they were ruthless and extremely dangerous."

"They were both," Herb said. "And that's why we had to destroy them."

"You destroyed them? But you just said this man was running them," the colonel said.

"If he's telling the truth, he's running the fragment that survived. He may also have recruited others. We neutralized the bulk of the Division's forces when they moved to attack our neighborhood, and then we destroyed their compound, scattering them."

The colonel looked impressed.

"If they have re-formed, they would become more dangerous under this man's leadership. And, as we know, there is more than one danger out there. To overcome those dangers, we have to become even stronger—with your help."

"Sounds like we have lots more to discuss as we start on the tour," the colonel said.

23

I stood just to the side of the wall and watched as the Mustang raced along Erin Mills Parkway and then lifted off. I had to admit to a little plane envy. Not that there was anything wrong with my Cessna, but it would be incredible to fly a plane like that—to have not just the speed and ceiling and range but also the machine guns in its wings. I'd love to be up in that and have Brett take a shot at me. I could swoop down and reduce him and those go-carts to flaming rubble.

The plane—with one of the islanders' pilots at the controls—did a quick flyby as it circled back toward the island airport. Their planes had been regular visitors to our neighborhood, and ours to theirs.

As I walked down the hill toward my house I thought about what the island colony had accomplished. Their planes impressed me, of course, but they'd done much more than take advantage of the air museum.

They had put sufficient land under cultivation to feed all three thousand inhabitants. They were all housed in a combination of the hangars, the terminal itself, a number of small island homes, and some new buildings they'd put up. Each had been subdivided so that every family had its own small living area. Once winter came, it'd be easier to heat them all.

We weren't so fortunate. Spread out in typical suburban homes, we were going to have trouble adequately heating them all. I knew there were already plans under way to house multiple families in places that had woodstoves or high-efficiency fireplaces.

Water collection and distribution was also easier for the islanders. They'd hooked up a generator to power a pump. It brought water from the lake for all their irrigation, drinking, and sanitation needs. Nobody was carrying heavy buckets. With our boundaries extending to the Credit River, however, we hoped to have a similar system created for us.

My thoughts were interrupted as I walked into our house and was greeted by the sound of crying. It was loud, almost hysterical wailing, the way Rachel or Danny would cry if they were told that something had happened to Mom or Dad.

My heart pounding, I raced to the kitchen and saw the social worker, Maureen, and Lori sitting at the kitchen table with Danny and Rachel. But it wasn't any of them crying. It was coming from another room. What was going on?

All four of them got up and came toward me.

"Where are Dad and Mom?" I asked.

"Your mother's in the other room," Lori said. She gestured toward the dining room, where the crying was coming from. "And your father—isn't he away with Herb on that overnight trip to the island?"

"Yes, but—"

"Your parents are okay," Maureen said. She understood my concern.

"What's going on in there?" I questioned.

"I'm going to take the twins to my house," Lori said. She took Rachel by one hand and Danny by the other. I would have expected Danny to resist having his hand held, but he allowed himself to be led away.

After they left I turned to Maureen. "Now can you tell me?" I asked.

She motioned for me to come with her. I stepped into the dining room and staggered to a stop. My mother was at the far end of the room with her arms wrapped around two young children. The older kid, a boy, was the one who was sobbing hysterically. He couldn't have been any more than seven or eight. On the other side was a girl, younger, maybe five, who was just staring blankly into space over my mom's shoulder.

They looked the same, like brother and sister, but I didn't recognize them. And I knew everybody in the neighborhood, or at least I thought I did. They must have been from one of the outlying communities.

Maureen walked over, bent down, and talked to my mother. My mother tried to get up, but the boy clung to her desperately. His face, his eyes were so full of pain that I had to work not to look away.

Finally he went to Maureen as she took him in her arms. The girl showed no reaction. It was as if she didn't register anything—not even her brother's screams and sobs.

My mother came to me as Maureen walked out, holding the brother with one arm and the hand of the little girl with the other. The cries deadened as the front door closed, but they were still audible for another few seconds, fading away finally to nothing.

"What happened?" I asked.

"Their parents were killed . . . right in front of them," she said.

"What?"

"They were killed by Brett."

"Brett? Brett was here?" I felt panic begin to rise.

"Not here. He killed them out there and then basically dropped the children off close to our gates and told them to come here," she said.

"But wh-why would he do that?" I stammered.

"He wanted them to deliver a message to us."

"What?"

"He pinned a letter to the girl's shirt and sent them to give it to us."

My mind spun. How could that be real? I must have heard her wrong.

"It's hard to believe that anybody could do that," she said. "He put a gun to their parents' heads and just shot them . . . right there while their children were watching. It's just . . . just . . ."

"Evil," I said. "There's no other word."

In a world where so much was beyond belief there was now a new horror for me to think of, and maybe it was worse, more evil, than all the others I'd experienced.

"What's in the letter?" I asked.

"That's what makes it all even stranger. He's demanding that we give him food and supplies."

"Why would we give him anything?"

"There's also a threat: that if we don't give him what he wants, he'll do more harm."

"We're ready for him," I snapped.

"It's not us he's threatening to harm."

I didn't understand, and asked to see the letter.

"It's, um, not here, Adam," she said.

"Where is it then?"

She hesitated. "It's with the judge."

I shook my head. "No it isn't, Mom. Why are you lying to me?" It wasn't just Herb who could read minds.

She didn't answer, but it was clear she was feeling guilty that she'd told me a lie.

"Did he threaten me and our family?" I asked.

"Yes."

"That's nothing new," I said. "But there's something else in there that is new, isn't there? Keeping it away from me doesn't protect me. I need to know what he wrote."

She looked like she was on the verge of tears. "The letter is addressed to you."

"To me? Did he address it to the little prince?"

"How did you know?"

"He called me that when he came and took me away that night and then on the radio in the plane. Can I see it, please?" As soon as I asked I almost regretted it. I wanted to see the letter, but at the same time I wanted my mother to keep telling me I couldn't see it.

She pulled it from the inside of her jacket. It was a manila envelope splattered with red—dried blood. She turned it over and there in a childish scrawl were the words *For Adam, the Little Prince*. She held it out to me and I hesitated before I took it in my hand. It felt heavy, almost hot to the touch, like I was holding all that anger, that evil, in my fingers.

"You can't believe what he writes, and you can't take it personally," she said. "It isn't true."

"Whatever he wrote is true to him."

I turned it over, trying to avoid touching the dried blood, and pulled out the letter. It was lined paper, the type that was in every school notebook I'd ever used. It was crudely folded and I opened it up to reveal the same stunted handwriting that was on the envelope.

> *Hello, Little Prince,*
>
> *I'm sure you're surprised to get a letter from me. After our little conversation in the airplane I wanted to make sure to write you now and again to let you know I'm alive and well. I hope you enjoyed meeting my two little mailmen—or should I say mailpersons because I wouldn't want to offend your great sense of political correctness? It's one of my life goals to someday live up to your standards, to be a little prince just like you.*
>
> *Strange thing is that while everybody in my life would have liked me to become more like you, instead you became more like me.*

Those words sent a chill up my spine.

> *It sounds like you really did enjoy killing those two idiots I sent with you to steal the plane. And they were idiots, weak-willed idiots. They died because they were too stupid to live, so they deserved what they got. Don't feel bad about killing them . . .*

Well, I know now you probably don't. You probably had to pretend that you felt bad, and maybe you did at the beginning, but you know you enjoyed it. The way you know you'd enjoy killing me. At least those idiots served a purpose. They gave you the taste for blood. You learned how sweet it is, how powerful it is.

But we can never be friends, Little Prince. There's only one way for this to end, with one of us dead. It's going to be you. But first I'm going to do to you what I did to those two kids today: I'm going to kill your parents right in front of your eyes. Then I'm going to kill you, slowly and painfully.

But business before pleasure.

I did as much as anybody else to help that neighborhood survive. I deserve some of the spoils from my efforts. Right now I have hundreds of mouths to feed. I demand some of the food that is being grown. My expectation is that a quantity of food will be left on the 403 on the bridge crossing the small overpass near Mavis Road at noon Monday, five days from when you receive this letter. I don't want much, just enough to feed a hundred men for one month. I'll leave that exact quantity up to good old Ernie to figure out.

If you decide not to do this, then I'll be forced to do something else. Those two poor little orphans you inherited today, well, I can make a lot more of them appear on your doorstep. Matter of fact, I can make two or three hundred of them appear. It's not hard to find people to kill. I'll send the surviving children *your way, and I know that you're all such good people that you won't turn them away. Your choice now—you can feed my men or you can feed orphans. You decide. I figure with Herb gone it's probably your mother and you making all the decisions. Does the committee still think they're in charge?*

I'd like to guarantee you that I won't attack the people bringing out the food, but you know my word isn't always the best. Besides, there are lots of other little nasties out here in the world, so make sure you send enough guards to take care of my food. I expect that you will be the one at the lead of this procession, Little Prince. I want you to lead this expedition— lead your subjects. I want you to be on the ground, not up in the air. I want you to clip your wings at least for a day. If I even see a plane in the air— either the Cessna or the flying lawn mower—then our little deal is off and I'll move on to the next step.

Your Pen Pal,
Brett

P.S. Don't even think about poisoning the food. I'll make sure to have a couple of the women and children we have as captives sample everything first.

P.P.S. Send Lori my love. Tell her that now I know you two have broken up I think about her often and it won't be too long before those thoughts become

more than thoughts. Monday at noon will come
sooner than you think.

I let the letter tumble from my hands onto the floor. If anything, I just felt numb.

"I don't know how he could do these things," my mother said grimly. I could see tears pooling in her eyes.

"I do," I said. "I understand him."

"He's not human—he's just an animal."

"He's more human than he is animal. Animals only kill to survive, to protect their young," I said. "Humans are the only ones who kill for pleasure."

"Only monsters kill for pleasure."

A monster, was that what he was? Could I ever become a monster?

"We'll radio over to talk to your father and Herb," my mother said.

Thanks to a huge effort by electrical engineers at each of the communities, we were now connected by shortwave radio to the island as well as to the refinery and hospital.

"I don't think you should do that," I said. "They need to focus on what they're doing. Besides, it isn't like they can do anything about it now. They'll be back tomorrow, and we have five days before we have to act," I said.

I bent down and picked up the letter. I folded the pages over and put them back in the envelope, careful again of the stains.

"I should take that," my mother said.

"In a bit. I want to look at it again."

"Word has already been sent to the judge and Howie.

They'll be here shortly. I don't know if there's any point in sharing the news with anyone else right now. I'll need you to show them the letter when they arrive."

I nodded. "Sounds good. I'm just going to go upstairs and lie down for a minute."

"Are you all right?" She reached out to touch my arm.

I tried to smile back at her. "If I was all right, then you would have other things to worry about! I just need to go crash for a minute, that's all."

She pulled me in for a hug. "It's going to be all right."

I nodded again, and that seemed to reassure her.

I went up the stairs to my room and closed the door behind me. I started to flop on the bed but then felt a wave of anxiety flow over me. I slid the desk against the door. Next, I looked in my closet and finally glanced under the bed. Nothing. I lay back on the bed and it groaned under my weight.

The envelope was still in my hands. This time I didn't care about the dried blood. I already had blood on my hands, and there was more to come no matter what we did.

Pulling the letter out, I stared at the words without reading them. It still looked like the homework of a sixth-grade kid instead of the manifesto of a monster.

And he *was* a monster—a monster I had to kill. And I had to do it without hesitation, without that split second of doubt, without thinking of him as a person. Then I realized that was the way Brett killed. No doubt, no remorse, no second thoughts. In order to kill him, to kill the monster, I'd have to be a monster, too. I'd have to join him. Not just for my own sake, but for the people of this neighborhood and beyond. I'd have to do it for those parents who wouldn't be killed, those children who wouldn't be orphaned.

And, strangely, maybe most of all I had to do it for Brett. There had to be some small part of him that was still human, still talking to him, a little voice bubbling up from below. He could suppress it, but he couldn't kill it completely. And that little voice knew that he needed to be destroyed.

I'd do it for Brett as well.

24

My dad and Herb arrived back first thing in the morning, excited by the prospect of new partnerships. But their excitement quickly turned to shock when an emergency committee meeting was called.

Judge Roberts read the letter out loud, then put it down on the table. There was stunned silence.

Brett had managed the feat of not being here but dominating the room. He would have liked that.

"This is just so awful, like a terrible nightmare," Councilwoman Stevens said, her voice cracking over the last few words.

I could tell she wasn't the only one close to tears. Herb, of course, looked like Herb—no reaction. I tried to mirror his blank expression.

"How are the two little children doing?" the judge asked.

"They're doing the best that can be expected," Mr. Peterson said. "They're staying with us."

"That's very kind of you," the judge offered.

"Kind or not, there wasn't much choice. My wife insisted, and now they won't let her leave their sight," he said.

"I'm glad they're being cared for," Herb said, "but we need to focus on the problem at hand."

"Yes, what are we going to do?" Ernie asked. "Do you want me to calculate how much food they want, get it together?"

"I think it would be wise for you to organize that end just in case we decide to give in to his demands," the judge said.

"I can do that," Ernie said. "It's unnerving to have him mention me in the letter." He paused and then looked at me guiltily. "Not that it wouldn't be worse for Adam . . . much worse."

"It's difficult for all of us," I said.

"So what do we do now?" Mr. Peterson asked.

"There appear to be only two choices. Either we give in and meet his demands or we don't," Herb said.

"And if we don't, then he'll kill more people, send us more orphans," Councilwoman Stevens said. "If we can believe him, if he'd actually follow through with his threat."

"He'll follow through," I said, and everybody looked at me.

"Adam is right, he will do it," Herb said.

"Then we have no choice," the councilwoman said.

"We always have a choice," Herb said. "If we allow Brett to dictate our decisions, then we're lost."

"So you're saying we shouldn't give him the food?" the judge asked.

"I'm not saying that either. Simply refusing whatever he wants is also allowing him to decide for us."

"Then what are you saying?" my father asked.

"I'm saying that we need to weigh the alternatives and make a decision that's in our best interests," Herb replied.

"In the interests of us or the people he's going to kill out there?" my mother asked.

"We can't be responsible for the lives of everybody. We've

become bigger, stronger, and more capable, but we're still just a lifeboat. We still can sink in the swells," Herb said.

"Herb's right," Ernie said. "We can only do so much. Our supplies are better but still limited."

"If nothing else, I have to give him credit," Herb said.

"Credit?" my mother asked incredulously. "For being a monster?"

"Yes, for being the monster that thought this through. Not just that he asked for something that was realistic but the way he went about it."

"Murdering parents in front of their children is something he deserves credit for?" the judge questioned.

"Not the action, but the thought behind it. I underestimated him. Up to this point I thought he was only capable of blunt, brute force. This is different. He thought about who we are, what we stand for, and he decided to use our kindness, our commitment to do the right thing, against us. His plan is subtle, well thought through, and almost impossible to defend against."

"Almost impossible?" Howie asked.

"Okay, maybe completely impossible to defend against. This threat is effective only because of what we believe in. What would Brett do if we threatened to murder innocent people?"

"We'd never do that," the councilwoman said.

"Of course we wouldn't, and he knows that," Herb said. "But even if he believed we would, how would he react? Would he give us something to stop us?"

"Of course not!" my mother said.

"Because *he* doesn't care. He knows *we* do. For all of that

I give him credit. It's important to know your enemy, and he knows us."

"While his venom is aimed at everybody, he certainly has a strong hatred of Adam," Mr. Peterson said.

"That hatred would be equally strong, if not stronger, if he knew I was alive," Herb said. "In part he only put this plan forward because he knew that if I were alive I would oppose giving in to his demands. He believes you are vulnerable to such a threat in my absence."

"So you are of the opinion that we should ignore him?" the judge said.

"Ignoring him is impossible, but I think that giving in is unwise."

"We have to make a decision based on weighing all of the consequences of both options," my mother said. "The option of ignoring him is clear. It will cause people to be killed."

"As will giving in," Herb said

"If we choose to comply, it will strengthen him," Howie added.

"He can use that food to attract more people to his side, to bolster his position as a leader. Brett as a leader of a larger group will ultimately cause many, many more deaths, perhaps even in this neighborhood."

"You still think he's going to attack?" Howie asked.

Herb was silent a moment, rubbing his temples. "It's a question not of if, but of when and how. His hatred has no boundaries. He is capable of all manners of evil."

"But if we don't comply, you believe he will carry out his threat. That more newly created orphans will appear at our gates," Howie said.

"Probably."

"And what will we do when they appear?" the judge asked.

"If we don't take them, they will most certainly perish," Herb said.

"Then we have to take them in," my mother said.

"But taking them in will only cause him to send us more. He'll only stop when we don't take any of them into our community," Herb said. "When we show we won't give in and we won't react."

"Then when children like the ones we took in yesterday appear outside the wall . . . we watch them die . . . or simply let them wander off," Howie said. "I don't think my guards could handle that. I don't think I could handle that."

"We could always just shoot them and put them out of their misery," my mother said.

Everybody turned to her in shock.

"Sorry. I am being painfully, awfully facetious," she said. "I just don't see any way out of this."

"There is no good answer," Herb said. "Only the answer we have to choose . . . together. Shall we put this to a vote, then?"

His suggestion was greeted by silence and people looking down at the table.

"It's just that usually we're able to find consensus," Councilwoman Stevens said.

"I don't think there's going to be consensus on this one," Howie said.

"I believe Howie is correct," the judge said. "And delaying it will not make it any less difficult. The strength of the committee is that no one person is ultimately responsible."

"I think people know which way I'm going to vote," Herb said.

Herb had spoken with such confidence. There was no shaking in his hands or even the hint of a quiver in his voice. It was like the urgency of the meeting had revitalized him.

"I am opposed to giving in to this extortion," Herb said.

"And I can't see any choice but to meet the demands," Councilwoman Stevens said. "To not do so would be to cause the deaths of many people. I can't have that on my conscience."

"I'm voting that way as well," Howie said. "Give him the food, at least this one time."

"This is a painful decision," the judge said, "but I am opposed to giving in, even this once. We have to stand strong."

Each person in turn voted—Mr. Peterson and my father voting to give the food—and Mr. Nicholas and Ernie voting against. Dr. Morgan voted for giving the food and my mother against. It was a tie vote.

"We are deadlocked," the judge said. "Perhaps we need to have further discussion."

"I haven't voted," I said.

They all looked at me.

"I am a member of the committee now, right?"

There was hesitation before the judge spoke. "You are a member as of the vote we took at the start of the meeting to make you a member, but I don't know if it's fair to make you vote on this matter."

"It isn't!" my mother exclaimed.

"I agree," my father said. "It's not right to make you responsible for this decision."

"It's not me. It's the members of the committee. Does it matter if I voted first or last?"

"It does when it breaks a tie," Herb said.

"Maybe we could vote again," the judge suggested.

"We could if somebody was going to change their vote," Herb added. "Is anybody prepared to change their vote?" He looked around the table. Nobody answered.

"I have a right to vote and I want to," I said.

As soon as I said that I felt a rush of regret. It was so much easier to just sit around the table but not have to take responsibility for what was decided.

"This is not the first time that Adam has had input into a decision," Herb said. "From the decision to form this neighborhood, all the way to expanding and helping establish other communities, decisions have been made with Adam being a driving force. I'm completely comfortable with whatever decision he makes, pro or con." He paused. "In fact, no offense to anybody around this table, but I think I trust his opinion more than that of anybody else sitting here, including me." He paused again. "Is there anybody who is not prepared to accept the decision of this committee?"

People shook their heads.

"Okay," the judge said. "Procedurally Adam is a member of the committee and has the right to vote. What's your vote, Adam?"

I took a deep breath before answering. "Both sides have merit. Both sides will lead to bad things happening," I said. "There's no right answer. But I do know what would be the worst outcome. Brett has put a question forward that has divided us in two. No matter which way I vote half of the people are going to think I'm wrong, that the other half is wrong or, worse, immoral or uncaring."

"Nobody will think that," my mother said.

"Yes they will," I said.

"He's right," the judge said. "Perhaps we have to make one more agreement: Whatever is decided, whatever way the vote goes will become the opinion of *all* people in the room."

"I don't know if we can change an opinion that easily," Howie said.

"Maybe I worded that wrong. Whatever is voted for, whatever Adam votes for, will become the direction we will all pursue, we will all agree with and support."

"I agree," my mother said.

"I think we all need to agree," Herb said. "We can't allow Brett to put a wedge between us. United we stand and divided we fall."

There was a nodding of heads around the table.

"Thank you," I said. "Thank you, all." I let out a big sigh. This wasn't going to be easy, but I knew what had to be done. "I can only imagine how awful it would be to find more orphans at the gate and know that deciding against sending out the food would allow the parents to be killed."

"So you're voting to give him the food," the judge said.

I shook my head. "No. We can't give in to him. I vote against meeting Brett's demands."

I could tell by the look in my father's eyes that he was shocked by my answer. He raised his hand. "I change my vote. I am opposed to meeting his demands."

One by one all of the other people raised their hands until every person in the room agreed.

"Then we have consensus," the judge said. "Now let's figure out how we're going to carry out that consensus."

I hesitated for a second, since the idea wasn't fully formed in my mind, but then I said, "Well, first, I think we should let Brett think that we *are* going to meet his demands . . ."

Confused looks went around the table. Then I forged ahead with my idea.

25

Somehow I made it through the next couple of days, busying myself with routine work, helping repair walls, even pitching in with some gardening. Anything to pass the time. I also spent time with Lori and the two orphaned children. Just this morning I found her at the park, watching over the kids. I plunked myself down on the bench beside her and we sat in silence for a few minutes.

Lori squeezed my hand and I looked over at her.

"Just seeing if you were still here," she said.

"I'm here, just thinking." I gestured at the two children on the swings. "More important, how are they doing?"

"He's doing better, but she still basically hasn't spoken since she arrived," Lori said.

"It's only been a couple of days. I'm sure she'll talk."

"Maureen says that might take months, maybe even years," Lori said.

"She's the expert," I said. "I'm glad your family has been there to take them in."

"My parents are already talking about adopting them, keeping them with us."

"They need somebody, and I can't think of anybody better," I said.

"My parents always wanted to have more than one child, so I guess it all works out in the end." She paused. "Of course we can't be doing that with all the children who might come here."

Obviously she'd heard.

"What else did your father tell you about the letter?" I asked.

"He told me about the threat. He told me that it was a lot about you . . . and that Brett mentioned me, that he threatened me, too."

"He hates me and he wants to hurt me by hurting the things that matter to me. My family . . . you. It's because of me that you're a target for him."

"It's not your fault. Besides, what are you going to do, break up with me to protect me?" she asked.

I wasn't going to admit I'd thought of that.

"I just can't believe the committee made that decision. I can't believe my father was in agreement," she said.

"He wasn't at first," I said. "He wanted to give Brett the food."

"Isn't there a chance that if we just give him the food he'll leave us alone?"

"No, he wouldn't. There's only one thing that will cause him to ever leave us alone, and that's his death."

We fell into silence. I knew what she wanted to know—which way did I vote? I also knew about the plans the committee had agreed to in the wake of the vote, but I was sworn to secrecy on those. I could have said anything or nothing to Lori right now. I wouldn't do that.

"I cast the deciding vote against giving in to his demands," I said.

She turned to face me, incredulous. "How could you do that?"

I hadn't expected her to say that, even if that's what she was thinking.

"I'm sure you and Herb and the committee have your reasons but I hope it doesn't mean more parents are going to be killed, more children witnessing their parents being murdered." Lori was on the verge of tears. "Look at those two kids."

I was looking at them. I'd been looking at them. I knew what she was saying, how she was feeling, but I couldn't afford to feel it myself.

"Do you even know their names?" she asked.

I shook my head. I didn't—and I didn't *want* to know. I stood up. "I better get going."

She grabbed my hand again. "Please don't . . . I'm sorry. I know it must have been a tough decision."

I pulled away, she let go of my hand, and I walked off. I didn't look back. I couldn't explain it to her, but my being away from Lori would protect her from Brett. And that would protect me.

Lori was the only thing that could soften my soul. Here I was, stuck between two options; either I was becoming too much like Brett—and how would I live with myself?—or I wasn't enough like him and I simply wouldn't be able to stay alive. I wasn't sure which was worse.

———

It took me a while to get home. I'd stopped in briefly to talk to Todd. I just wanted him to joke around with me, help pretend none of this was happening. Instead that's all he would talk about. I told him how I was feeling, how I was honestly feeling, about the vote and the plan. He told me not to worry because he would be going out with me in the lead car. That wasn't something anybody else had talked about, but it did make me feel better.

He also told me that I had to be sure to keep him not only alive but perfect, because he had an obligation to the girls in the neighborhood to stay pretty to help fulfill their fantasy lives. I promised him. Delusions were sometimes better than reality.

I left his house and walked around the mostly empty streets of our neighborhood for another hour. I can't say I did a lot of thinking. It was more like I did a lot of not-thinking.

When I got home, Herb, Howie, and my mother looked up from our kitchen table. Herb gestured for me to come and join them. On the table was a detailed map showing the eastern part of our neighborhood, the bridge where the exchange was supposed to take place, and the area around it.

I listened as they talked more about the logistics of where people were being moved, how they would be positioned, and how they were going to attack. The plan was basic. We were going to bring out the "food" as Brett had requested. I'd be leading a big group, large enough to discourage Brett and his doodlebugs from attacking us, but it would be only one of three other groups. We would be surrounding the men Brett was sending to pick up the food. We'd try to kill or capture this group, get information about their base, their new compound. And then the real attack would happen, in which we were going to try to wipe them out altogether.

What Brett didn't know was that this time we weren't going to be alone. At least we hoped we weren't. It wasn't official yet—nothing had been formally agreed to—but we were going to call on the other twelve "colonies" to provide us with help.

Brett's letter and the appearance of the two orphans had overshadowed the fact that my father and Herb had come back that morning with an agreement in place among the different colonies, the communities that the island colony had befriended over the last several months. If it hadn't been for Brett, that agreement would have been cause for celebration throughout the neighborhood: We weren't alone anymore. It wasn't just us and a few even smaller places desperately banding together with us. We were now aligned with twelve other groups, including a large industrial complex that had been able to maintain some level of manufacturing, and a steel mill—not operating but perhaps capable of being put back into operation.

There were great distances between some of us—the farthest was almost a hundred miles away—but we were linked by the ability our neighborhood and the islanders had to fly between the colonies. Those flights would allow us to share resources, trade commodities, and offer mutual defense from outside aggression.

According to the agreement, if one colony was in danger, the others would provide fifty armed guards. If each colony complied, that would be six hundred extra personnel. That was a force that could have taken on the Division even at the height of their power. The doodlebugs certainly weren't that big now—Brett had asked for only enough food to feed a hundred men for a month. Even if he had double or even triple that number, we could still take them on and win.

"Is your father back yet?" my mother asked.

"Not that I know of." He was out on a test flight of the Cessna, now that we'd made a critical new adjustment or two to the plane.

"There's nothing to be worried about," she said.

Up to that point I hadn't been worried. "I know it's complicated to refit the Cessna like that," I said.

"But a very good thing," Herb said. "Adding a little sting is a good thing."

A gun had been mounted on the Cessna and could be fired by the pilot or copilot. It would be reassuring to be not just a sitting duck—a flying duck—in the sky waiting for people to take potshots from the ground. My father, along with Mr. Nicholas, the engineer, was now out on a flight seeing how the gun mount would affect the plane's handling. It was worth the possible complications. At least we'd be able to fight back. Now if only we could arm the ultralight.

"It's going to make me feel better knowing my husband is up in the air when my son is leading the group out there to deliver the ransom," my mother said, and turned to Herb. "I really think it should be somebody else leading the way, though."

I spoke before Herb could. "There's no choice. Brett'll probably know if I'm not at the front. And we can't have Dad too close. Brett told us not to have a plane in the sky."

"Adam's right on both counts," Herb said. "I'm sure that as soon as the group leaves our walls he'll have eyes on us."

My mind drifted back to the letter. It still sat on the top

of the night table in my room. I'd claimed it as my own since it was addressed to me, but I hadn't even looked at it since it was read out loud to the committee. Maybe there was something in there that I'd missed. I'd go over the letter and ask Herb to be there when I did. Maybe it would become obvious if there was something more we needed to know.

"I still can't help but think this is nothing more than a trap," my mother said.

"It might be, but we ourselves are laying our own trap," Herb said.

It was a conversation we had had many times over the past couple of days. But before anyone could respond to Herb, there was a pounding on the front door of our house.

All four of us jumped to our feet and ran to the hallway. Instinctively we also all went for our weapons, but before we could react any further a trio of guards from the wall burst in.

"There are five of them!" one of the men yelled out.

"Five of who?" my mother demanded.

"Children," came the swift reply. "They're at the gatehouse by the bridge . . . It's the same as the others . . . Their parents have been murdered."

26

By the time the children had been brought up to our house, most of the crying had stopped, replaced by silent, shocked expressions. The five children were from three families: two sisters, ages five and seven; a brother and sister, who we guessed were a little older; and a teenager named Thomas.

Thomas explained exactly what had happened in dull, blunt terms, sounding almost as if he were bored or tired of telling the story. Of course he was just in shock. The way he described things was almost as if he had been watching a movie and hadn't been there.

He and his parents had been down by the river, on the far side but basically in sight of our guard station on the other side. A man who later identified himself as Brett swept in with five other men and overpowered them. His parents tried to reason, talk, explain, and finally beg, but nothing worked. Brett had shot them right in front of him.

Thomas gave the details so painstakingly that most of the people who heard turned away. Howie had started to tear up, and my mother worked hard to keep calm.

I didn't look away. I listened and forced myself to picture it all in my mind. All of the evil. I had to.

The guards reported that they'd heard the gunshots. There were two shots, and then two more, and then a final two—all in less than twenty minutes. It had been less than another thirty minutes before the children showed up, stumbling across the bridge over the river. Thomas had been carrying two of them—the little sisters—and the other two clung to his sides. He said he didn't know any of them or their parents. They were bound together only by the tragedy that they'd all experienced. Somehow those families had managed to survive all the dangers of the past few months, managed to survive against the odds. They couldn't prepare for such an act of unprovoked evil.

The children had been driven forward by Brett at gunpoint, the littlest girl with a letter tied around her neck.

The letter was simple and short.

In case you thought I wasn't serious. See you soon.

There was no need for a signature.

Thomas stood up and moved toward me from the far end of the room, his eyes locked on mine. I felt a sense of uneasiness but didn't look away.

"You're Adam," he said, his voice hardly a whisper.

I nodded.

"Can we talk?" Before I could answer he said, "But not here."

I got up. Every eye was now on us. Even two of the other children were looking in our direction.

I had to say something.

"Thomas and I are going for a walk."

I could tell from the expressions of my mother and Maureen that they were surprised and concerned. My mother looked like she was going to say something but instead just nodded and mumbled something about being safe.

"They'll be all right," Herb said in my defense. He motioned for us to leave.

"We won't go far," I said as a final reassurance.

Thomas and I left the house behind, and I felt myself wilt as the pressure was relieved. I had a big question: How had he known I was Adam? Nobody had mentioned my name. I had just sat off to the side of the room and listened.

"He said I was supposed to give this to you," Thomas said. He dug into his pocket and pulled out a crumpled note.

I took it and went to read it, but he stopped me.

"He said it was just for you . . . a secret . . . that he'd do something to me if I didn't get it to you or if anybody found out."

"He can't get you here," I said.

"You have to promise!" he pleaded. "He said if I didn't deliver it that he'd . . . he'd . . ."

He burst into tears and I put my arm around him. "I promise I won't let anyone else know about it." I stuffed it into my pocket. I'd read it later, in private, where my reactions would be my own.

"What happens now?" Thomas sniffed. "What happens to me . . . to us . . . to the others?"

"We'll take care of you. You'll stay here."

"Really? Why now and not then?" he asked.

"I don't understand."

"We tried to get in once. My parents said it would be safer

inside. The guards on the walls said we couldn't, that they'd shoot at us if we didn't leave."

"They wouldn't have done that," I assured him. "They were just trying to get you to leave, that's all."

It had been one of the hardest things for our guards, to send off innocent people, to tell them to leave, that they couldn't help them. And then I thought it through another step. "Did you think our guards were going to shoot you when you were walking toward our gate right now?"

He nodded, and his eyes started to fill with tears again. I could only imagine how terrifying that walk would have been—away from a group of people who had just killed his parents, under a threat he'd be shot if he didn't, and toward another group he thought was going to kill him.

"We're not like that," I said. "He is."

"He told me he killed my parents because of you."

"It wasn't because of m-me," I stammered.

"I know," he said. "He did it because he wanted to, because he enjoyed it." He paused. "I saw it—he *wanted* to kill them."

"You don't have to talk about any of this, not to me."

"I can't stop thinking about it! I can't stop seeing it."

I wanted to tell him it would go away, but that would have been nothing more than a bad lie.

"What grade are you in . . . Or, I mean, what grade would you be in now?" I asked.

"Ninth."

"My brother and sister are in fifth grade. You're going to become like a big brother to them because you're going to be staying at our house, with us."

Thomas just looked at me with dull eyes.

"And I'm going to make you a promise. You're never going to have to worry about Brett getting near you again. I'm going to . . . take care of it."

"You're going to kill him?"

I looked at Thomas and nodded.

"Yes."

27

It was almost four o'clock in the morning. I couldn't sleep, so I slipped out of the house and started walking the perimeter fence. In my pocket was the note from Brett that Thomas had passed on to me. I couldn't believe how a single piece of paper could weigh so much, could feel so heavy. I hadn't shared it with anybody—not the content, not the fact that I'd been given it.

Of course there wasn't one person in the neighborhood who hadn't heard about what had happened. Five more orphans, six more dead parents. Brett's name and deeds were on the tongues and minds of everybody. He couldn't have been more present if he was living among us.

All along my walk I'd nodded to or had a brief conversation with guards stationed at the wall. I'd had to answer the same questions in one form or another at least a dozen times. If my hope was to get away from the situation and clear my mind, this was the worst plan possible.

Up ahead I saw Howie with three other guards. He started toward me.

"I didn't expect to run into you out here," Howie said.

"I couldn't sleep, so I thought I'd go for a moonlight stroll. You?"

"Sleep is never easy for me, so I thought I'd inspect the troops," he explained. "I think they needed it. There's a lot of tension on the line. It's ramping up every night."

"We won't have to wait much longer."

"At least the break gave us more time to plan, prepare, and get in some reinforcements," Howie said.

"We basically had this plan in place in two days," I said. "The waiting is always the hardest part."

"Maybe that's why he gave us five days, to make it harder," Howie suggested.

"I never thought of that," I said. "I'll ask Herb what he thinks."

"If you hurry, you can catch him. He was here just a couple of minutes before you."

"I guess he couldn't sleep either," I said.

"I don't think he ever sleeps, but that's not it. He's going around talking to every person on the wall. He's giving them confidence, trying to reduce the tension, eliminate the doubt." Howie pointed. "He went that way."

I started off and Howie stopped me.

"How's the kid Thomas doing?"

"He was asleep when I left. He's bunking with Danny."

"I heard that your family is taking him in and that it was your idea," Howie said.

"I just thought of it first, that's all." I knew I should have checked with my parents before I'd made that offer to Thomas, but he did need a place to stay and people to take care of him. Besides, having him close was good for me.

"Either way, it was nice of you. Caring."

Caring wasn't the only reason, but I couldn't tell Howie

that. Having Thomas nearby gave me a chance to see this living reminder, to hear the stories, to think about what Brett had done and what he would continue doing.

"I better get going if I want to catch up to the old man."

I went away quickly. I passed by the first two towers on the North Wall, exchanging a couple of words with the guards and confirming Herb had just spoken to them. I moved right along the base of the wall. It was solid cement, and double my height. It was the most secure fencing we had, and I felt protected in its shadow.

If I could have seen over it I would have been able to see the smooth, empty lanes of the highway and the forming community to the north. Of all of our new neighbors, that community had been the slowest to come together. Fields were being cultivated with winter wheat and some hardy greens, and security was being organized, but the people there hadn't been able to fashion a complete wall and Howie had reported that their attempts at perimeter guards were the least developed. Because of that he'd put his best guards on this segment of our walls. If we hadn't been so occupied with the pending exchange with Brett we could have invested more time in helping them. I'd feel better, more secure, once they were a more solid force.

To the left, the west, was one of the small buffer communities and the highway. If danger was to come, it would be from the city, in the east; that highway heading west would be our escape route.

To the right, the east, were the gate and the guardhouse over toward the Credit River. That's where we'd be passing in two days. We'd probably be walking into a trap that Brett had waiting for us. I could only hope that he didn't know that a trap was being set for him as well.

I heard laughter coming from the next guard tower and suspected Herb was there. As I approached there was more laughter and I recognized Herb's voice. He saw me and waved, offering a smile.

"So it looks like everybody is out tonight!" Herb said.

"Maybe you two could stay here and we could go home and get some sleep," one of the guards joked. I knew her—Joanie—the way I knew everybody else. She was a decent person, took her job seriously, and was somebody who could be counted on. She had two children and a dog and a husband who was also a guard on the wall. They usually were on two different shifts so that one of them would always be home to watch the kids. I wondered if either or both were assigned to any of the away teams and how the children would cope if something happened to their mother or father. Hopefully one of them would survive—hopefully both would survive.

What a terrible thing to have to think about. Terrible because it was true. No matter what happened, somebody was going to lose somebody they cared for. I just had to hope it wasn't my parents or me or Herb or Todd and his family or the Petersons. But was that like wishing that somebody else was going to die?

Herb shook hands with everybody and we started walking again.

"So what brings you out tonight?" Herb asked.

"Couldn't sleep. And you?"

"Too much work to do. My father used to say there'll be plenty of time to sleep when you're dead." Herb laughed a little. "I guess he's been sleeping well for the last forty years. Hard to believe it's been that long and the time has passed that fast. I know you might find this difficult to believe, but at one point I used to be your age."

"That *is* almost impossible to believe," I said. "Actually, there is something I wanted to talk to you about. I was wondering about Brett setting the drop-off five days after he sent the message. Why would he give us that much time?"

"Perhaps he wanted to make sure we had time to meet his demands," Herb suggested.

"He knows how we operate, so he knows it wouldn't take us more than a day or two to decide and prepare. There has to be another reason."

"It might be taking him that long to set his trap."

"Then why didn't he get it all set before he sent the message? He set the agenda and the time. He showed us today that he has no problem finding more people to kill to send a message."

"Or messages," Herb said.

Messages? Did he know about the note Thomas had given me?

"It could be more psychological than anything else," Herb continued. "Waiting is hard. It allows uncertainty and fear to spread, causes people to divide and decisions to be second-guessed. All that gives him control."

I thought about the promise I'd made to Thomas about not telling anybody about the message, but if nothing else I'd learned that many promises couldn't be kept.

"How did you know there was more than one message today?" I asked.

"I couldn't think of another reason why that boy—"

"Thomas," I interrupted. "His name is Thomas."

"Yes, Thomas. I couldn't think of another reason why he would need to talk to you privately. What was the message?"

I pulled it out of my pocket and handed it to Herb.

"My reading glasses are at home. What does it say?"

"Brett wants to meet me, person to person, out there on the other side of the bridge. He said if I was a real man I'd meet him and that either he'd kill me and leave the neighborhood alone or I'd kill him and it would be over."

"You know that's just a lie," Herb said.

"I know that killing him is the only way this will end."

"You aren't really thinking of doing what he's asking, are you?" Herb questioned.

I shook my head. "It's just a trap. He'd just kill me."

"No he wouldn't," Herb said.

"He wouldn't?"

"No, he wouldn't *just* kill you. He'd torment you, torture you, hurt you in a way that was so cruel and painful that you'd beg for death."

"I'd never do that!" I snapped. I felt offended that he'd even suggest that.

"Adam, there is no limit to the pain that can be induced through torture. I know . . . I've been on both sides of the equation," Herb said. "And giving in to such pain is not a sign of weakness; it's just human."

I didn't know what shocked me more, that he'd been tortured or that he was admitting to having tortured somebody.

"There are so many things that a government can sanction and a conscience can allow before finally saying no. I found that out the hard way," Herb said. "I just know that if it came down to a choice of dying or being captured by Brett, I'd save one bullet. I'd kill myself before allowing him to have me."

"You can't be serious."

"Completely. It would be the way of denying him what he wants most."

What Herb was saying seemed to make some sense, but still I shook my head. "I don't think I could do that."

"Did you ever think you could do any of this?" he asked, encompassing the neighborhood with his hands. "Did you think any of us could do any of this?"

"It is hard to believe."

"Then you have to believe me. Fight to the end if you have to. But if there's no way out, then escape the only way you have left: put a bullet into your head before you let Brett get his hands on you."

Slowly I nodded.

"Come on and let me walk you home."

"I'm not going to go out there to meet him," I said.

"I know. I think we both need to go home and get some sleep. We have to have our minds clear for what's still to come."

28

There was a countdown clock in my head. In less than twenty-four hours I'd be leading the team out of the neighborhood to where we were going to meet Brett. I stood at the Erin Mills Parkway wall. The road had been closed down completely awaiting a special landing. What was a long, wide landing strip for an ultralight or even a Cessna was tight and tricky for a bigger passenger plane— even if that plane was a relatively small antique four-propeller passenger plane.

I wasn't sure whether I should be relieved or uneasy that it was my father at the controls. He was a great pilot, but it was a really old plane. How could we be sure that they'd been able to check it out completely? It wasn't like there would be any mechanic alive who'd made a living servicing planes that old.

While the road itself—the runway—was clear, there was no shortage of spectators. Hundreds and hundreds were waiting to see the plane land and to greet the visitors when they arrived. Our lives had become so insular. Most of the residents of the neighborhood hadn't left it in the past six months, never ventured beyond the walls.

People lined both sides of the road, peeking out at the

runway over the top of the fences. It reminded me of a crowd waiting for a parade to pass by. There was a feeling of excited expectation. It was also something like that day in the beginning—in the strip mall's parking lot—when people were waiting for food to be distributed and eating ice cream from Baskin-Robbins before it could melt.

"It feels like a big birthday party or something," Howie said.

"They're just happy to greet our guests," my mother added. "It's not like we've had many visitors lately."

"I thought the whole idea behind the wall was to avoid having any guests," Howie joked.

"Unwanted guests," my mother said. "These are very wanted, at least judging by the bouquets of flowers some of your neighbors have brought."

I'd been confused about that. "Where did they even get all those flowers from?"

"Mr. Gomez has been bringing them in. The scavenging teams have been under orders to bring in certain flowers for transplanting into the neighborhood."

"You'd think they'd be more worried about finding food and other things we really need," I said, although it might be time for me to get Lori another bouquet.

"We really do need flowers," Herb said.

That surprised me. He must have noticed from my expression.

"Lots of things are important that aren't about just surviving, Adam," he explained. "Flowers are to some people what fairness, justice, laughter, and love are to others. You might grab some for Lori."

There he was, inside my head again.

"I think it's such a good sign that people are able to have something on their minds other than making it from one day to the next," my mother said.

Maybe this little street party did make sense, although I thought it should have started by now, they should have arrived. I looked at my watch.

"They left a bit later than planned," Herb said, reading my unspoken question.

"And they are taking a circuitous route," Howie added. "It's better that they not be seen by anybody we don't want to see them. We'd like our alliance to remain a secret."

"Do you think he's watching?" I asked.

"He or some of his men are probably not far outside the walls. Hopefully anything they see won't make sense to them."

"How many people will be coming today?" I asked.

"An even hundred guests will join us."

"I didn't think their plane could hold nearly that many people," I said.

"Your father will be making two trips to bring them here," my mother explained. "Fifty per trip."

As part of our self-defense agreement, she explained, the islanders were providing us with a force of a hundred armed guards. They'd stay to defend our walls when our forces went out on the attack against Brett and his force.

"I just wish we knew more about what was waiting for us," I said.

"We're not totally blind. You and your father have been making regular flights over the meeting spot," Herb said.

"And you know how much we can miss from the air," I said.

"We've also had two small away teams in the field, one led by Quinn, both of them practically living out there," my mother said.

"With your father in the air, Quinn's the best man we could have in that position," Herb said.

I couldn't argue with that, and quite frankly I was so much happier to have my father up in the air instead of on the ground outside the walls.

"Quinn knows their tactics and strategies better than anybody who wasn't ever part of them could," my mother added.

"I know there are still some who don't trust him or even like him," Howie said, "but I know better."

I agreed. It was strange to believe that our safety was at least partly in the hands of a former member of the Division. But he was maybe the only person who hated them more than I did. Unless it was an act and if that was the case he was the best actor in the world. I didn't believe that. I liked Quinn and I'd trust him with my life. I guess I *was* trusting him with my life. Mine and hundreds of other people's.

I caught sight of a flash in the sky. "I see a plane," I said, pointing toward the south. "But it isn't a passenger plane . . . too small and moving too fast." I suspected it had to be one of the Mustangs.

We watched as it closed on our position. It quickly became more visible—it *was* one of the Mustangs. It was probably acting as a fighter escort for the passenger plane, keeping it safe. That meant my father couldn't be too far behind.

It swooped over top of us and wiggled its wings in greeting. Its presence made me feel happy and proud and hopeful all at once. I couldn't help wondering if one day our country could be what it was before—this time maybe even better.

As quickly as it came, it passed, then banked off to the east. I scanned the sky to the south and at last spotted the other plane.

There wasn't much wind, so my dad could come in and land in either direction. The direction he was heading made sense. It was farther away from anyplace where Brett might have been.

"He's really low isn't he?" my mother said.

"Low so he won't be seen from so far," I responded.

The plane got closer and closer until we could hear it. The waiting crowd responded by getting quiet, as if they didn't want to disturb my father's concentration or scare him away.

His wheels were down and he was coming in slow. He couldn't be that much above stall speed. I noticed the nose of the plane come slightly up—he'd pulled back on the yoke to change the attitude—as it just nudged over the far wall.

What I hadn't mentioned to my mother was my concern about the width of the road. He had clearance between the fence and center light poles, but a sudden cross breeze could have pushed him sideways. Clipping a wing would destroy the plane and everyone on board.

"He's coming in perfectly," I said. Those words more for my mother than anything else.

It was a shiny silver bullet with four engines, two on each wing, with their propellers just a blur. There was a shriek of rubber on asphalt as the wheels hit. He stuck it, no bounce back into the air. I could picture him going through the procedures for landing—imagined him pushing the throttle in, pushing down on the brakes, making sure it didn't slide to the right or left but stayed center.

My images were broken by the roar of the crowd as everybody burst into applause when the plane raced past us. Anxiously I followed along as it slowed down—I could smell the burning rubber—and it came to a stop at the end of the runway, well short and clear of the end wall. It had been a picture-perfect landing.

In seconds the plane was surrounded by a throng of people. We ran forward to join them, and the crowd allowed us to pass until we were right beside the plane. The door opened and a little folding stairway was lowered to the ground. A head popped out and the crowd just went wild, the screaming and cheering almost deafening. I found myself cheering along in spite of myself.

The first person—a woman who was wearing camouflage clothing with a rifle slung over her shoulder—stepped onto the stairs. As the crowd pressed forward she looked almost frightened, then confused, and then a gigantic smile burst onto her face as she realized the cheering was for her and the crowd was wildly friendly. She was greeted with handshakes and hugs, and a couple of bouquets were pressed into her hands. With each new person exiting, a new round of greetings was exchanged. My mother, Herb, and the judge, who'd come out of the crowd, were the formal welcoming party.

I slipped through the crowd and around the line leaving the plane and waited beside the door until the last passenger came down the steps. Then I went up the stairs, ducked down, and climbed into the plane. The door to the cockpit was open and I caught sight of my father. He saw me, waved, and motioned for me to come. I had to duck down again to enter the cockpit.

"Not as fancy as my usual plane," my father said.

"But a lot fancier than the Cessna or the ultralight."

"Definitely—and, believe me, I'm not complaining. This old craft flies pretty well. Are you interested in finding out how well?"

That's what I had been hoping for. "It would be great to fly back with you."

"You could come back as my copilot."

"I'd love to! When do we leave?"

"We need the runway to be cleared, and we need to get fueled up. While that's happening why don't you tell your mother you're going with me?"

"I'm on it."

———————

There were almost as many people waiting to watch us take off as there had been to witness the landing.

"Push forward on all four levers simultaneously," my father said.

With both hands I fed more fuel into the engines and the roar got louder. My father released the brakes and we started to rumble along the roadway.

"Full throttle," my father ordered.

I pushed the levers the rest of the way and the engines screamed out in response. We rapidly gained speed, rolling along the road, and my father pulled back on the yoke—the one in front of me moving in tandem—and the plane lifted off. I couldn't see them or hear them but I was sure a cheer went up from the crowd. I felt like cheering myself.

"This retracts the landing gear," my father said as he moved another lever.

We gained elevation and headed straight south, toward the lake.

"It's a Boeing," my father said.

"You've flown Boeings before."

"This is a Boeing Stratoliner, which is sort of the great-great-great-grandparent of the 777 I usually fly," my father said. "It has four Wright GR-1820 engines, a length of seventy-four feet, a wingspan of over a hundred feet, normal capacity of forty-four, and a cruising speed of two hundred and twenty miles per hour and a top speed of two-fifty."

"So it's pretty much like the Cessna in terms of speed."

"There are similarities and differences but enough similarities that you can take the controls. Right now, it's yours."

"Really?"

He took his hands off the wheel, and I put my hands on the yoke on my side.

"Continue on this heading until we get to the lake, and then take us to the east," my father said.

I pulled back on the yoke to gain more altitude in preparation for the turn. The lake quickly came up beneath us, and I worked the rudders and pedals to execute the turn. I was cautious, wanting to get the feel for the plane.

"That's it, nice and gentle. You're doing well. Colonel Wayne has offered me the chance to be the full-time captain of this plane."

"That's amazing!"

"And as the captain I would be allowed to choose my copilot." He paused. "I guess I should tell you that you're not just flying this plane right now; you're auditioning for a new job."

"You're joking, right?"

"I would never joke about flying. You'd be the youngest co-pilot in history to ever fly one of these. You get to achieve the dream of being an airline pilot faster than anybody would have imagined. So are you interested?"

"Of course I'm interested!"

"It would involve a lot of work. This plane may seem like something out of an old Hollywood movie, but it's just about the most sophisticated airplane in our corner of the world right now."

I laughed. "I can picture the whole thing being in black-and-white instead of color, but I'd like to be part of it."

"We'd be responsible for transporting people and equipment and supplies between the colonies. It could be as many as a dozen flights per month."

"That's a lot of air time."

"It will be. Correct your heading, please, to bring us around more until we're going almost due east."

I made the correction, executing the bank until the controls showed I was bang on the forty-five-degree mark on the compass.

"If you take the job, I'd put you through the same routines and practices that I would when a copilot was assigned to my flight crew. I'm not going to go easy on you."

"I wouldn't expect it . . . and I won't need it," I said.

He laughed. "I like confidence. We'll also be training a

flight engineer and working to develop an entire ground crew to service the plane."

"Have you talked to Mom about any of this?"

"We've talked about me taking the job. She understands what it means for me to be in the air."

"You are in the air with the Cessna," I argued.

"This is different. Not just because I'm in the air but because I'm needed. This will be a job that will really make a difference. It's important. We need to pull the colonies together, to move the alliance forward, to facilitate training, to be able to get armed support from one place to another if needed."

I knew what he was saying was completely true.

"They don't have anybody else who can do it. In time we might find another pilot or somebody I could share the job with, but for now it's me and hopefully you. I'm hoping everybody will be happy about all of this."

"I'm happy. I know how much being in the air means to you. How much it means for me, too. I'm just worried about flying that much and still doing the things I have to do on the ground."

"There are many people who can do most of the things you do on the ground, but there are only a few of us who can fly. And I think it would be better, safer, for you to be up here with me instead of alone out there," my father said. "Up here is the only place where I feel completely safe."

"I understand. It's the same for me," I said.

"You don't have to go out there tomorrow," he said.

"I do have to go. There's no choice, not for tomorrow, but maybe after that . . . maybe," I said.

"Okay, I can respect that," he said. "Funny, I flew off that morning to Chicago and you were still a boy. When I came back you were a man. I have trouble believing you're still only sixteen."

"I have the same trouble sometimes," I admitted.

"The past six months have changed you so much."

"They have changed all of us," I said.

"It didn't just change me," my father said. "It broke me."

I hadn't expected him to say that, and I didn't know what to say in response.

"I know I'll never be the same man I was. I'm just so sorry that I wasn't there for my family when they needed me."

"You walked halfway across the country to get back home."

"That's what broke me," he said. "I'll never be the same again . . . except for up here in the air."

I understood exactly what he meant.

Soon enough, the island was on the horizon, the airport and the runway visible.

"I'm going to take over the controls again," my father said. He placed his hands on the yoke as I surrendered the instruments. "Don't worry, though, you'll be landing her soon enough yourself."

Maybe being in control would be just part of who I was from now on. Whether I wanted it or not.

29

It had been a long day and we'd been late getting back home. We'd flown in the second group of guards and had to go back to the island to drop off the Boeing and pick up the Cessna and fly it back to our neighborhood.

My father and I had occupied the same small space for hours, but on the return flight we hadn't talked much. Well, except for things that had to do with flying. It was like we'd said too much at the start and neither of us knew what to do with it. It was an unspoken sort of agreement not to go any further, and it seemed to work.

Getting to sleep was never easy, but tonight it was going to be pretty well impossible. I had so many things crammed into my head.

I thought about what it would be like to live somewhere else, somewhere Brett couldn't reach me. I felt like running away and taking my family and my friends with me and—

But there was no place to go, no place to run.

I rearranged the pillows, punching them down with my fist to try to find a comfortable place to rest. I really did need to sleep. I needed to be as sharp as possible for tomorrow. After that, well, I didn't even know if there was going to be anything beyond tomorrow. I had the strangest thought: if I got killed I wouldn't have to make any more decisions, be troubled anymore about what to do or what had happened—and that was almost reassuring and calming.

But no, I couldn't allow myself to think that way. Or maybe I could. The key might be to just not care if I lived or died. Was that how Brett felt? If he didn't care about other people's lives, did he care about his own life?

My bedroom was pitch black except for a little ray of moonlight coming in through the window and settling onto my desk. The letter from Brett sat there and looked like it was practically glowing. It was just another way for him to haunt me, to taunt me, to rob me of sleep. It felt like even the moon was against me.

I got out of bed. I was going to put the letter away in a drawer where I couldn't see it. Instead I picked it up. It felt heavy, and there was a tingling that seemed to vibrate into my fingers and hand. Instead of opening the drawer I sat at the desk. I couldn't put it down. I needed to read it one more time.

I struck a match and put it to the wick of a candle. It fluttered and then caught. The candle was handmade—someone in the neighborhood had started to create them out of beeswax—but the light was good.

Hello, Little Prince . . .

What had I ever done to him that he should hate me so much? I flipped through the sentences.

I want you to lead this expedition.

How could I have any doubt that this was a trap that was being set for me? He wanted me out there so that he could try to kill me. Thank God there were going to be many other people out there. Then again, he knew we'd do that; he'd even taunted us to send more.

I'd like to guarantee you that I won't attack the people bringing out the food, but you know my word isn't always the best.

Why would he do that? He'd have to know that we would send out enough people to protect the party. My mother would never allow me to go out there unless I was protected.

He would expect that we were going to try to set a trap for him. In fact, by giving us five days he was almost inviting us to set that trap. That could only mean that he was setting a trap to trap our trap. My head started to hurt. This was too many levels of things to think through. I had to go back to the basics: My role in this was being the bait. I was the cheese in the trap, and we hoped we'd catch a rat and that he wouldn't get away with the cheese and devour it.

I thought about what Herb had told me—take your own life if he catches you, don't let him have the satisfaction of killing you.

I'd almost felt insulted when he said that. Now I realized that it was something I could do. Just like waiting was hard, waiting to die would be even worse, especially if that waiting involved being tortured and tormented.

Of course it still wasn't too late. In the morning I could say no to going out there. That would make my mother and father and Lori happy. Todd would cheer me on and probably be thrilled that it meant that he didn't have to go either. None of them wanted me to do it, even if they thought it was the right thing to do. In the end, though, didn't I have to try to do the right thing even if there was a cost, a price to pay? I just had to hope that the price wasn't my life.

I didn't have to be a victim, but I also didn't have to be the one who killed Brett. But still, I *wanted* to kill him. What a twisted, bizarre thought. Just six months ago, I spent my time being concerned about good grades and fantasizing about Lori. Although I still did fantasize about her, now my other fantasy was about killing somebody. And if our trap worked I might have that chance.

The thing was, something just didn't seem right about Brett's letter.

He had to know that we were going to try to trap him.

So why would he put himself in that situation? Why would he risk the lives of some of his men? Maybe he didn't care if their lives were forfeited. It wasn't like he cared about anybody. Still, it would have been a waste of resources. Even if he didn't think of them as people he still wouldn't want to have them taken away from him.

I looked at the letter again, although I didn't know what I was expecting to see that I hadn't seen the last twenty times I'd looked at it.

Then I read the final line, the final taunt.

> *P.P.S. Send Lori my love. Tell her that now I know*
> *you two have broken up I think about her often and*
> *it won't be too long before those thoughts become*
> *more than thoughts. Monday at noon will come*
> *sooner than you think.*

That made no sense other than he was trying to get me too crazy to think. But really, the only people who were at risk were those who were going to be part of the away team.

The people behind the wall were safe. He had to know that Lori was going to stay in Eden Mills, that no one would let her be there when we turned over the food.

Then it came to me, and I saw what Brett was planning.

He was going to attack the neighborhood.

I felt a rush of adrenaline throughout my entire body. I had to talk to Herb, and I had to do it now. I blew out the candle and the room was dark again. As soon as my eyes adjusted to the only light being the thin rays of the moon I got up.

Quietly I opened my bedroom door and left, letter in hand. I already had both guns strapped on, one on my hip and the second on my leg. I already had my knife strapped on. I already had my shoes on. I went down the stairs and to the front door. There were no other sounds, no signs of anybody else being awake. For a sick, terrifying second, I thought that Brett was already in the house, that he'd silently killed my family and now he was coming for me.

I froze in my tracks and felt my chest tightening and my breath becoming labored. I moved my head from one side to the other, scanning the darkness, trying to pick out one shadow from another.

"Calm down," I muttered under my breath. "You're alone . . . he's not here."

I wanted something to break the silence. I wanted one of my parents to come to the bedroom door and just call out to me. Their bedroom door remained closed. They were sleeping—of course they were sleeping, and I wasn't going to wake them up to ease my paranoia. This was all part of Brett's plan, to get so far into our heads that we couldn't think straight. It had taken me this long to figure it out, and I wasn't going to let him drive it from my head now.

I slipped off the door's chain lock, and went outside. I pulled the door shut again and checked to make sure it was locked. Funny how being outside felt safer than being in my own house behind that locked door. Out here I could see things coming.

The air was still and cool and dry. There wasn't a sound. It was as silent as the house. I knew there would be guards patrolling throughout the neighborhood, but right then I was completely alone. It could have been that I was the only living person in the world. If I was, there would have been nobody to hurt me.

Or protect me, or love me. I wasn't alone. I was surrounded by all the people who I cared for and who cared for me.

I padded across the driveway, skirted the vegetables growing on our lawn, and glided down Herb's driveway and up the walk to the front door. As I stood there I wondered what to do next. It wasn't like I could pound on the door to wake him without waking everybody else in the nearby houses.

Was there any chance he'd left the door unlocked? I reached for it and the door suddenly opened up. I jumped back in shock.

"Adam, it's all right, it's me."

It was Herb.

A shudder went through my entire body.

"You might want to put that away," my friend said.

I looked down. I was holding my gun. All in one motion without even consciously realizing it, I'd pulled it out from the holster and aimed it toward him. It was like looking at somebody else's hand holding a gun.

"Sorry," I said. I lowered it and carefully tucked it back into its holster. "I didn't mean to wake you."

"I wasn't asleep. I was watching out the front window. This must be important," Herb said.

"It is. We have to talk. We have everything wrong."

30

I brought my Omega to a stop at the gate, and the procession behind me came to a stop as well. I was leading a convoy of three other vehicles—another car, an old van, and a stake truck loaded with boxes. All four vehicles had a driver and a person in the passenger seat. Anybody watching would, we hoped, assume that the boxes on the truck were the extorted supplies. Instead they were filled with rocks and formed around a hollowed-out middle that contained ten of our people, heavily armed with rifles, shotguns, and RPGs.

Like a good scorpion, we had our sting in the tail.

"So are we doing this or what?" Todd asked.

I looked at my watch—11:28. "You got someplace you're hoping to go after this?" I asked.

"I have hundreds and hundreds of places I'm hoping to go. I'm a busy man, and in a lifetime of bad decisions this one stands out as perhaps one of my worst."

"It's not too late. You don't have to come along."

"Are you kidding? And let you have all the fun?" Todd asked.

I tapped my horn a couple of times to get the attention of the guards on the gate. The two of them struggled to swing it open. It was big and heavy, and they were used to having a lot of people to help them. Now, with the advance parties already sent out, we were seriously undermanned along this whole part of the wall—so undermanned that we couldn't possibly withstand an attack of any significance. And it was this way because of my suggestion.

"Do up your body armor and put on your helmet," I said to Todd.

"Yes, Mother." Todd pulled up the zipper and tightened the belts. "There really isn't enough headroom for me to wear the helmet," he complained. "Besides, it messes up my hair."

"Would you like your hair parted with a bullet? Isn't part of the deal that I'm supposed to keep you pretty? Put it on."

He grumbled, then slipped down in the seat and put on his helmet.

"Being low is good," I said. "Those doors will protect you from most gunfire."

The doors of the Omega had been reinforced with metal, and sand had been poured into the frame to offer further resistance to bullets. It was reassuring, but I also knew it couldn't stop a large-caliber weapon or a close-up shot. And all the extra weight cost us some speed. My car—which never was very fast—was slower than ever.

We eased out through the gate and were immediately onto the bridge.

Todd slumped down even farther. "Didn't you say we weren't going to be fired at?"

"We won't be. At least if I'm right about all of this," I said.

"And if you're wrong?"

"Then the helmet isn't much protection from an RPG and

your hair getting messed will be the least of your problems," I said.

The cement railings on both sides of the bridge blocked our view of the water and valley below. In my rearview mirror I watched as the other three vehicles came out after me and then the gate swung shut, locking us out. Now it really did feel like it was too late.

"Do you think we're being watched?" Todd asked.

"I'd be shocked if we weren't."

"So an attack could come at any time," he said.

"Not if I'm right."

"I wish you'd stop with the '*if* I'm right' part. It's not particularly comforting," Todd said.

"So you'd like me to pretend that I'm certain, that there's no way I could be wrong?"

"That is correct. I want complete certainty, a vote of confidence—a big, beautiful, wonderful lie if necessary," Todd said.

"Okay, in that case, I am one-hundred-percent certain that I am correct, and you therefore have nothing to worry about whatsoever. Take off the helmet, undo the vest, ride on the roof of the car if you want."

"You know, that would have been much more convincing if you hadn't added in that part about the roof. But really, you are right . . . right?" Todd asked.

"I hope so."

"And if you're not?"

"At least it will be over quickly," I said. "You won't even see it coming. If he's gunning for me, then he'll be aiming at my car."

"Great, just great. If you were really my friend, you would have insisted that I didn't come with you because you couldn't bear to risk my life."

"I guess I'm not as good a friend to you as you are to me for offering to come along," I said.

"Apparently. Why didn't we have this discussion five minutes ago on the other side of the wall?"

As we moved away from our neighborhood, the roadway became more littered with abandoned vehicles. All had had their gas tanks emptied, most had been stripped down, and many had been torched, nothing left but charred metal skeletons. On both sides we were boxed in by the high cement and metal walls. At one time they were innocent noise barriers designed to protect neighboring homes from the drone and roar of the highway. Now they were perfect cover. Anybody pinned in between the walls, like we were at the moment, could be fired on from both sides. We were in what Herb called a perfect kill zone. It was better to be on the outside of a zone like that firing in, instead of inside firing out.

I took a glance in my rearview and saw that, even with the Omega moving slowly, I was leaving the other vehicles behind. That wasn't smart. I eased off the gas pedal to let them gain. We needed to stay tight.

"Are the other teams in place?" Todd asked.

"They're under radio silence, but I have to assume they're out there where they're supposed to be."

"I guess that's reassuring."

"Only if I'm right. If I'm wrong it's really, really not reassuring at all," I said.

"Comforting lies only, remember? I'd hate to get out and walk back, but I will if I have to."

I started laughing, which was something I hadn't expected to do today. Having Todd along was a good idea. Or a really bad one.

"Brett and his men would have seen the support teams go out as well, right?" Todd asked.

"They were so large that even in the dark they would have been hard to miss."

I continued to drive around the vehicles abandoned on the highway. There were lots of them, but between the three lanes and shoulders on both sides there was always a path. I figured they'd been cleared wherever they had formed a complete block.

"Do you see them?" Todd exclaimed.

"See what, where?" I demanded.

"People. There are people up ahead!"

I scanned the horizon and caught sight of movement. It was three or four people, and they had obviously seen us as well. They were running away.

"It looks like a family," I said. "They're probably afraid of us and just looking to get away."

The words had no sooner left my lips than they disappeared through a place where the fence had crumbled. Instinctively I changed lanes to get to the far side of the road away from where they'd escaped. Just because they were afraid of us didn't mean that we shouldn't be afraid of them.

"Train your rifle on the gap as we go by," I said.

Todd aimed his rifle out the window, using the door frame to steady it. If somebody shot at us, Todd might be able to get off a shot or two as well. He probably wouldn't hit any-one, but it might make them duck or take cover. I gave the car some gas and we whizzed by the opening without any-body taking any shots. Todd let out a big sigh of relief.

"You know, in thinking this through, it probably would have been better if Herb was here with you," Todd said.

"He's got a more important place to be. Just like my mother and father and Howie."

"So I'm basically your fifth choice," Todd said.

"Not really, but my parents wouldn't let Danny or Rachel come, and Lori had other things to do, and Ernie was busy at the store," I joked.

"You really make a guy feel appreciated and—"

He was interrupted by a call over the radio. "Green, green, green!"

31

I cranked the wheel of the car and slammed on the brakes so that we skidded to a stop. The other vehicles behind me did the same. I spun around, pushed down on the gas, and pulled away from the others. They didn't need us, and we needed to get back as quickly as possible.

"What if they see us turning around now?" Todd demanded.

"They'll just think we got scared and are racing back to the safety of the neighborhood. It's too late even if they did figure it out."

Without having to wait for the others, with no more need to stay in a tight convoy, I passed the abandoned vehicles like a skier going through a slalom course.

I had to work to control the adrenaline coursing through my veins. We were heading back to the neighborhood and running straight toward the danger.

We hit the stretch of the highway that we'd cleared when we had harvested vehicles. I pressed down harder and we picked up speed. The needle on my speedometer edged up to over sixty miles an hour—as fast as this car had traveled in a long time and definitely as fast as it could travel now! I hazarded a glance in the rearview mirror and saw the other vehicles well behind but still coming.

We hit the bridge and I realized that the guards hadn't opened the gates on the other side. I laid on the horn—my dinky little horn—and hoped the racket would alert them to action.

"Slow down!" Todd yelled.

I started to press the brakes when a little gap appeared and the gate started to open. It widened and we shot through, almost scraping against it.

Up ahead, the road was active with guards and vehicles that seemed to be everywhere. I slowed down but kept moving, weaving through the people. I wanted to get to the wall. As soon as we couldn't drive any closer we jumped out of the car. I reached back in and grabbed my rifle, and we raced to the wall.

The section was already lined with armed people, four or five of whom had RPGs. Many had on body armor and riot helmets like Todd and I were wearing—gear my mother had held in reserve from the police station. Others had put on motorcycle helmets. Not perfect, but better than a baseball cap.

The wall had been reinforced with dirt and chunks of concrete that had been hacked off of other walls and piled up behind it. It was like a series of little hills that had been constructed in the last few hours using shovels and wheelbarrows as well as Mr. Peterson and his tractor. They'd started working just at daybreak as soon as the committee made the call. Every available person, from old people to kids, had been part of it. The hills were made not only to give people perches to fire from but also to make the wall strong enough to withstand an RPG strike.

I scanned the crowd, looking for my mother or Herb or Howie, and then remembered that both my mother and Herb were already elsewhere. My mother was leading the group on the south wall, and Herb was in charge of the group on the north. Both groups had gone out early, heading east, where they could be seen leaving the neighborhood, and then had spent the last five hours sifting back through the trees, crossing the river, and getting into position.

I caught sight of Howie standing atop one of the piles and scampered up after him. He'd know what was happening. While he barked out orders, I waited and looked down the stretch of highway. It was open, empty, blocked by us at the end and bordered on both sides by the high concrete walls that hid my mother and her squad on one side and Herb and his squad on the other. Inside, ringed on three sides, was the kill zone.

"Aren't you going to say hello?" It was Lori.

"I d-didn't know you'd be here," I stammered.

"I was assigned to this wall. Everybody is assigned somewhere."

"I just wish you weren't here," I said.

"Ha, nice to see you, too."

She was wearing body armor but nothing on her head. "Take my helmet," I offered as I went to remove it.

She placed her hand on mine. "Don't even think about it. How would I ever live with myself if something happened to you because you gave me your equipment?"

"And how would I live with myself if something happened to you because you didn't take it?"

"Don't worry, once the action starts my head is going to

be pressed against the ground and hidden behind the wall," she said. "Can you make that same promise?"

I knew I couldn't—but still it didn't seem right.

Howie and I locked eyes, and he came to my side. "Quinn reported there were approximately two hundred and fifty of them," he said.

"I didn't expect that many."

"We all thought there'd be fewer. They're mobile and closing quickly."

"Is there any possibility that another group is unaccounted for and is going to hit us from another direction?" I asked.

"Our scouts report no activity except coming from this direction."

"That's good."

It was better than good. With all of the guards being deployed on this section, we couldn't withstand an attack on another part of the neighborhood.

"How long before they arrive?" I asked.

"We'll see them soon. They're coming straight along the highway at full speed," Howie said. "I still don't know how you knew this was going to happen."

"Lucky guess."

"But why would you even think this could be their plan?" Howie asked.

"Herb told me about people not really changing who they are," I said. "Brett isn't subtle: he goes big in whatever he does. When I went back through his letter I realized he even told us the time and place of the attack. Today at noon at our neighborhood."

"How did you know he was going to come from this direction?"

"Once I knew the plan, then I figured out that this was the only place that made sense. He'd have to be coming from the opposite direction that we've always expected trouble to come from, the opposite direction from where we'd send out away teams, so not from the city but from the country."

"Which is why he tried to draw off our forces by asking the drop to be made to the east, toward the city," Howie said. "But still, how did you know to expect the attack to come right along the highway?"

"Herb figured that part out. This is our soft spot, because the community to the north hasn't developed as far as the rest of the neighborhood. And with those go-carts we'd seen before, he figured they'd be coming along a roadway. We finally pieced together that the reason he wanted five days was to allow him to move his doodlebugs across the river."

"And that meant a forty-mile detour on the first bridge north of here," Howie said. "I get it now."

"They're coming!" somebody yelled out.

My eyes, and everybody else's, looked down the open stretch of road. It was still deserted, but there was a noise—sort of like the buzzing of bees. It was getting louder, and then the little dots appeared in the distance.

"Everybody down!" Howie yelled over the bullhorn. "Everybody down!"

All around, people dropped so that they were hidden and protected by the wall. I had dropped as well, but I peeked over the top to see. The little go-carts came, more and more, until they filled the entire width of the highway—six lanes on both sides—and they were charging toward us. I trained my rifle on one of the riders in the middle lane. He was too far away and his face was masked by a shield, so I couldn't know if it was Brett. But knowing him the way I thought I did, he would have been in the first line. I had a one-in-twelve chance it was him. But if it was, I had him squarely in my sights—if I fired, he was gone. But, of course, I had to fight the urge to fire—I had to wait until they were all in the trap, in the kill zone.

The noise picked up as they closed in, taking up all the lanes and going on and on and on.

Then it came: muzzle blasts from the go-carts.

"Incoming!" Howie yelled out.

Flashes of light and trails of smoke came twisting toward us. RPG rounds were coming! I crouched down farther but kept my eyes on them as the first three shot over our heads. I swiveled around as two went over the wall and onto the pavement, skidding along before exploding. The third hit the gate, and smashed pieces of cement and wood shot out of the cloud of smoke and into the air before my eyes. Anybody who was anywhere near there, well, they were gone now.

There was a massive explosion that shook the ground and then I was pummeled with pieces of dirt and rocks and bits of concrete that bounced against my visor. I looked up and saw that the whole top of one section of the wall was obliterated. Thank goodness the bottom remained and the chunks of concrete behind it held strong.

I turned to Lori and she looked up. Her scalp was cut and blood was flowing down her face.

"More incoming!" Howie yelled.

I threw myself on top of Lori, shielding her with my body as another grenade shot over the top and exploded just behind us, and I felt my back being pummeled with more rocks and hunks of dirt and concrete. I pushed myself up. They were almost on us—why hadn't we opened fire yet?

I pulled up my gun, ready to fire at them, and there was another explosion! It was much bigger than the others, and the whole far end of the highway just vanished in a cloud of smoke and dust. I knew what that was—it came from us. We'd blown up the highway behind them, trapping them in the kill zone.

"Open fire, open fire, open fire!" Howie yelled.

On both sides of me people started firing. Heads and weapons popped up over the walls on both sides of the highway, and gunfire was directed into the kill zone. Some of the little carts skidded to a stop; others spun around, crashing and flipping into the air.

Out of nowhere one of the Mustangs swooped above, passing so low I ducked my head. It raced over, its .50-caliber machine guns firing, ripping into the carts, the people, and even the pavement.

It was gone in seconds, leaving behind a path of devastation that was as wide as one lane of the highway. Then the other Mustang roared over, guns firing, blazing a trail of destruction the width and length of a second lane. How could anything survive that?

"It's your father!" Lori screamed.

I looked up just in time to see the Cessna pass over so low that I felt like I could almost reach up and touch the landing gear. The plane's gun started to fire repeatedly as my father strafed a third lane of the highway, punching bullet holes into anything and anyone in its path. He, too, was gone in seconds.

Almost all of the go-carts had stopped moving, but that hadn't stopped the fire. Muzzle blasts and bullets were flying into and out of the kill zone.

An RPG shot out and hit one of the walls, shattering it into a million pieces and opening up a gigantic hole. Five of Brett's men jumped up from behind their carts and ran toward the hole—two were cut down, and the other three ran back to take cover.

"Cease fire!" Howie yelled. "Everybody cease fire!"

I hadn't fired a shot yet, so there was no need for me to stop anything. Others lowered their rifles, and the sound of shots slowed down until finally there was silence from our section, followed by the other two walls falling quiet. Some stray shots came from the go-carts, then slowed down and almost came to a stop. If they didn't stop completely, I knew we'd start firing again.

Up in the sky the two Mustangs and the Cessna circled, doing big loops around us. They were close enough to be seen but far enough away to avoid taking fire. If they came in again they'd put an end to any resistance.

"Attention . . . attention!"

It was Herb's voice coming over a bullhorn from the wall. I tried to track the voice—where was he?

"Please put down your weapons so we can talk . . . Nobody else has to die today," Herb called out.

I swiveled around and caught sight of him close by, almost at the corner of the two walls over from me, just his head peeking over the top.

There was silence. I could only hope that they were listening. At least there were now no more shots.

I surveyed the scene. Many go-carts were tipped over or destroyed, riddled with bullets. The asphalt was littered with bodies. Some had been hit by the .50-caliber fire from the planes and been almost cut into pieces. Black smoke was rising from the go-carts that had caught fire. The smoke was thick and mixed with the odor of spilled gas and, of course, the bitter, acidic smell of gunpowder.

"I need to speak to your leader!" Herb called out. "Brett, are you still alive?"

A chill went through me at the mention of his name. I hoped he wouldn't answer—that he *couldn't* answer. But then came that familiar voice.

"Good to hear from you, Herb. I've never talked to a ghost before!"

"I'm alive and still kicking . . . no thanks to you."

"I thought you'd take my men's attempt on your life as a compliment. I guess if you want something done right, though, you have to do it yourself!" Brett yelled.

"How's that working out for you today?" Herb taunted.

"Not as well as I'd expected."

I could hear him clearly but couldn't figure out where his voice was coming from. I looked through the sight of my rifle, scanning for him. I knew he wasn't far, but there were many places to hide. It was now so quiet and they were both so close that Herb had put down the bullhorn and Brett hardly needed to raise his voice.

"So what now?" Brett asked. "Are you going to surrender?"

Herb laughed. "Nice to see you haven't lost your sense of humor. Surrender is something *you* need to consider . . . all of you."

"I'm the only one making that decision!" Brett shouted. "How about if you just back off and let us go and we won't bother you anymore. You have my word."

"You told us yourself what your word is worth, Brett."

"Come on, Herb, you really don't want a lot of prisoners, and we're not going down without a fight."

"If you fight, there won't be any prisoners. You're trapped with no place to run."

"We'll take more than a few of you with us," Brett replied.

"You can try, but I'm just going to call back the planes. They'll make pass after pass until none of you are left alive!" Herb said.

There was no response. Was Brett thinking over the offer or was he just buying some time while he was planning something?

"So if we surrender, what happens?" Brett called out.

"We'll tend to your wounded."

"And then what?" Brett asked.

With that last response I was certain I'd found where Brett was hiding. There was a little bit of motion from behind a cluster of go-carts close to the front. I trained my rifle right on the spot.

"Some of your people will be let go if they cooperate with us," Herb replied. "Some might even be invited to join our neighborhood, like we did with Quinn."

"And what will happen to me?" Brett demanded.

"You're going to stand trial."

"I think we all know how that's going to end, so that doesn't sound like much of a deal for me."

"Best I can offer."

"Give me ten minutes to think about it, talk it over with my men."

"You just told us you make the decisions, so there's nobody to talk it over with. You stand up now, hands above your head. I've already radioed the planes and told them it was time to come back," Herb said.

I looked up and tried to find the planes. The Cessna was off to the south on its own and the two Mustangs were in formation. It looked like they were cutting their bank short, getting ready to come in and make another strafing pass.

"It's now or never," Herb called out. He was back on the bullhorn. He was now talking to all the men out there, not just Brett. "This is your last chance. Surrender or you will all die . . . Get to your feet . . . weapons down and hands up. Last chance."

I looked back over my shoulder. The Mustangs had made their turn and were now coming back, straight toward us. If they weren't called off within thirty seconds they'd be right on top of them again and just cut them to ribbons.

A man stood up, hands in the air. And then there was a second and a third and fourth. The man closest to me was splattered with blood, his left arm holding up the right, which was badly mangled and on a strange angle. More and more of them stood up, some staggering, obviously badly wounded. Still, there had to be more of them alive than that—and what about the planes? They were still closing in, bearing down. Somebody would have to call them off soon or they'd be shooting people who just wanted to surrender.

Another man stood up. I recognized the form before I saw the face. It was Brett! I saw a dark stain on his left leg. It extended from the calf and leaked down to his shoe. He'd been hit.

"Everybody, lay down your weapons and put up your hands!" Brett bellowed.

There was a gap of a few seconds and then others got to their feet, hands in the air.

The two Mustangs banked and veered off to the side. Thank goodness they'd been radioed in time.

Soon there were dozens and dozens of men on their feet. Some had their hands in the air, others on their heads. Several were held up by others, an arm or two around their shoulders. There was much to see, much to study, but I wanted to look at only one place, one person.

I brought my rifle back around until it was trained squarely on Brett. I was sighted on his side, a place where the body armor was thinner and my bullet could penetrate. In fact it would enter in through the side, slow down as it passed through his body, bounce off the other side of the vest, and ricochet back inside. If it didn't hit any major organ the first time, it was almost guaranteed to rip up enough on the return trip. There would be nothing Dr. Morgan could do to save him.

Brett came forward, the one leg dragging as he walked. His hands were on his head. I felt my finger tightening on the trigger. There he was in my sights. I could squeeze off a round and it would be over. He'd be dead. There would be no more fears, no more threats to my family, to me, to Lori. There'd be no chance of him talking his way out of this, of somehow getting through the trial or escaping to come back at us again and again and again. It wouldn't be like the last time, when he was there and I didn't pull the trigger. If I had pulled it then, many people would still be alive now. If I didn't pull it this time, how many more might die?

I took a deep breath and then held it, the way I'd been taught to shoot. I'd just squeeze my finger, move it the slightest bit, and it would be over. I could claim it was an accident and nobody would doubt what I said.

"Adam."

I felt my finger tingling, almost itchy, wanting to—

"Adam!"

I looked over at Lori, who was standing right there, saying, "It's over . . . it's over."

It wasn't.

She placed a hand on the barrel of my rifle, lowering it. Then she put her hand on my shoulder. "It's over. You don't have to do it."

My instincts told me she was wrong. It wasn't going to be over until Brett was gone, until Brett was dead.

"Everybody, hold your fire!" Herb called out to our people. "Aim your weapons to the ground. I'm going out!"

Every eye turned to see him stand up. He climbed over a place where the wall had been partially destroyed. What was he doing? He didn't have to go out there. They had surrendered, so just let them come to us, one by one.

"We're going to provide for your wounded," Herb called out. "You'll all be treated with mercy and in a fair manner."

Brett stepped forward. "I want you all to listen to him! He's telling the truth . . . You can trust him."

All along the stretch of highway those who were still alive and able to walk started to move forward, stepping and staggering or dragging themselves around and through the go-carts and the bodies. They all still had their hands in the air or, like Brett, on the top of their heads.

Brett moved toward Herb. And then I saw Brett smile.

I brought up my rifle and aimed, but before I could get a shot off, Brett whipped out a pistol from behind his back. As if from far away, I heard the sound of the shot. Then my finger moved and I pulled the trigger. Brett spun violently, staggered to the side, and then toppled over. I barely registered that the whole top of his head was gone. *He* was gone. Dead. But then my gaze turned to Herb, who lay on the pavement, blood pouring from his chest.

32

"Hello, Adam."

Reluctantly I looked up. It was Dr. Morgan standing above me.

"How are you doing?" he asked.

I wanted to give no answer or just tell him whatever he needed to hear so that he would leave me alone. But, really, what was the point of lying? Here I was sitting on the highway with my back against the wall, the evening dark becoming deeper as the sun disappeared below the horizon.

"I've been better," I admitted.

"Mind if I join you?" he asked.

I shrugged. "It's a big wall."

He sat down on the pavement beside me. As we sat there a mother and daughter walked up and placed a bouquet of wildflowers on the ground. Their bouquet joined hundreds and hundreds of others that had been placed there over the past three days to mark the spot where Herb had died.

He was dead.

I'd seen it with my own eyes, but I still didn't believe it. I'd thought he was dead before, yet he'd risen as if from the grave. Part of me still expected him to saunter up, talk to me, and explain what the next move was going to be. There was nobody to do that. Not for me and not for anybody else. All of us were now alone together.

"I was glad when things went well at the follow-up on Brett's compound. Nobody wounded on either side," Dr. Morgan said.

"That ended better than anybody could have expected," I agreed.

I had been not on the ground but up in the air in the Cessna with my father, along with the two Mustangs. The hero of the day had been Quinn. I'd been told that he'd calmly taken the rifle off his shoulder and the pistol out of his holster, put his hands in the air, and walked into the compound. He had convinced the fifty men who remained— some of whom he knew—that we'd treat them fairly. That combined with the massive show of force—over four hundred armed people surrounding their position and the planes in the air—convinced them to surrender without a shot being fired.

There were also almost forty men, women, and children— people held as slaves—who had been rescued when the compound was captured. It was a collection of people who had skills the doodlebug crew needed, including eight people who were mechanics. They'd been the ones who had made the massive fleet of go-carts. All of the prisoners were offered the choice of simply going free or joining one of our neighborhoods. All who chose to join would make us stronger.

And we'd be stronger in other ways as well.

Going through the remains of the attack and then the stored supplies at the compound, we had gained over four hundred guns, close to seventy-five RPGs, and almost a hundred thousand rounds of ammunition—not to mention food, supplies, and the go-carts that were spared or could be salvaged. The spoils had been split between the different neighborhoods that had participated, but the vast majority stayed with us.

Still to be decided was what would happen to all of the captured members of the Division. They were going to be interviewed one by one about the role each had played and what they might be likely to do from here. Some would simply be released outside the neighborhood, while others would be granted amnesty and allowed to join us if they chose. Others were going to have to be imprisoned—or worse. I wouldn't be part of any of those decisions, even if I was a member of the committee. They'd go before the courts we'd established and be tried by a jury of their peers, innocent until proven guilty, the way it had been before and would be again.

"I'm just glad it ended when it did. I don't know how we would have dealt with more wounded if there had been another battle," Dr. Morgan said.

"You already have enough casualties to deal with," I said.

"I guess it's better to tend to the wounded than to bury the dead. Even if they are the enemy . . . or were the enemy," he said.

"We just have to make sure that that's the end of the Division."

"It's gone. No head, no body, and no base," Dr. Morgan said.

"That's what my mother said as well."

"That's who I got that line from." He smiled. "Had Brett

managed to break through the walls, he would have left a trail of death and destruction throughout the neighborhood. I can't even imagine the carnage he had planned."

I could imagine it. I'd seen it months ago at Olde Burnham.

"I wonder what Herb would have said about all of this? I suppose he'd have come up with something reassuring and a little bit mystic," Dr. Morgan said.

I laughed, and that surprised me, but Dr. Morgan was right—it would have been both.

"You know you had no choice, killing Brett."

"I know."

"You can't have any regrets," he said.

"I just regret I hadn't been smart enough to do it one second earlier. If I had, then Herb would still be—"

"Don't even say that!" Dr. Morgan said, cutting me off. "There were hundreds of people watching, all of them with guns, and nobody saw it coming."

"I should have. I should have shot him as he walked toward Herb."

"Shot him before he pulled the gun? Shot him in cold blood?" Dr. Morgan asked.

I shook my head. "My blood wasn't cold."

"And neither was your heart."

"I should have killed him. As soon as he stood up I should have pulled the trigger."

"That's not who you are. That's not who *we* are, what we stand for, and you know that."

I did know it, but that didn't change the way I was feeling, and I didn't think I'd ever feel any different no matter how long I lived.

"Your parents are worried about you," he said.

"That's what parents do."

"Everybody is worried about you."

"I don't want to worry anybody."

"It's more than that. With Herb gone, you're needed even more."

"Needed?"

"Yes. Everybody knows what you've done; everybody knows that none of this would have been possible without you. There's not a person in this neighborhood who isn't grateful, who doesn't owe you a debt that can never be repaid."

"That debt was to Herb. We survived because of him."

"I think if Herb were here he'd disagree with you, but you probably don't believe that." Dr. Morgan groaned as he got to his feet. "I have something for you." He pulled an envelope out of his pocket. "It's from Herb."

I looked at the envelope. My name was on the front in his handwriting. For a split second, for just that instant, I thought Herb was still alive.

"He gave it to me two weeks ago. He told me to give it to you after he died."

"But he couldn't have known he was going to die."

"He did, though. He knew, because I was the one who told him," Dr. Morgan said. "I made the diagnosis. He was dying."

"Dying from what?"

"Cancer. It was aggressive and inoperable. I couldn't have saved him even if I'd had the full resources available from before the blackout."

"Did he have long?" I asked.

"It's hard to say . . . two months, maybe six. When you're dealing with somebody that stubborn . . ."

Dr. Morgan trailed off, and the two of us remained there in silence for a long time.

I hadn't understood why Herb had gone out to face Brett in the open. I'd kept going over it in my mind. Walking by himself toward all of those people with guns, having no backup plan. He *always* had a backup plan.

Now it made sense. Getting killed *was* his backup plan.

"I knew he wasn't well . . . the shaking hands . . . the tiredness . . . but I never imagined he was dying."

"He didn't want anybody to know, and I had to respect his wishes. He said that it would have been a distraction and that people needed to be focused, to be confident."

That sounded like Herb.

"I don't know how he could go on the way he did," Dr. Morgan continued. "He wouldn't even take medication to control the pain. He said he needed his mind to be sharp, his thoughts clear."

That sounded even *more* like Herb.

"I've got to get back to the clinic to do rounds with the wounded," Dr. Morgan said. "By the way, I haven't read the letter, because it was meant for you . . . I just hope it brings you comfort."

Dr. Morgan walked away, leaving me alone with the letter. I turned it over in my hands, knowing what I should do but unsure if I could do it. Maybe it would be better to go home and open it with my mother and father there, or even have Todd or Lori with me. It would be good just to have somebody there.

Ironically, if I could have chosen anybody to be by my side when something like this had to be done, it would have been Herb. And I guess, in a way, he *was* with me, right there in my hands. I turned the envelope over, opened the flap, and pulled out the letter. It was one sheet, folded over. I unfolded it.

> *Adam,*
>
> *If you are reading this, it means that I'm dead. Not "gone" or "lost" or "off to a better place." I always hate when people talk like that. I'm dead. Simple as that. I don't know the specifics of my death, but I know that it was fast and clean whether it was because of an accident, by the hand of another, or by my own hand. I wasn't going to allow this illness to rob me of my dignity. In the end, however it happened, it was my choice. I knew that I was never going to live long enough to see the sun coming up again on the country that I devoted my life to, but in this I was going to have some control.*
>
> *Life always seemed to hand me something that I was supposed to be doing. And those things put me in a position where I didn't have the time to settle down with a wife and raise kids. It wouldn't have been fair of me to expect anyone else to have shared my life in that way. If I ever had had a son, though, I could have only hoped he would have been like you—except maybe a little better-looking.*

I broke up laughing.

*Make sure you tell that joke to Todd. I still think
the poor lad is afraid I'm going to yell at him to get
off my grass. You tell him he's free to go on my front
lawn—or what's left of it—anytime he wants.*

*The thing I admired most about you was your
sense of honor and fairness. You got that from your
parents. They are about the best people I've ever met.
You all have to stand tall and stand together. You
need them and they need you. The whole neighborhood, and beyond, needs your family and what you
stand for.*

The dim rays of the sun still filtering over the horizon were
fading fast, and I had to angle the letter to get enough light
to keep reading.

*Our enemies—known and unknown, people like
Brett—would believe that our greatest weakness
was our humanity. It isn't. It's our greatest strength.
It is the glue that holds us together, the rock on
which we stand. Thank you for helping me to
understand that. Thank you for helping me to
believe in the future even when I had nothing
to go on but your faith.*

*I have a little secret to tell you. I suspected that
Brett was planning to attack the neighborhood after
distracting us with the food exchange. I would have
said something if I'd had to, but I was waiting for
you to figure it out for yourself. And you did. I knew
you would. You proved to me and to others that you*

have what it takes to be a leader. I hope you proved
that to yourself, too.

I don't want you to grieve for me. There's no time
for sadness. Even if you're feeling it, you have to put
it away. People need you to be a leader today and—
more important—tomorrow. But right now, you need
to go and find that girlfriend of yours, give her a
hug, and take her out on a date. Bring her some
more flowers like I told you to. Tell her how you feel
about her. Among all that's going on, it's not just
okay to feel love and hope for the future, it's essential.

With great respect, hope, and love,
Herb

My whole body shuddered and I felt the tears start to form
in my eyes. All I wanted was the chance to thank him, tell
him how much he meant to me, how much I was going to
miss him, too. He had been like a second father to me, especially when my own father had been on the outside, walking
back across the country to his family.

Folding the letter back into the envelope, I had a sudden
urge to get back to my house, to be with my parents. But before I could do anything more, I heard a gigantic gasp from
the guards and other people nearby.

I jumped to my feet trying to see in the dusk what had
happened, find the danger, and then I realized what had happened: I was bathed in light.

The lights on the highway had come to life. All along the
highway as far as I could see, the giant lights hanging from

their tall poles were shining bright, and we were caught in their glow. People all around me stood with their mouths open, silently staring. Somehow, somewhere, somebody had done something to make this happen.

I was mesmerized by the yellow glow. It was amazing, beyond words. I heard some people laugh, and there were a few shouts of joy, and then another gasp as the lights flickered and went off.

A collective moan rose around me, but I felt like laughing instead. It was going to be okay. Somehow the lights had come back on for a few seconds. Someday the lights were going to come back on for good. There was always hope. Life would find a way.